DARK PARADISE

To Kim,
Write great characters & settings
4-ever!

GENE DESROCHERS

Gene Desrochers

ACORN PUBLISHING

SCWC SD 37
17 Feb. 2023

Dark Paradise
First Edition

This story is a work of fiction. References to real people, events, establishments, organizations, or locales are intended only to provide a sense of authenticity and are used fictitiously. All other characters, and all incidents and dialogue, are drawn from the author's imagination and are not to be construed as real.

Cover design by Dane Low at E-Book Launch

ISBN-13: 978-1-947392-19-9 (Hardcover)
ISBN-13: 978-1-947392-16-8 (Paperback)

For Mindy

CHAPTER 1

Saint Thomas filtered into view as I peered out the Saab 340's window. White-washed shorelines dotted the west-end, distant palm trees bent, but never broke, in the off-shore winds. To the south, forty miles away, St. Croix crouched close to the horizon shrouded in hazy impressionist strokes. Along with St. John, they made up the U.S. Virgin Islands. If the world were flat, these islands would be the edge.

Antonio Lopez de Santa Anna, the eighth president of Mexico, took his third political exile in St. Thomas after losing more than half of Mexico's territory in the Mexican-American War. In my personal history, my plane trip home to St. Thomas would be known as Boise Montague's first emotional exile, after my stunning, but predictable, defeat in Los Angeles.

Most Saint Thomians were of African descent, brought over as slaves to harvest sugar cane. I suppose that's another difference between Santa Anna and me. He came from an elite Mexican military family. I came from African slaves and Europeans making babies together.

I'd let myself go since Evelyn, my wife, had been murdered a year ago. Other than twenty extra pounds, baggy eyes from lack of sleep, a wild afro, and a sand-papery face, I looked great. Hazel eyes against high-yellow skin and jet-black hair gave me an exotic look, but people had trouble figuring where I fit into the racial divide. Someone who studied racial history would call me quadroon, or one-quarter black.

Pulling my lips back, I threaded a piece of dental tape between every tooth. I dragged the floss up and down three times on each side to the gum line. I kept my teeth as clean as a surgeon's hands. Most dentists recommended a cleaning twice a year. My teeth were polished every three months. I'd never had a cavity. As I pulled the floss out from between my back lower molars, I grinned. The sunlight caught the white enamel and my teeth glowed in the plastic window. No tragedy could stop me from maintaining flawless dental hygiene.

Murdered. The word stuck in my mind like a rock stuck in a drain. I couldn't prove it. The cops thought Evelyn's death was an accident. The police threatened to arrest me for interfering in their so-called investigation.

The scent of mascara and lavender assaulted me. "Señor Montague?" the flight attendant whispered, her bronzed, Latina features hovering inches from my face.

Had I been speaking to myself out loud or something? I'd never had a flight attendant mention me by name.

She tilted her round chin and smiled at my consternation with practiced ease. "We are deplaning, Mr.

Montague." She handed me my seat assignment slip that must have fallen on the floor.

I tried to push out of my seat to get a better look, but my seatbelt held me fast. All the seats in the plane were empty. Besides the captain and staff near the entrance and my flight attendant smiling at me with concerned patronage, I was the only person left. I tried to recover my cool.

"Hey, uh, call me Boise."

"I prefer Mr. Montague. You know, it's mi favorita. All the romance and so forth," she continued.

"I'm sorry?" I said.

"The greatest literature the world has ever known," she paused dramatically, then continued, "*Romeo and Juliet*, in any language. Shakespeare was a genius, no?"

"Yes, wonderful. Good old Willy. I'll get out of your hair now ma'am." I pushed past her and hurried down the air stair.

The heat slapped me like James Cagney smacking a woman in a gangster film. Waves of hot air oozed off the black tarmac. I turned in a circle, taking in my surroundings. I'd returned to my birthplace for that feeling of belonging somewhere. The smell of salt in the air, drifting clouds always in the sky, the oppressive heat. I felt right about my decision.

A vast ocean surrounded the airport. Brewer's Bay lay to the west, waves calmly lapping the sand. To the north, the Mahogany Run Golf Course rolled along below a giant block of rust-red stone my parents had claimed was a cistern. Nothing much had changed.

A person would have trouble finding St. Thomas on a world map. But, for hundreds of years, as went the Caribbean, so went the destinies of the most powerful nations on earth: France, England, and Spain. These little rocks were the hidden cornucopia that fed the beast of imperialism. St. Thomas possessed one of the finest harbors in the region, which made it a merchant's paradise. And, because of its remoteness to any mainland nation, it was notoriously difficult to enforce laws.

Questionable characters migrated to these U.S. territories in search of wealth and freedom. The freedom to enslave, steal, smuggle, rape, and kill. To seize the obvious benefits of the United States' financial assistance, but have the geographic and cultural distance that allowed easy, unfettered corruption. I needed to get lost in that unwanted riff-raff of humanity. I belonged in that world.

For now.

***

I found a room in a local dive, dumped my luggage on the floor, then lounged about for a day, giving me time to reflect and gather my bearings.

Without my wife, my tether to a personal life had severed. Back in L.A., I worked as a private investigator for law firms, but the meat of life, relationships, dried up like flowers in the Mojave Desert. I hunted down evidence that exonerated our clients or helped win huge sums of money for plaintiffs in everything from personal injury suits to copyright infringement. If you needed it, I found it.

Evelyn did her save-the-world environmental lawyering and I brought in the money. Until her sudden death.

I got some life insurance money; socked it away.

Every non-working second, I tried to prove that Evelyn's death was no accident. The Los Angeles County Sheriff agreed to look into the evidence I found, but ultimately, they didn't really care to solve the case. I couldn't do it alone and when I pushed too hard, they had threatened me with incarceration.

Which led me back to the islands. I listened to the crickets chirp outside my motel window, crying out their love songs, lulling me into sweeter dreams. For the first time in months, I slept through the night.

Showering in the grungy motel bathroom, I headed to my old neighborhood at the base of Bluebeard's Hill. I walked, just as I had growing up here. Years of driving in Los Angeles made walking feel like a luxury.

I had a plan. I would reacquaint myself with people who could help me re-root myself to my childhood home. A comforting relationship with a long history would get me on the road to recovery. My first stop and highest hope would be my former best friend whom I hadn't seen since I'd left town at the tender age of twelve. Roger Black.

CHAPTER 2

Roger's house looked like a neglected drunk on a bender. A tattered piece of red cloth caught on the rusty front gate fluttered in the hot breeze. Crates of cardboard and Styrofoam were stacked inside the gate. Brown paint flaked off as I ran my hand along the exterior wall. I trotted up the stairs to the front door.

My stomach churned. I had forgotten to take my goat pills--as in, only a goat would be crazy enough to eat pills this large. They calmed my colon. Running my hand through my brillo-pad hair, I realized the flight down from Miami jostled me around so much, that in my nauseated state, I had forgotten a dose. In my pocket I found a couple loose pills and popped one. Swallowing it dry caused me to gag twice. Roger must have a cold beer in that house for his old friend.

Some amber varnish stuck to my knuckles when I knocked. I blew it away, looking over my shoulder at the deserted road. The potholes had been filled. That had never happened in all the years I'd lived here.

I knocked again, shifting from foot to foot as the aching in my ass ascended toward my lower back. I hated wearing watches. My wrist always itched.

Thank God for smartphones. Mine said it was ten in the morning, but that couldn't be right. In the settings application I switched off airplane mode and the correct time popped up. Almost two in the afternoon on March thirty-first. The time of year mattered little because St. Thomas only had one season: hurricane season. As winter became spring and summer approached, the temperature changed from hot to hotter to scorching.

After a safe thirty seconds, I knocked again, but louder in case Glor, Roger, or Guillermo were back in the kitchen or out on the rear porch.

A tall, white manor stood up on the hill. It rose stately above the rest: a wooden watchtower. It was the same house Presidente Santa Anna had occupied while in exile.

The current owners had enough sense to keep the sign in front freshly painted red, but hadn't done so much with the house itself. Two swords crossed beneath the pirate font. It read: "The West Indian Manner, A Guesthouse." The vintage wooden sign curled at the edges like a parchment page from a treasure map.

I rocked from heel to toe and back again as I clenched. How would I find Roger if he'd moved stateside? Needing to take a leak, I made my way around the ugly white office buildings that had been stacked in front of our homes by a land developer named Payne and Wedgefield in the nineties. I hustled down the elongated steps, through the grassy asphalt, and up to Lucas's house.

This was a harder knock. Lucas and I had ended things badly. We were young and both angry about different things. Saying good-bye for good as pre-teens wasn't easy. I hoped he'd forgotten those growing pains and would at least tolerate seeing me. I reached the top of the stairs and was greeted with an open door.

"Hello," I called into a cavernous room full of boxes.

A male voice called out, "Yeah, wha' you want?"

I saw no one.

"I'm an old friend of Lucas Beauregard. Just comin' by to say hi," I hollered, edging my foot over the threshold.

"No one here by dat name," came a gruff reply from behind the boxes.

"Any idea…"

An aged man emerged wearing a ripped Pittsburgh Pirates hat balanced on a gray afro. "He ain't here."

"I got that, sir. You see, I just want to locate him. He was Adam's grandson. I used to live there." I pointed to a vacant lot on the hill.

He sauntered over to the doorway smelling like Aqua Velva aftershave. His brown eyes gazed up at the dirt lot while petting his mustache.

"All right. What about Lucas?"

"I just want to see him, you know, say hello. I moved to St. Croix when I was twelve and he was thirteen."

"Mi-son, you ain't ol' enough to be dat old," the guy laughed.

"Yeah, I have a youthful face, but seriously, we were buddies."

He pulled a soiled handkerchief out of the back pocket of his cut-off jeans and slathered it across his forehead. He adjusted his scrotum. "Adam die five year ago."

"Wow, I can't believe he lived that long. He was old when I was a kid," I said.

"Yeah, well dey sold da house to somebody from da nort'side. Some Frenchie or da odda." He finally looked at me. I couldn't help shifting and squirming. "Da bat'room ova der." He pointed back to the right.

"T'anks," I said, scurrying off.

I returned with a big, tired smile on my face. "What about any of Lucas's aunts or anything? This place isn't that big, you gotta know some of these people? You local, right?" I said this, knowing that questioning his knowledge of the local people would bring out the desire to declare his allegiance and knowledge for life on the island.

"Hey, hey, I know da Beauregards. Nobody who from dez parts don' know dem, check," he said.

"Okay, so can you tell me where to find Lucas," I said.

"I don't know Lucas, but da lady who have me doin' dis, she work right der." He pointed at a house that had been converted into an office building.

"T'anks, da man," I shot back, falling into a bit of the island dialect.

"All right," he said as I almost stumbled down the narrow brick stairs.

I looked back, thinking of asking if he knew anything about Roger's situation. He held his crotch with a look of complete satisfaction thrown skyward, so I left him alone.

Chapter 3

A bell tinkled as I entered the offices of the Virgin Islands' Historical Society. Three desks positioned around the walls all faced the center of the room where a bronze sculpture of a coral reef encircled by a dozen fish stood. A human figure struggled to climb out of the reef. One upraised hand stretched toward the room's ceiling as if a rope would descend and pull him out, freeing him from the beautiful oppression.

"Can I help you, sir?" asked a short-haired woman seated behind a mahogany desk to my right. Although she must have been at least sixty years old, she had smiling eyes that enlivened the room with academic wonder. A good librarian who seemed eager to help a research-minded seeker of knowledge.

"Yes, I'm looking for Lucas Beauregard. The man in his house said someone here might help me."

She gazed at me for a long, searching moment. "Do I know you?"

"I used to live here when I was young. I spent a lot of time in Lucas's house as a child," I said.

"Where did you live?"

"Up the hill a little further in a white house," I said. "Do you know Lucas?"

"Excuse me, yes, I'm his aunt, Iris Adamson. That's mine and my sister's house. I haven't seen Lucas's mother in twenty-six years."

"Yeah, he was always in there with his grandpa and great aunts."

"They're all dead. Well, one's in a home, but she's senile. Lucas isn't around here much. He got an apartment down by Fortuna and works at the Island Rentals rent-a-car place right when you turn onto Veteran's coming out from airport road. You know where I mean?"

"I know the place. Sign's faded?" I spotted the sign when I'd left the airport. The place had been there forever.

"That's it," she nodded with motherly approval. "You don't look old enough to be Lucas's friend."

"He was a bit over a year older than me, but didn't matter much at the time. We were tight."

I looked around at the books dusting on the shelves. Original documents stuffed into cases sat on the floor scattered about the room.

"Did you know Roger, who lived over there?" I pointed to the north wall.

"Glor's boy?"

"That was his grandma," I said.

"He was hers. His mama was never around much and I have no idea about a father. I know they moved away a while back after some bad things happened to that poor family." Iris peered at her computer screen and clicked the mouse three times. "Not sure I want to tell you about those things…not if you were friends with that boy. What did you call him?"

"Roger. Will Lucas tell me?" I asked.

"Lucas doesn't talk much. Something went wrong up here." She tapped her temple. "It's like he never went past when you knew him. He doesn't talk about anything before yesterday much, really ever," she shook her head wearily.

"You might be the only source left," I muttered.

"What?" Her forehead creased with age.

"I said, you might be the only historian worth a damn on this rock."

"You lived on the hill?"

"I did."

"Were you the ones with all the cats?" she asked, wrinkling her nose.

I nodded.

"Father hated your cats. Ever since, I've disliked cats too."

"That's too bad. They're good bullshit detectors," I said. "Would you mind telling me what you know about Roger?"

She scratched her head and let out a long, reluctant sigh. "He got into illegal dealing. Drugs. He got into it deeply and wholly. It took him to the grave. He died around Christmas two years ago."

My breath quickened as I felt a sharp pain run through my right arm like a moving needle. My thumb twitched. I put out my hand and found a chair in the corner. Roger dead? Impossible.

He'd never had any interest in that life. We played stickball, rode bikes near the baseball stadium, snuck into games on Saturday afternoons. The convenience store with its treasure trove of sugary goodies like Hubba-Bubba and ring pops, our only vices. Once, Roger washed blood out of my hair when an older boy pegged me with a rock in the head after a baseball game. I didn't want my mother to know or she'd have whipped me. He washed it out and kept the secret.

The familiar feeling of home I'd experienced on the airport runway disappeared, leaving a gaping wound in my chest that fluttered with each breath. "Drugs?" I muttered.

"I'm sorry, what did you say?" Iris got up, went to a water cooler. She handed me a tiny paper cup. It felt cool against my fingertips. "Drink this," she said as she gently pushed my hand toward my lips. I tried but dribbled some of the water onto my shirt. The cold wetness startled me.

"I…did he try to get out of that life?" I said, hoping his soul cleansed itself before death.

"Don't think so. He was deep in, like I said. He wanted to run things. He was not savage enough in his heart for that, but he wasn't a good person either," she said. "I hear he's buried down by Frenchtown."

Iris adjusted the waist of her flowered skirt then circled back around her desk. As she sat down, her face lit up. "Now I remember you! You gained some weight, right?"

"Yeah," I said, patting my protruding gut. I was probably twenty-five pounds over ideal weight. Stress. "I got more buff, just in the wrong places."

She laughed. "Nah, mi son, we all put it on over the years. You also have a nice chest."

I waved good-bye on the compliment. The sun warmed the back of my neck as I stepped outside.

Roger and I hadn't seen each other or spoken in seventeen years. Yet without him, St. Thomas was a foreign land. I pushed the hair away from the scar on the right side of my head where that boy had hit me with a rock after the ball game.

Jet lag notwithstanding, trudging around in the ninety-degree humidity felt freeing. I walked through Charlotte Amalie, past the whorehouse, right next to St. Peter and Paul Catholic Church on Dronningens Gade, also known as Main Street.

I entered the iron gates and whitewashed concrete walls of the cemetery. After thirty minutes, I found his tombstone. It read: "Roger Black, January 26, 1983-December 24, 2011." While there, I visited my grandparents' graves as well.

CHAPTER 4

After eating a burger along with three large Guinnesses at a local bar, I dropped four quarters into a yellow newspaper dispenser in front of the post office for *The Daily News*. The caption "A Pulitzer-Prize Winning Newspaper" appeared below the title and the familiar blue border. A photo of a handsome, goateed man skipping double-dutch style as two women held the ropes and smiled at him occupied the center section above the fold. On the back page I located the phone number for classified advertising.

"Where are your offices?"

"We located on Estate Thomas. You know?" said an annoyed female voice.

"Yeah, over near Havensight?"

"Yeah," she said.

"T'anks." I clicked off.

Roger didn't count. In my drunken stupor, the injustice magnified. I needed to find out if anyone, anywhere, cared that my friend died because if not, justice was even more remote here than in Los Angeles. Roger was murdered.

Fact. In Los Angeles, a compelling argument could and had been made that Evelyn's death was accidental.

Maybe once I sobered up I wouldn't care about Roger anymore. Maybe my caring got used up when Evelyn died. So, while I was drunk, I intended to follow my swollen nose to *The Daily News*. Figuring out what happened to Roger felt more real than pushing papers in an office or selling textbooks or running down details on some divorce settlement. Evelyn would have told me to stop and get real, but I had no one to answer to anymore. I could do as I pleased.

The newspaper, which covered the U.S. Virgins, plus Tortola, had been around since 1930. I'd grown up reading snippets of it, mostly the funny pages and movie listings, before moving to the states. Seeing it on the nightstand in my dumpy motel room and hearing the crickets chirping away outside gave me a degree of comfort I hadn't felt in a long time; certainly not since Evelyn had been killed.

I believed she'd been murdered. The Los Angeles Police Department disagreed. That disagreement intensified right before I left California.

There might even be a warrant for my arrest out there if the downtown homicide division chief had his way. I planned to stay away as long as I could, but there was no telling when the urge to go back and finish my investigation would overwhelm good sense.

For now, I'd focus my attention on Roger Black. However, it would all have to wait until morning as I was nauseated. I stumbled to my hotel room and crashed on top of the sheets, the overhead fan humming gently in the dark air above my bed.

CHAPTER 5

A distant lawn mower powered up, followed by a rumbling bus with a poor excuse for a muffler chugging below my balcony. I struggled to a sitting position. Rubbing my eyes, I tried to remember exactly where I was.

My so-called balcony consisted of a screen door with a fourteen-inch tiled area just wide enough to hold my girth. Reacquainting myself with my surroundings, I tumbled out of bed and squeezed outside. Leaning on the balustrade, a couple jagged pieces of concrete flaked off and plummeted to the ground. To my right, the lawnmower screeched as the blade caught a rock on the uneven patchwork of weeds that qualified as a lawn.

Better go inside. I shut the sliding glass door, showered, shaved, and dry heaved. My gag reflex had intensified over the last six months. I enjoyed few mornings without retching whatever tiny amount of water, alcohol, or food remained undigested.

I brushed the taste of bile out of my mouth, wandered downstairs to the kitchen area. They fixed me an egg sandwich and coffee with milk. I headed out at nine-fifteen, squinting at an address and phone number on a scrap of paper.

The Daily News wasn't what you'd call an investigative journal at first glance. Based on its Pulitzer Prize boast, it must have achieved some level of competence.

I arrived at a dirty building with barred, frosted windows. An uninviting look. The brick work had chipped and the mortar had eroded, so it needed pointing. Once inside, I leaned over a deserted Formica countertop.

"Hello?" I hollered.

Behind me, the door I'd entered through opened. A very tan redhead showing signs of aging from many days spent in the sun entered carrying a laptop bag and shouldering a camera. A red Carnegie Mellon University baseball cap that looked like it had been run over by a garbage truck covered part of her tough, but beautiful face. She looked me over like I was a mongrel who'd wandered in begging for table scraps.

"You need something?" She dropped her stuff down on the cushioned chair next to the counter.

"Uh, yes, I wondered if I could get some clippings or microfilm or copies or whatever it is newspapers give for issues two to eight years old. Are they digitized yet?" I stammered.

"Seriously, what do you want?" She pulled her Ray-Bans off and the gray-blue of her eyes stunned me for a moment. Using her sunglasses, she tapped my shoulder. "Hello?"

The faint odor of cigarette smoke assaulted me when she got close.

"Clippings, you know, news from the past," I said.

As she slipped the glasses into a case from her purse she said, "Yes, but you implied that something here was digitized." She pursed her thin lips. "This newspaper went online three years ago, so, the last three years are available online in the archives section if you buy a subscription. You a subscriber?"

"I don't have a subscription," I said defensively.

"Figures. This is why my job is constantly in danger. Everyone expects news for free." Her fine hair moved in a blur as she shook her head derisively while she rummaged for something in her bag.

"Hey, I'm happy to buy a subscription. I support journalism," I said. It sounded lame.

We both flinched as a thunderous banging rang through the room as something or someone hit the other side of a door to my left.

She threw her hands up, exclaiming, "Not again!"

"What? What's that?" I said.

"Calling the cops," she sang out. "They said they're gonna start charging us if this happened again," she whispered.

Another, more urgent banging erupted through the room. The reporter had her cell out.

"Wait," I said. "Is it really that dangerous?"

"No, just annoying." She pressed a button on her phone. "You believe this? Now I'm on hold. I could probably walk over to the police station faster. He'll probably take a dump on the floor by the time we get back."

"Who's he?" I prompted.

She blew out an exhausted sigh. "God damn it! This shit's wasting my time." She slammed the phone against her thigh and screamed at the screen. "Fucking answer, you pricks!"

I leaned against the door listening for the other side. It was quiet.

"Do you have a key?" She stared at me, then held out the keys: a gold one between her thumb and middle finger. "Not dangerous, right?"

She nodded, holding the phone to her ear.

The lock clicked open and a man burst through, knocking me into the wall. He spun around three times showing amazing nimbleness, for he looked to be at least sixty--wild white hair ala Einstein shot off his brown scalp in all directions. He wore a dirty, threadbare tweed suit, complete with elbow patches and a name-tag pinned to the jacket pocket that read, "Professor David Tyfoe."

"Where am I?" Tyfoe hollered. "Where you got me locked up?"

The reporter had stepped behind the counter, evidently not entirely believing her statement that this man was not dangerous.

"Maria, I need a handi-wipe. Get me one, pronto." When the reporter--who may or may not have been Maria--didn't move, Tyfoe's voice rose two octaves. "Now!" Her eyes became moist.

"Are you still on hold?" I asked. She nodded, her lips pursed as she fought back tears. She moved further back against the wall behind the counter.

David put both his paws on the counter, slapping it like a disgruntled customer I'd once seen in a bank. "Are you listening? I need a handi-wipe! What kind of assistant are you?"

I tapped his tensed shoulder, feeling the dustiness of the tweed beneath my finger. "Hey David?" He turned to face me; his brown irises seemed to pulse with manic energy. "I can get you handi-wipes. In fact, I'd like to take you out for a meal, if that's okay. What do you say?"

His mustached upper lip curled into an entitled snarl. "So long as we don't eat at the UC. The food there is for dogs." He gripped his lapels using the swift tug of a man straightening his suit for a night on the town. "I'll have a meal at Victor's."

"Sure, we'll go to Victor's."

Maria, or whatever her name was, shot me the universal sign for *no* by waving her hand back and forth across her throat and mouthing, "It's not open this early," from behind David's right shoulder.

"Hey, uh, David, perhaps we should pick another spot?"

He threw me another sneer along with an arched eyebrow. "Firstly, my moniker is Professor Tyfoe. Thirdly, young man, what is your name?"

"Boise Montague, sir."

"Very good, Boise. Victor's then, let's go." He formed a triangle using his arm and held it out to me. I shrugged, stuck my hand through, and tossed the keys to Maria over my shoulder. He escorted me out the door and hailed a cab.

As we started to get into the cab, I ran back inside after asking them to wait. The reporter was gathering her belongings and starting up the stairs into what I assumed was the main office area.

"Hey, wait," I tugged on her shoulder. She spun, a can of mace attached to her keychain held ready. "Whoa! Hey, easy tiger!" She glared at me, letting out a breath of relief. "I wanted you to come eat with us. What do you say? Meal on old Boise?"

Her serious demeanor held for a moment, then she cracked a smile. "All right, I'm prepared. What could go wrong?"

We trotted back outside to the waiting cab and piled in.

"To Victor's, my good sir," Tyfoe hollered at the driver as we flopped into the back seat.

After the meal, which we had to wait to eat because Victor's didn't open until eleven, Tyfoe insisted on staying in Sub Base.

"I shall journey back to the university from here, my friend. What did you say your name was?"

"Boise, sir."

He stuck out his hand after blowing his nose into a mint green handkerchief. "Well, Boise, I'm available for dinner, let's see." He pulled a crumpled stack of paper from his pocket, examined it, then returned it. "Yes, yes, on the last Thursday of April, my docket is open. How's that sound?"

"Sure," I said, knowing I'd probably never see this man again and, if I did, what were the chances he'd remember our dinner plans?

He leaned into the window of the waiting cab and sneered at the reporter, who had continued to let him call her Maria during lunch, "T-T-F-N Maria. Don't forget you owe me a business letter for Professor Humbolt by the end of the week."

She nodded.

As I re-entered the cab, Tyfoe waved vigorously before licking his palm and running his fingers through his frizzy mess of hair.

"My name's not Maria," was the first thing she said as we drove back to *The Daily News*.

"What is it?" I questioned.

"Dana. Dana Goode."

"Victor's is great," I said. "That place has been there a long time."

"It's an institution. At least the Professor has good taste. Was that really in your budget or do you need me to pay you back for my meal? I mean, what were you thinking?"

She started to pull cash out of her wallet but I stuck out my hand.

"I meant it, meal's on me. I have insurance money that'll last me at least a few months to a year, even with an occasional trip to Victor's. It's something my wife used to do. She'd invite some homeless woman to join us for a meal. Used to piss me off, but, well, I guess there's not much in this world a good meal can't fix, right? Maria is it?"

We arrived in front of *The Daily News*. Dana insisted on paying for the cab ride and I let her.

"I still owe you for that meal," Dana said as we picked our way to the back of a room full of desks, only a few of which were occupied.

I shooed the thought away with a wave of my hand, "Pshaw. We're all good. Dana. Fits better than Maria."

"Cool, all right. See ya later. Thanks for stopping by."

"Really?" I chimed.

"No! I really owe you. The way you handled that guy, he's always sneaking into our basement. You also saved us money on the cop call. I'll give you twenty minutes." She adjusted her Carnegie Mellon hat, pulling some strawberry hair that had escaped back through the loop.

"Very generous," I chuckled.

Her mischievous nature sparkled in her gray eyes. "I'm intrigued by a man who will take a smelly, unstable bum to dinner and convinces me to join the party. You could be fun."

Squinting at her, I tried to make sense of this woman. She was bold. Her clothes and demeanor told me that before we even spoke. A flowing, cotton wrap covered a very practical, cream-colored tank-top featuring a sparkling tiger swirling and growling. She wore tight jeans that tapered around her slender legs. Her shoes were a weird, platform-type sneaker made of baby-blue canvas and white, vinyl trim. She was a small woman, but the funky sneakers made her taller, lending her more authority.

"If I remember correctly from this morning, it sounds like your research goes back a ways--so we have to pull out the box files and search manually through the old papers."

We trudged down to the room where we'd first met. Standing outside the door Tyfoe burst through, I knew his entrance was something I'd never forget.

"Do you know how he gets in there?"

She adjusted the strap on the African-style basket purse she seemed to keep on her shoulder at all times. "Nope. He's got some way of getting in. When you're homeless, you have a lot of ingenuity for breaking and entering," she said, opening the door we'd left unlocked after freeing the professor earlier. "Anyway, I don't want to think about Tyfoe. What's your research about?"

I ducked to keep from hitting my head. I stood a solid five-six and my panama hat scraped under the concrete doorway. White boxes lined the linoleum floor, stacked upon wooden pallets that looked like they were pilfered from a grocery store.

"Are you an archivist?" I asked.

She threw her head back and laughed. "That's a good one. Organization's not my strength. What's the story about?"

"A friend of mine was killed in a gang incident."

"Was he in the gang? Most of the gang stuff is inter-gang politics, but sometimes it spills out to the civvies."

She pulled some gum out of her large purse and offered me a piece.

"No thanks," I said.

She removed the paper wrapping and popped a piece in her mouth. I could smell the mint as she chewed.

"Was your friend in a gang or doing drugs?" she asked.

"Probably both."

"Nice. Sounds like a good friend."

"He was. I hadn't seen him in many years." I wiped a drop of sweat off my forehead. "You guys have AC?"

"You're not up on the crisis in the newspaper business, are you? Where are you coming from?"

"I'm just an innocent citizen looking for information," I said.

She threw her head back and laughed again, but this one was more contrived. "Innocent. I don't think anyone's innocent and human interactions are mostly about power and potential violence. That's why I always carry these."

She pulled out the red cylinder of mace covered in imitation jewels she'd brandished earlier. Next she pulled out a silver and black box that looked like it could pinch you.

"Yes, I see that you take defense seriously. Women should do that."

"See, I was right to be wary of you. Military?"

"No, just lived in L.A." I said with a wry smile.

"The mystery deepens. Quick, what brand is my taser?" After sticking the mace back into her purse, she held up the pincher-box, covering the label with her unmanicured hand.

"I really don't want to play games. Is it possible to see the clippings from about four years ago?" I said.

"Answer the question," she shot back.

"Taser's the brand," I said.

She frowned dramatically. "You are absolutely no fun." She kept the Taser in her hand and started motioning toward the boxes with it. "So, this is where…"

"Do you think I'm going to try something?"

She stopped and swung around in an athletic manner like she'd grown up with older brothers. "You're too slow to even make a move on me, Jabuti."

I glared at her. "I'm sensitive about my girth. You mind not teasing me about that? I'm generally in shape, it's just lately I lost interest."

"It's not a comment about being fat. It's about being slow. Jabuti's a tortoise. Do you play the flute?" she asked and winked.

"Are you flirting with me?"

"I prefer girls, but I've tolerated men now and again."

"Flirting doesn't mean we're going to get together," I said.

"You're cute. Lose a couple pounds, the ladies will swoon for those green eyes and that caramel skin. You could wear a nicer t-shirt too, just sayin.'"

"Thanks for the fashion tips, Anna Wintour," I mumbled.

She motioned again toward the stacks of boxes.

"Each pallet represents a five-year period. Each box has two months in it. We publish six days per week. What years do you want?"

I looked at the medium-sized room with no windows and fluorescent lights. My heart ached as I thought of sitting on my knees, fingers covered in black newsprint, searching for Roger's mug in these time capsules.

"This is all that's left of him," I muttered.

"What was that, Jabuti?" Dana asked.

I weighed my next question, knowing that I would be letting a reporter into my inquiry. I had a good feeling about her integrity from her no-nonsense attitude. I hoped my instincts were correct.

"Dana, you're the one who had a story in today's paper about the governor, right?" I had read a story by her in the paper I purchased. I felt good about being in her hands.

"A story with my name on it. What was left of it." She said the last part with a mix of resentment and sarcasm.

"I'm trying to find out details on the death of this childhood friend of mine. I just got back on island. I went by his house to see him and it was deserted. A neighbor said he died and pointed me to his grave."

My eyes became hot marbles burning inside my head. Why'd my only friend have to become a drug dealer and end up dead? Why hadn't anyone told me? It hit me. I'd abandoned him. No one told me because I moved away with barely a glance back. I never visited. Never called. Never even tried Facebook.

I raised my eyes to the paneled ceiling, fighting the tears I didn't want to shed in front of this stranger. Blinking profusely, my next words came out in a high-pitched, choked tone.

"The date on the grave was December 24th, 2011. Can you point me to that week?"

Dana looked away at a stack of boxes, respecting my privacy. For this I already liked her.

Instead of the usual question people asked about whether I was okay, she continued along our original line of discussion as if nothing were amiss.

"Are you talking about Roger Black?"

"Yes!" My exclamation magnified in the confined space. "You wrote a story on his murder, didn't you?" I asked, happy my instincts had led me to her.

"I wrote stories."

"I knew it! I mean, I had a feeling you were the one who covered his case."

"Why?" she asked.

"Just a feeling. Just a feeling." My instincts were working. I felt a jolt of adrenaline that I'd somehow found someone who had real information on Roger.

"Well, there aren't that many of us, so the odds weren't long. You don't need to be down here. Let's go up to my desk."

We reached the more humane existence of the main reporters' room. The uninviting opaque windows diffused the bright spring sunlight. I yawned. The Folger's instant coffee I'd slugged down at seven was wearing off. A giant clock that hung above the reporter's bullpen like a watchful eye read 8:45AM.

Below the clock, like the black grease on a footballer's face, was a faded black-and-white sign that read, "The news never sleeps."

"Boise, I'm a reporter. I get paid to notice things. Can I tell you what I notice about you?" Dana asked, taking some of the bluster out of her repartee.

"We need to go have a drink if you are going to do that," I quipped.

"I'm taken."

"I didn't mean that. I'm not hitting on you!" I forced myself to maintain eye contact, but I couldn't help noticing a tiny bit of black bra and tanned skin.

"I know, but it's hard not to have a little fun at your expense. Relax."

"Sure thing, Ms. Goode. I'm relaxed." I leaned against the wall and crossed my feet like I was waiting for the bus.

She dropped into her squeaky wooden swivel chair. "Go take that crappy chair from Givens' desk." She pointed at an even more abused reclining swivel chair the next desk over.

I pulled it beside her and sat down, almost losing my balance in the process, but righting myself. I leaned forward to offset the busted springs.

"You seem nervous, a sign that whatever it is you're looking for here is out of your league," she continued.

"I respect your journalistic observations, but I'd really just like to look at anything you have on Roger."

"Okay, let me set you straight on a couple of things, Mr. Montague. I'm a reporter, not a journalist. Journalists write and I guess journal about things. I report. I see what happens and report exactly what I see as close to the original, objective event as I can. A word camera."

I nodded.

"Now, the second thing is, if you want to see Roger Black's file, you've got to abide my observations because as a reporter, they're all I have in this life." She leaned back and laid her hands in her lap.

We stared at each other a while until I finally spoke. "Okay, Ms. Goode, tell me about myself."

"You're depressed. I don't mean that in the typical sense, as in someone says you're depressed, but they mean you're unhappy. I don't know what you are, but I know whatever you should be feeling, you're pushing down that feeling like a button you've permanently got your finger on."

I nodded at her. "Okay, observation accepted. May I see the file?"

"Eventually you'll nod off and let your finger off the button unannounced. Then, boom." She spread her fingers apart like I'd seen the kids in Emancipation Park do with the exploding fist bumps they used to greet each other.

She unlocked a drawer to her left, took out a manila file folder, and placed it on top of the papers already littering her desk. A photo of a four- or five-year-old girl with a smattering of teeth and curly brown hair sat on top of the file. Dana snatched the photo away and dropped it back into her desk drawer.

I picked up the file. "You know, my parents didn't give me tons of wisdom, but a few gems stayed with me. 'Let people be who they are' was a good one."

She laced her fingers together, put her hands over her head, and cracked her knuckles. "I like it. Sounds like something a ten-year-old girl once said to me."

I pointed at the desk where I'd gotten the chair. "Can I sit at," I snapped my fingers, "Giver's desk and read this? You're not going to let me take this with me, right?"

"Her name's Givens. Yeah, sit there. I have some reporting to do."

She pulled her laptop out as I plopped the file onto the chair and rolled it back to Givens' desk. The file was thin, which was good and bad. Good because I was still weary from the flight and didn't relish digesting vast sums of information. Bad because less information meant fewer leads.

"Is this everything?" I asked after skimming the file for three minutes.

She ignored me, staring at the Apple's screen with the intensity of a cheetah. I started to say it again louder, but thought better of it, since the first thing she'd ask was whether I'd carefully read what I had already.

Roger died in a violent manner on a Saturday night. Christmas Eve. A photo appeared in the top left of the article with his red-tinged black hair in loose curls blowing in the wind. He'd been a good-looking guy. The picture captured that mischievous look ever-present in his devilish smile.

I was no better. In fact, I was usually the one who decided to take things a little too far. Back in the day, Roger would come up with some prank like sitting on the flat roof of a building behind his house where we'd use our homemade sling-shots to shoot paperclips or bottle tops we scrounged from the dump at cars moving along a couple stories below. I'd lose interest after twenty minutes because we'd get no reaction and suggest we move onto something more exciting, like flinging small chunks of concrete.

Roger, not wanting to look like a wuss, would go along. As the size of the chunks grew, one of us would hit a car too hard. The brake lights would blaze up, halting traffic, forcing the other cars to honk, and bringing an angry driver out of his vehicle to see a scratched paint job or cracked back window.

We'd duck, then peek over the ledge to see the driver staring up at us like a CIA agent. We'd scramble away, laughing as shouts crawled over the roofline along with more honking. Roger would declare I was nuts. I'd say it was fun, to which he'd grudgingly agree.

Further along, the article said Roger was shot, then stabbed. Seven stab wounds to go with the gunshot to his upper back. The gunshot started the job, the stabbing finished it. It sounded like someone really wanted him dead.

***

My wife, Evelyn, had been killed by a car while she was riding her bike through the Ballona Wetlands on the coast in Los Angeles County. She'd fought a large land developer by the name of Richard Elliot, who kept saying he only wanted to develop a small portion of the wetlands into a housing project to alleviate the constant housing shortage in Los Angeles.

The county had given in.

Five years later, Elliot asked for more land to build another housing development. Evelyn, a curvy, fierce brunette with a passion for environmental protection, had started the Ballona Wetlands Protection Project (BWPP) specifically to stop this man. It became her life. Shortly before her death, she won a massive victory to stop further development for ten years.

The police believed it was a hit-and-run accident by a scared citizen who meant no harm. Had the driver stopped and called 911, that person might have saved my wife from a coma and eventual death.

I forced my attention back to Roger's undeniable murder. Black ink stained my fingertips. I wiped them on my shorts. According to the article, Roger was survived by his mother, Jacinta Black, his aunt, Lydia, and his older sister, Claudia. I hoped that wasn't everyone who'd survived.

"Do you have a copier or a scanner?" I said.

Dana continued to stare at the screen. I got up and tapped her shoulder. She jumped, as if coming out of a trance.

"You okay?" I asked.

"Fine, just on a deadline. What do you need?" she said.

Before I could answer, she leaned over to her purse and pulled out a pack of cigarettes. "Gonna have a smoke. Want one?"

"No, I want to make a copy of some of the articles in your file. I could scan it too, whatever's better for you," I said.

As she cupped her hand around a match to light her cigarette, a slender bald guy who walked like his spine had been fused strode through the door.

"Do I smell sulfur, Goode?" he shouted, charging toward us. "How many times I gotta tell you no smoking in the newsroom?"

Dana waved the match out, the unlit cigarette hanging from her bottom lip. Smoke drifted off the tip of the match into the man's face. He blinked behind his glasses, coughing. He didn't wave it away. He remained focused. Intense.

"Hey, boss." A theatrical grin broke across Dana's face. "Meet someone I'm working with on a story."

I stuck out my hand. He shifted his gaze up from Dana to meet my eyes. His demeanor instantly turned warm and pleasant as he gave me a too-firm handshake.

"Walter Pickering. I'm the editor of this fine newspaper. And you are?"

"My name is Boise, Mr. Pickering. I'm helping Dana out with a story. Nice to meet you, sir."

"No, no, sources are the life-blood of a newspaper, so please, call me Walter. You are a source, correct?"

"I guess I might be, sir. We're still hashing out the details of my knowledgeableness on our story," I said.

"Splendid. Excuse my gruff attitude, but you understand that the law prohibiting smoking inside work environments has now extended its reach all the way here to the islands. We don't follow all the mother-land rules, but I like this law."

As he said the last sentence, his eyes locked with Dana's. A tense silence followed, which I broke.

"Uh, where's the bathroom?"

"Why that's in the southwest corner, over there," Walter pointed.

"Thanks," I said, happy to escape the workplace tension.

I pushed the knobless door open, threw the tiny clasp inside across. A single-person bathroom with an old-fashioned pull towel dispenser and a white bar of Dove soap streaked black from so many hand washings. I prayed the black came from newsprint.

I stood over the toilet. A cute, little sign placed next to a spider plant in the window read, "If it's yellow, let it mellow. If it's brown, flush it down." I chuckled, thinking of the sign we used to have in our bathroom growing up. It had a flower in each corner: "In the land of fun and sun, we don't flush for number one."

I'd never seen wells or heard of the island having any ground water, so every drop of rain had to be captured in cisterns. I leaned against the door, my wet hands dripping down the white washed wood, as I pressed my ear against the doorjamb. I heard small clicks. I opened the door a crack and peeked out. Dana tapped away. Walter must have retreated into his office.

Dana looked up. "Did mommy and daddy scare you?"

"I'm going to read the rest of the file and be on my way. What about copies?" I asked, holding up the papers I'd left sitting on Givens' desk.

She dropped her gaze back to her laptop and simultaneously pointed to the far corner.

"My code is six-six-six," she said.

I made copies, read the rest of her file, and said good-bye. Goode had lost her words. Right as I was about to hit the street, she came out behind me.

"Just walk," she said.

She glanced around periodically. We reached Market Square where vendors stood upon a red concrete stage surrounded by columns, hocking all sorts of agricultural goods. She pulled me to a wall behind a parked car, out of earshot of the milling shoppers.

"We have an agreement, you understand?"

"I'm sorry?" I said.

"Remember Walter asking if you were a source? Well, you are. You're my source on this. Are you going to be investigating…things…as your source of revenue?" She questioned, her gray eyes boring into me.

"I don't know. I've been here for one day. Roger's a friend. No one's paying me for this."

"You must have other friends. What makes Roger so special?"

"I learned to ride a bike next to this guy. I spent my youth flinging rocks and playing stick ball with him," I said.

"Roger Black…" she stopped and looked around again. "He…interests me too, okay?"

We stared at each other like islands on the ocean, looking across a calm surface with many living secrets beneath.

"You're not going to tell me why you have a thing for this murder?" I said.

"Sure. I wrote the articles, interviewed the witnesses. It looked open and shut. A gang guy gets whacked for doing gang shit. Simple. Too simple. I've been in this game a long time. This story never added up, but I've had other things to do. The case went into storage, but not all the way. For two years, I've felt like I bullshitted my way through." She paused to survey the scene again. A stray mutt with matted hair trotted by. "St. Thomas isn't Eden, but this one felt like the end of innocence. I felt like figuring out the right answer could at least give us back some semblance of trust."

"Do you mean that Roger's death led to other things around here?" I asked.

"Murder's not a little thing. Even in a place the size of New York City, one murder can cause massive changes. Murder happens when someone's decided a person can no longer be dealt with and the only solution is to get rid of the problem," she said. "It's like one of those knots in your fishing line where you try to untangle it, but can't, so you take your knife and slice through the whole mess. You sacrifice the line so you can start fishing again."

I put my hand on her shoulder. "Dana, I'm hungry, is there a point to this?"

She looked around again and swallowed. "Do you know about our governor?"

"A little. I read your article from a couple days ago," I said. "Well written."

She met my eyes. "Gimme a fuckin' break Boise. I'm here to expose things. That article was political garbage just to fill space and keep our advertisers comfortable. It pays the bills." She pulled out a copy of *The Daily News* and pointed at the caption below the title. "What's that say?"

"A Pulitzer-Prize Winning Newspaper," I intoned.

"Let's walk," she said.

"Look Dana, I respect your professional goals, but I'm here to help a friend."

"He's not your friend, Boise. When was the last time you and Roger spoke? Did you know his gang handle? Did you know who his wife was?"

I grimaced. "I thought your article said he had no wife OR kids?"

"Exactly my point. What you know about your friend is from an article I wrote in a hurry without all the facts."

"He was my friend," I said. "Are we done?"

"I'm sorry. That was insensitive of me. You need me and I need you. The governor…" she paused and looked around again, but no one paid attention. The smell of urine drifted into my nose. "The governor's a bad guy. He used this murder to justify a local war on drugs. He runs this place like it's his own private domain."

"The U.S. owns this island," I said.

"You think the U.S. government puts our business high on its list of priorities? We're imperial backwash. Our citizens don't have a vote, so what's the motivation? As long as Abbey James doesn't start shooting people in the street..." she shrugged. "Please, if you find anything, I need to report it."

"Why'd you point out the Pulitzer Prize caption?" I asked. "It makes you seem selfish."

"We're all selfish. You feel bad that you weren't here for your friend. You need to find the killer for your own peace of mind. I want you to know that I have skin in the game outside of helping the people."

I tilted my head back and felt the tropical sun bake my face. I pointed my chin at the market stage. "There used to be planters with palm trees on the corners."

"Things change, Boise. Here's my card. Call if you need more info or have something for me. I'll help you on this." She looked at me hard, her eyes piercing mine like needles. "I know we were just covering with Walter when I said we're working together back at my office, but I wouldn't mind finding out what really happened. This place needs people like you. Depressed, half-bearded handsome men who feed the homeless are hard to find."

CHAPTER 6

The cinderblock motel would have bled me dry. If I was going to continue living off my dead wife's insurance payout, I needed more permanent, cheaper accommodations. I'd spent the first week here eating and drinking beers. The skin around my stomach ached from pushing against my jeans. Sucking in as I walked toward Bluebeard's Hill alleviated some of the discomfort.

The sun shone bright in my eyes as I pulled my rolling luggage along behind and flung my puke-green duffle bag over my shoulder. Like a battering ram, my bag banged against the shoulders of tourists who wandered in and out of glittering shops, faces turned up, oblivious to everything without a duty-free sign on it.

Thirty-six steps made of brick and concrete over arched openings used for storage in colonial times got me to the entrance. In my youth, I'd played hide-and-seek inside those same passages. They still smelled of bums who slept there at night.

A glorious, Spanish-era wrought-iron chandelier hung overhead as I stood in what I supposed was the lobby of the West Indian Manner. An ice machine hummed behind the counter to the right as I rang the welcome bell.

"Hello." A copper-skinned woman with petite breasts called out from the bottom of the steps leading to the second floor. She sauntered around the counter like a mermaid gliding through water. "I help you?"

"Yes. You have any rooms?"

"How long you visitin' for?"

"I don't know," I said. "How about indefinitely, depending on the price? Do you have a monthly rate?"

"We have rooms rented out by da week. I's one-fifty a week. We give new linen and sheets a week. If you wan' twice a week service, add twenty-five. We need a deposit of t'ree hundred."

She turned around to get a key off its hook. I leaned over the counter to glance at the ledger. There weren't many names on it.

"I don' know if I can afford dat," I said.

"You local?"

"I used to live up behin' here. Da house gone now," I said.

"I could give you a local discount. One-twenty-five wid two times a week service."

I nodded.

She called out, "Marge, we got a cust-a-ma." She turned back to me. "I Lucy. Marge and me a couple, you know, lesbian. You okay wid dat?"

"Yeah, no problem," I said as a burly woman in a muumuu appeared.

Lucy glanced at my check-in slip. "Show Mr. Montague to room eighteen. Come down for a drink lata, Mista Montague, my treat."

She opened the door next to the check-in booth, revealing a large, mahogany bar. Three customers hunched over amber-colored beverages in the dark room.

"T'anks, I will," I muttered.

Marge barely glanced at me. No wonder Lucy greeted and closed the sale before Marge appeared. Lucy accepted a hundred and twenty-five dollars, plus the deposit, from me.

I trudged up another sixteen stairs after Marge.

We walked in silence. It seemed Marge wasn't particularly keen on speech. Later I learned that she wasn't mute, but had an abiding belief in making noise only when absolutely necessary. When she made noise, you listened.

Marge flipped on the ceiling fan and left. I dropped my bag on the shag carpet. A window looked out on the town below. I felt safe in this Spartan room for the first time since I'd discovered Roger was gone. Light-colored stains dotted the beige carpet. Paneled faux wood adorned the walls--a throw-back to the seventies.

I tried not to think about my tiny, vanished, seventies house. Every time I turned around, my hopes for signs of my old life were dashed like ships on a reef.

I pried open the splintering wooden louvers. Lazy palm fronds swayed in the yard below. I laid back on the golden sheets and fell into a dreamless sleep.

CHAPTER 7

The next day Dana sat at her desk, eyes stuck to the laptop as usual. Appropriating Givens' chair once more, I parked it in front of Dana's desk. Her eyes twinkled mischievously.

Two other journalists were in residence. One whispered on the phone, glancing my way suspiciously every now and again. The other rested his feet on his desk. His bald head glimmered under the fluorescent lights. He wore a long-sleeved shirt and slacks despite ninety-degree heat. A desk fan blew right at his face. He squinted against the blast as he read what appeared to be a 2015 Virgin Islands Water & Power Authority report.

"Hey, Boise!" Dana yelled.

"What! Don't yell. I'm right here." I said. "Too early for that."

"I said your name twice before I yelled. I was about to shake you," Dana said. "What are you doing here?"

"I got you doughnuts." I produced a pink paper bag and set it on her desk. "Got a half dozen," I said, taking a glazed for myself. "Not sure what you like."

"I'm avoiding sugar." She held up her coffee mug. "Diet Coke." She whistled and the two reporters dropped what they were doing. Each examined the bag, snatched two doughnuts, and returned to their desks.

"I like the way you think. I trust the ones here," she said. "We'll try to meet discreetly, but no promises. Being discreet takes a lot of extra time. Time I don't have." She reached under her desk. "I bought you a gift."

She handed me a brown paper bag. A cheap looking flip phone lay in the bottom.

"Is there something you haven't told me, Dana?"

She smiled, took a sip of Diet Coke. "What did you glean from the file?"

"Your file has a lot of fluff. Did you write a piece for *People*?"

She smacked my hand playfully. "You take that back. Sometimes you have to put the mark at ease and sit back," she said. "Start with what's in the file. There's stuff there. Think of it as your job interview. If you get something based on that info, I'll feed you more."

"What's this gig pay?"

She reached under her desk, brought up a long red wallet. A fresh one-dollar bill appeared in her hand and she slid it across to me.

"Is there more where this came from?" I asked, slipping it into my pocket.

"Lots more. In fact, I can promise, if we get to the bottom of this aquarium, there's at least one more of those with your name on it."

"How can I refuse such an offer?"

"Bring me a story, and quick, Jabuti."

CHAPTER 8

The sea air battered against the side of my face. Foam rose and fell like snow on tiny mountain tops. Dana's file listed Roger's attorney, so I headed there in hopes of getting more information.

Passing the newer courthouses, I circled up around the Danish buildings lining the end of Main Street. Bluebeard's Castle towered overhead, nestled among flowering greenery. The burnt-sienna roof of Roger's house poked out of the bushes below Bluebeard's Castle.

A flight of stairs wound up the side of a two-story building to a sign that read: "Miguela Salas, J.D., Attorney at Law." The lettering was plain, even humble, making me wonder why Roger hired a woman.

Roger didn't like women, even when I knew him. He'd resented his mother for moving in with an alcoholic drug-addict down the street and leaving him in the care of his overly-protective grandmother and macho-man grandfather. He complained all the time that she never gave him any money.

He once grumbled to me when he came out of his mother's house, "I fuckin' hate dat woman. I hate she. She stupid." He'd been rubbing his eyes frantically wiping away tears.

That's strong stuff to say about your own mother. When his sister attempted to play with us, he shooed her away with a kick in the ass.

"No girls," he hissed.

Hell, we even spray-painted those exact words on the outside of our clubhouse, a lean-to we'd set up using discarded pieces of galvanized metal and wood scrapped from a junkyard down the street after Hurricane Hugo. I knocked after looking over my shoulder. I could see all the way down the street to the large Lutheran Church I'd attended until third grade. A lone drunkard in ragged clothes and tattered shoes lurched toward a fast-food chicken stand. Otherwise, the street was deserted. I knocked again, noticing a doorbell button low down on my left. I pressed it but heard nothing. Moments later, the door lurched open. A middle-aged Puerto Rican woman with chipmunk cheeks appeared. She had a dissociated look on her face.

"Yes, can I be of service?"

"I'm here to see Ms. Salas," I said, grinning like a weather man.

"Yes. What do you want?"

"I'd…may I come in?" I asked.

"No."

Well, with her winning personality, I saw exactly what Roger must have seen in her: a woman who didn't care what anyone thought--a.k.a. the perfect lawyer.

"Is there a reason you didn't answer when I knocked?" I asked.

"Yes," she said, her eyes vacant as an eight ball.

A moped puttered by, slowed at the corner, zipped off.

"What do you want?" she repeated.

"Oh right, I was just admiring your door and your sign's font. I like it."

After a beat, she shut the door in my face. I knocked. Knowing she was inside and knowing not many people had the guts to ignore someone standing outside their door for long, I waited.

Finally, I yelled through the door, "I'm Boise Montague. I just want to ask a few questions about someone who passed away a while back."

Nothing happened. From my battered wallet I extracted Evelyn's photo. Dropping down, I slumped on the steps. In the photo, Evelyn was waving me away because she didn't like having her picture taken. Her black hair blew backwards revealing her slender neckline and milky skin. Her lips sparkled red from a lip gloss she'd applied moments before. In the background you could make out the Santa Monica Pier.

"What are you doing?"

Salas was standing at the top of the stairs, hands on her ample hips. Her short-cropped hair swooped about her forehead in the wind. The haircut made her tea-colored face look fatter than it actually was. I stashed the photo away.

"Who were you looking at?" she persisted.

"Nothing. I'll get off your steps." I started to descend.

"If you tell me who you were looking at, I'll tell you what I can about Roger."

"How did you--"

She held up a crumpled piece of note paper I recognized as my to do list for the day and some of the notes about people I'd looked up online.

"You dropped this," she said.

The sky darkened as I contemplated sharing my wife and our marital history with this cold stranger.

"I'm trying to figure out what happened to Roger Black. Why he died. I mean, beyond him just being part of the gang-slash-drug world here," I said.

She stood unnaturally still, one hand on her hip and one frozen in the air holding the fluttering sheet of paper. Rain fell. Heavy drops pelted us. She remained still, so I climbed the stairs between us and snatched my note away, stuffing it back into my pocket.

She spun on her flats and I followed her into the office. A lone banker's lamp illuminated her paperwork and an iPad and a laptop sat atop a large mahogany desk. Compared to the ones I'd frequented as an investigator in Los Angeles, her legal office was spartan. Absent were the large beige and red tomes numbered like encyclopedias.

"Where are your law books?"

"My questions first, then I'll discuss Roger to the extent I am comfortable. You may answer now."

She sat, looking at me like a petulant puppy.

My memory felt sluggish. I visualized our stairway encounter in the rain, feeling the gusting wind and watching my note flap like a flag. Then it came to me.

"It's a photo of my wife," I replied.

"You looked like you were trying to remember who she was," Miguela said.

"Something like that I suppose," I replied.

Her brown eyes bored into me. It felt like she could see my blood vessels and naked skull right through my skin. Uncomfortable with the silent interrogation, I glanced away.

"Are you going to confess that she's dead or that she left you for another?"

"She did not leave me!" I startled myself with a shout that ricocheted off the walls in the tight room.

"I'm sorry she's dead," she said.

Three deep breaths, counting them.

"I'm going to look at my screen again so you don't feel uncomfortable composing yourself. This wound is still fresh. Did she die in the last year?"

"Just over a year ago."

"Today is April ninth. Did she die in March or February?" she asked.

"She died on March twenty-second. Do you want the fucking time of day?" I asked.

"No, not now. You appear distraught. I'm pushing your emotional boundaries."

"Yeah, you could say that. You got any beer?"

"No. Mr. Montague, this is my office, it is not a bar, grill, or restaurant. I have bottled water. Would you like some?"

I leered at her. "Sure, esquire. Whatever's handy."

She handed me an ordinary bottled water bearing a local brand. No doubt somebody using a label maker and tap water to charge everyone four-fifty. It declared something about being from a spring in Jamaica.

"Can you please tell me about Roger now? Quid pro quo," I said while twisting the top off my water.

"You know Latin?"

"It's from a movie," I said.

"I don't watch movies."

"What do you do?" I asked, realizing I was thirsty and taking a swig. Rain *tink-tinked* on the galvanized roof, providing a soft background symphony to our jagged conversation.

"Yes. I listen to music and work." Miguela opened up a desk drawer to her right and held up a large pair of headphones plugged into her iPad. "This is why you cannot knock on my door and get an answer. When you ring the doorbell, that light comes on and I can decide whether I wish to answer."

A large red light resembling a police siren hung above the door.

"It really gets my attention, but sound does not. I have another question for you."

I groaned. "Hold on, you never told me anything about Roger."

"No, I answered another. My turn." She waited, clearly not willing to give any ground on this.

"What is it?" I said impatiently.

"What was her name?"

"Can we stop talking about my wife?" I said. "Ask me something else."

She stood up. "It was nice meeting you, Mr. Montague. I have work to do. Perhaps we'll meet again." She held out her hand in a businesslike fashion.

"Her name was Evelyn."

"Okay, your turn. Ask about Roger," she said, pulling a black file folder from her desk.

"Is that his file?"

She shoved her laptop aside, closing the lid. She placed the file on her blotter.

"Yes, it is." She tapped the file with her index finger. "Black is for dead."

"Could I look at it? It would save us having to do so much talking," I said.

"No. Mr. Montague, most of what is in this file will not bear on your, what should I call it? An investigation. It is still considered confidential by me, if not the law."

"Okay, talking it is. Could you tell me about him? What was your impression? What kind of a guy was he? Did you like him?"

"Yes, those things are not in the file. See, we need to talk. Roger was not a good man in a moral sense. He was driven to have money. He was avaricious, but more than that, he wanted respect. He thought money was part of it, but not all of it. I have no doubt that Roger had many enemies. He did not like killing, but to advance his business, he would do what was necessary. In his case, sometimes that meant doing unsavory things."

"Did that make representing him challenging?" I asked.

"No," Miguela said.

"So, you knew his business from the beginning?"

"I work and live in this neighborhood. Everyone knew Roger's business, if you paid attention." She paused for effect, "Mira," she muttered the Spanish word for *look*, "he wanted to be famous as much as allowable and not go to jail."

"Did he owe you money when he died?" I asked.

"Yes, a lot," she said. "I got a little out of his estate, but I came out on the short side of that transaction. My motive for killing Roger was not strong."

"Anyone else come to mind with motive or not?" I said.

"Why 'or not?'" she asked.

"Motive's not always obvious and sometimes people die by mistake. For example, he could have been killed by friendly fire during a battle between gangs by his own deputy," I opined.

"So you think he was stabbed seven times after being shot in the back by a friendly?"

"Just an example," I admitted. "So, anyone who jumps to mind?"

"Yes," she stared off, slipping on her headphones. She clicked a button after opening her laptop again. I sat for a whole minute, contemplating my next beer as rain pattered. Here wasn't here anymore. The St. Thomas I knew died long ago, even longer ago than Roger. Maybe I'd changed so profoundly in California that the whole world felt like a strange land. I heard a noise through my fog.

"Mr. Montague? Mr. Montague? Can you hear me?" Miguela asked.

"Sorry, I'm here."

"Here are the people I'm willing to give you who are relevant at this time."

She handed me a paper. Four names. "Do you have any idea where I can locate these people?"

"Yes." She leaned over, typing rapidly, very rapidly, into her computer. Exactly twenty seconds later another page printed. She reached behind herself without looking and handed it over.

"Nice trick. Behind the back printing," I joked.

"I think our interview has concluded," she said, standing. Her chair rolled away from her legs and bumped lightly against the wall.

"Well, uh, yeah. Thanks. If I need a little more background, can I call or stop by again?"

"Yes, you may do either."

My hand hung in the empty air for a couple seconds until I realized how silly I looked and dropped it to my side. Another quirk of Ms. Salas. The wad of paper in my jeans felt like a large tumor expanding in my pocket. Roger's death was becoming a project.

CHAPTER 9

The V.I. Daily News bustled with reporters darting in and out of Pickering's office. He sat bolt upright behind a dark mahogany desk. A wooden business card holder in the corner blended into the décor like a knot in a tree. Through his wide-open door his subjects came and went. He surveyed his kingdom.

"Hi, Mr. Pickering. I'm looking for Dana. You remember me? Boise. She left me a message to meet her here yesterday."

He squinted. "Riiiight, the new source. Hello, Boise." He pumped my hand without standing. "What can I do for you?"

"Dana? I was looking for her," I repeated.

"Yes, she's at the police station. She wants anyone looking for her to meet her there. Good luck, I have reporters waiting to talk to me."

Pivoting, I almost plowed into one of said reporters. Apologizing, I scurried out the door. I thought about what we could do to gain access to the files on the victims. One idea after another entered my thoughts, but I discarded them as each scenario presented a trace and capture likelihood that resulted in me having an even more screwed up life than I had when I left Los Angeles.

My personal cell buzzed. Wondering who would call me at this point, I pulled it out. None of my friends had heard from me in over a year because I could not take the human reminders that Evelyn would never go out with me again. The sympathetic, and sometimes pathetic, looks I got from friends whenever they took me out to "have a good time" ensured I'd never have a good time. In fact, being in a good time made my pain flare. I wanted to be left alone or, better yet, find myself distracted by a problem that had no ties to my California life. I clicked the red *ignore* button on a number I didn't recognize.

Then, the flip phone Dana had given me rang.

"There's a killer here who I believe came from the Southern U.S. to kill black people. We're mostly black, so the pattern goes unnoticed. Or maybe it's because they're the poor. Either way, it's happening and our governor and police chief are turning the other cheek. Why? Because we don't have any real detectives here and they don't want the tourists freaking out like the navy."

"The navy?"

She sighed. "Yeah, back in the eighties, the navy stopped taking leave here because a bunch of seamen were killed and nothing was ever done. Put a big hurt on the economy for ten years."

"Where are you?"

"Watching from a safe distance. I bet you're wondering why I had you meet me here?"

"Dana, I'm hung over, so spill it."

A yellow brick building loomed in front of me. "POLICE" in black stenciled letters covered a white, plywood sign bolted to the right of the entrance.

"You are going into the police station and you're gonna figure a way into the chief's office. I have it on good authority that the tourist-sensitive cases are kept in a file cabinet behind his desk, or who knows, it might be even easier than that."

"Sneak attack, huh?" I said.

"You said you wanted to help. Do you want to help?" Dana hesitated, then continued, "I spoke to Mike Howard, a contact in L.A. He knows you. Said you're a gun-slinger with a conscience. Is he right?"

On the other hand, what did I have to lose? No one I cared about was left except my mother. I counted her as someone I cared about mostly because she gave birth to me and reminded me constantly of how much she had sacrificed to bring me into this world.

My ass hurt. I popped a pill in my dry mouth. If you've ever had colitis, you know sometimes you have to take a dump very suddenly, like a big bubble swelling inside you that needs to pop. Bolting inside the police station, I demanded the bathroom for real.

Chapter 10

Inching out of the bathroom, no plan for what to do, I glanced around the booking area while the receptionist ignored me and clicked her gum simultaneously. I sat, pulling out my flip phone and started a text.

"Na-ah," the receptionist said as I started to type.

After slipping the phone into my pocket, she continued to stare at me. "You need somet'ing?"

"Uh, no, no, not yet. I'm waiting for my wife. She's parking." I pointed out the glass door. The receptionist frowned at me. A phone rang, but not the land line. It sounded like a cell beneath her desk. She answered it, but I couldn't hear her.

"Oh, so what about the sign?" She ignored me, whispering into the receiver. Hanging up, she marched into the waiting area.

After adjusting a couple chairs she mumbled, "Stay right there. I back soon. Five minutes."

She walked toward the bathrooms. Her huge rear end arched so wide she tapped the walls of the hall with each step. I looked at the door leading into the inner offices. It was ajar.

My phone buzzed. A text said, "Go, dummy." Tiptoeing past the receptionist's desk into the office area, I came to a door marked "Chief of Police." The door was unlocked. Files rested on top of the desk, open. Evidently, the chief thought these killings were related because they were in files of the same color. I snapped photos on my phone of as many pages as I dared from each file. The toilet flushed.

Dana waited in Emancipation Park a few blocks away. "Did you get it?" she asked.

She scrolled through the photos, her face lighting up while she nodded her approval.

"Good start, Boise. Good start," she said, texting the photos to herself. "Let's go."

"Is she a source?" I asked.

"I don't reveal sources. I won't reveal you either. Regardless, we are in this together now, so if you ever expose someone I work with, I will expose you." She glared at me, like a poker player trying to read a bluff. "Understand?"

"I'm hungry. Breaking into high ranking officials' offices gives me cravings." I grinned at her serious countenance. "You're buying."

CHAPTER 11

A "Do Not Disturb" sign hung on my doorknob while I wallowed in self-pity for days, drinking beer from an ice bucket. April sixth, my birthday. When it came and went I managed to ignore it, but it snuck back up on me like a red ant. I didn't hate it for the usual reasons: getting older or fearing that no one would care. I hated it because when we were happy, Evelyn made a big deal of it.

One year she bought me the Gorillaz vinyl, a rap-rock-electronic style band of animated hoodlums who made the best music this side of Led Zeppelin. She hated rap and didn't much care for rock. She loved ballads by Celine Dion and cheesy love songs by Manilow or Michael Bolton.

She had spent our dating years teasing me about my typical-guy choices in music, but once we were married, that changed. From then on, every birthday, she would find and go to any concert for me and dance out to the music as if it were the best she'd ever heard.

Since she passed, I'm reminded I'd never been that selfless. I vowed to spend every birthday listening to ballads by Bolton and other Vegas stylings from Tom Jones and Dionne Warwick, after volunteering at a local environmental cause. It was better than drinking beer for hours while I lamented the shattered remnants of my life.

Putting down the beer, I picked myself up to check both phones. A dozen missed calls on the Dana Phone. I had to find something environmental to do and upload some of Evelyn's horrible music to the replacement phone I'd bought after smashing the last one to bits on dirty gravel in the Ballona Wetlands. Did I still want to continue this birthday idea despite what I'd learned investigating my Evelyn's death?

A loud knock filtered through my hazy consciousness and the swirling sounds of the ceiling fan.

"Do not disturb!" I yelled. "Go 'way."

More pounding, this time for a full twenty seconds. "Boise, I know you're there." Dana. "Don't make me come in fa true. I have Lucy out here and she will let me in."

"Go away. Makin' plans. Gotta plan." I croaked.

"Boise, we can smell your breath from out here. Open up, or we're coming in," Dana said.

"Suit yourself," I said.

Another swig of bucket beer, now warm and flat, then a loud belch quaked from my gut. The door creaked open.

"Je-sus! Boise, I gon' evict you if you don' let me clean dis place!" Lucy cried.

I grunted. "If you don't like the smell in here, leave."

Dana sighed. "Boise, we have a shitload of work piling up. Things are moving and I need you."

I opened the door and wandered down to the community bathroom.

Upon returning, I said, "All right, but not till the day after tomorrow. Do you know some environmental organization I can volunteer at today? Clean the beach or save the orcas or something?" I looked back and forth at their faces: the faces of children watching a drunk parent.

Lucy handed me a towel. "You even know you naked?"

Wrapping the towel around my waist, I repeated, "I told you to go away."

I plodded over and flopped onto the bed as Lucy left the room.

"I need your help today. Can you help me now and do your world-saving tomorrow? Huh?" Dana shrugged, both palms turned up.

"Boy, you are dramatic. What is it?"

Lucy returned, dragging a vacuum cleaner along with cleaning gloves. Dana motioned at Lucy. "It's okay, Lucy doesn't care about our top-secret business. Just tell me what you want," I repeated.

Dana let out a heavy breath as Lucy started the vacuum cleaner. She sat beside me on the bed. "Boise, I'll make sure that you can do a beach clean-up or whatever other crazy thing you desire tomorrow if you do me one solid today. Now, can you take a shower and meet me downstairs?"

CHAPTER 12

As we trotted down Main Street, Dana smiled at my disheveled appearance. "Did you move back here just so you wouldn't have to dress nicely?"

"What do you want me to do for free today?" I asked.

She pulled a single greenback from her purse and waved it at me. "Here, not free."

Snatching the bill, I said, "Does this mean I should have business cards printed?"

"You ain't limin' no more. You workin' freelance for da *Daily News*. Do you know how to take care of yourself?"

I stared at Lincoln's picture a long moment before crushing the fiver and stuffing it into my pocket. "Irrelevant. What are we doing today?"

Dana pulled a file out of her worn, leather satchel. "There's mention in here of only one specific address. These guys have the stench of racism based on names I've run across before. The location puts them on the side of the hill inhabited by our citizens of French and Danish ancestry. I'm hoping to catch these guys at home today. Everything else in here's written as if they are worried about the official report giving too much away, so it was hard to even piece this much together," she said. "Always, always keeping a lid on things for the tourists."

"I got the motive for hiding this stuff, but even in police reports? Seems excessive."

"Yeah, well, it's all political. You have a lot to learn about the government here," she said. "This is me," she pointed at a beat up dark blue Nissan Sentra.

"I hope we don't have to make a quick getaway."

"In that case, let's take your car." She glared at me. I got in.

She threw the standard transmission into reverse and ripped backwards, looking in the rearview mirror. I tensed and spun around to make sure no one was there. Before I could turn back around, we shot out of the parking lot. Gripping the edges of the cloth seat, I squeezed my eyes shut and said, "I guess a quick getaway won't be so hard after all."

CHAPTER 13

We jostled down a pock-marked hill, a blend of concrete and asphalt arranged in no discernible pattern. The steep slope ended at a stone wall surrounding a clutch of dilapidated houses on the other side. Weeds dominated the landscape as if the owners had been gone for a long time. However, the façade of one house had a fresh coat of paint and its galvanized roof glistened waxy silver.

We could turn right or left, but Dana didn't move. She shifted into neutral and applied the emergency brake. Tall blades of grass waved against the hillside. A tattered truck hauling surfboards in the bed rattled by and rambled down the hill to the right.

"What are we doing?" I asked.

Dana shushed me as she consulted a map. "I know it's not this far. We must have missed the turnoff back there by that house at the top." She threw the open map on my lap as a car honked then swung around us, also headed down to the right.

"Maybe we ought to spend the day at the beach," I suggested.

Dana flung around in a wide u-turn. Her car groaned in protest as we headed back up the hill.

"There!" She pointed to the right, her forearm almost hitting my nose.

Another overgrown property rested on the hill right above the road. The corner house featured crumbling concrete with rebar sticking out in some places. We swung onto the smaller lane, even more narrow and poorly paved than the hill down to Hull Bay. Tall blades of grass obscured our vision in both directions.

The blades were not like the friendly kind found on lawns throughout the United States. They resembled a true tropical species featuring tiny serrated edges. As a kid, I'd return from exploring my backyard covered in tiny cuts until I learned how to slip through the stuff without letting it slide along my skin. It dominated the countryside.

"Where are we going?"

Dana stopped the car and snatched the map off my lap.

"Are we working together on this?" I pulled the brim of my straw fedora lower to shield my eyes from the glaring sun. "Remember you asked for my help, right?"

She still said nothing, looking up the road then down at the map. She pointed at the map. "Do you think this is where we are?"

I looked at her finger. Many of the roads in St. Thomas were unnamed, but somehow she had gotten a more detailed road map that included lanes without any numbers or street signs.

"Where'd you get this?" I asked.

"I know someone at the post office," she said. She poked the map again. "Do you think this is right? Here's

Hull Bay and there's the intersection where we stopped before making the final turn down to the beach."

I looked at the map with more focus this time. "Looks like it to me."

"You mind walking uphill?"

She reversed to the end of the road then headed down the hill, all the way to Hull Bay. We parked on the sand adjacent to the boat ramp. This wasn't a powdery beach from the magazines. Boston Whalers dotted the shore and men untangled nets as they worked the sea.

Trapaco Point jutted out to the east. It separated Hull Bay from Magens Bay, a beach frequently featured on tourism magazine covers. To the west, the land moved in more gentle slopes and houses dotted the hillside. After a steep drop below the houses, another beach, this one gray with rocks and squawking sea gulls, lay deserted due to a reef surrounding the water there. The end of the reef, about half a mile out, stopped just inside another point. Small yet shapely waves peeled out of the water and rolled onto the shore.

A surfer rode a wave into the channel. As the wave petered out way inside, he dropped squarely onto his board. From experience, I knew he was being careful not to dip his feet into the shallow water for fear of scraping himself on jagged coral.

Recalling another life when I managed to paddle all the way out there to ride those same waves, I imagined the molecules of water beneath the boards that had travelled through the mouths of whales. A giant network of conductive material joining the entire planet. Surfing had made me feel connected to the world like nothing else. Nothing except young, naïve love. Maybe surfing was love.

"Hey! Boise, we gotta go, you done wave watching?"

For some reason I felt like sharing, so I said, "Surfing. Probably the only good thing my dad really ever did with me that made me feel like his son."

Dana looked like she didn't know what to say.

I shrugged and started back up Hull Bay Road. She followed. As we retraced our drive on foot, we skirted a small shack that passed for a bar and restaurant. Trees canopied the establishment and the faint sounds of a basketball game emanated from a television inside.

I wanted to go in, sit and watch the game, and sip some brews. Instead we walked right on by, trudged up the hill, returning to the road we'd passed on the way down.

"What are we getting into here, Dana? Like specifics."

She sneezed, yanking a tissue out of her satchel. "I don't really know, just an address mentioned in the file."

"How do you have an address? That street doesn't seem to have a name. And why are we all the way down here."

"Like I said, I know someone at the post office. Looked it up for me." She sighed with some annoyance. "It doesn't matter. We want to get a look at who lives up there, perhaps get a photo of them. If no one's around, we want to get in, snap some photos, snoop around, get the hell out. I parked down here so if they spot us, they can't get my license plate. It'll be obvious if I park a strange car nearby. People like this get suspicious easily in my experience."

We walked in silence. After twenty minutes, Dana offered me a drink from her water bottle.

She snatched the bottle back mid-drink, causing water to dribble down my shirt. It felt good and we laughed. We finally arrived back at the small lane with the crumbling house on the corner where we'd turned around before heading down to Hull Bay. I was beginning to huff and puff.

"The house is somewhere up this road," Dana said. "See how deserted it is? If we parked here we'd stick out like a lizard on a snow bank."

The paved part of the road ended and morphed into a rutted dirt mess. We passed a couple houses on our way in, then nothing for the last five hundred yards.

"Are you sure this place you found in the file is out here?" I couldn't see a thing over the bush grass.

"We need to keep quiet from here out," she said.

I grunted my assent. Then I saw it: above us on the right, a fenced yard and what looked like a mini-compound with metal louvered windows in two stories.

"This has to be it," she whispered. I could smell stale coffee on her breath.

"Now what?" I whispered back. "You have a plan, right?"

"Stakeout. We watch and see if anyone leaves or arrives."

"In that case, the bush over there would give us a fine vantage point," I suggested.

We crawled into the tall grass. After what seemed like an eternity, but was probably only forty minutes, a Ford mini-van jostled past us, bumping to a halt in front of the locked gate. A white guy climbed out. From underneath his white t-shirt I could make out the edges of a large tattoo. A bright red "Make America Great Again" hat covered his tanned head.

He opened the gate, then searched up and down the road presumably for oncoming traffic. He opened the van door and hauled several paper grocery bags out before heading inside the house.

After another twenty minutes, he emerged. Two Rottweilers and a German Shepherd circled around him. They barked and charged for the open gate. Dana squeezed my upper arm, her hand like a vise. He charged ahead of the dogs and slammed the gate shut.

"Ah, ah, ah." He stood with his back to us. I breathed a hushed sigh of relief. "Not now boys. Shit in the yard. I'll let you out later."

The man turned and looked through the vertical bars. "I got work to do."

The dogs stared through the bars for a couple minutes, right where we were laying. We held our breath. Their big amber eyes and wet snouts remained locked on us until they started sniffing each other's butts, marking the yard and relieving themselves. I mouthed at Dana, "What are we doing here?"

She hunched her shoulders. Stakeouts always seemed so exciting in movies, but only because they cut out the long stretches of boredom.

Pinpricks were edging down my hands from leaning on them when Baldy finally sauntered out again with a short surfboard under his arm. After dropping the board into the mini-van, he wrapped and locked a chain around the gate. A sign on the gate read: "No Trespassing. Bad Dogs Present." He maneuvered a tight three-point turn and took off down the road, a light mist of dust hanging in his wake. The dogs barked for a moment, then retreated toward the back of the house.

Dana started to get up. "Wait!" I said in a loud whisper. "Sometimes they come back." Sure enough, we heard the sound of the van crunching back up the unpaved lane. He darted back inside and came out with a duffle bag he tossed into the passenger seat before tearing off more urgently.

We waited a full five minutes this time. "See, told you I needed you on this," she said and clapped me on the back.

Dana pulled a pick kit out of her satchel.

After a long time, the padlock popped open. I held my hand over the lock before she could remove it. "What is this place?" I asked.

She pointed at the door to the house. "See that?" Above the door a sign read, "Faero."

She continued, "I really don't know, but it sounds like some commune for a bunch of white supremacy nut-jobs who think that as original descendants of the Danish settlers from a voyage in 1672, they're the rightful owners of this island. There was a time they had stationed themselves in St. Croix. I rooted them out, but they vanished before our crack police could apprehend 'em."

"They stupid enough to put a sign on the front door announcing who they are?"

"Zealots, that's what we're dealing with. People who believe slavery made the new world what it is and our current descent into the bowels of history is due to freeing the slaves and letting one of them become President of the United States, among other things."

She waited. I didn't remove my hand. "Go on," I said.

"Look, they think we should be a sovereign nation of white people living on beaches and drinking piña coladas served by people who say 'yessir and nosir' all day long."

I glanced around for the dogs. "Where'd those beasts get to?"

She pointed to a clearing edged by some bushes. "There, but they can't see us. Just keep quiet."

I released the padlock. We pushed the gate open. The front door was secured with two dead-bolts and a regular doorknob.

"Can you pick those?" I asked.

"It would take hours. I'm really not confident hanging here for that long," she whispered.

We snuck around the back of the house. The smell of dog shit hit me full force. I'd just stepped in a mound. Dana giggled, then held her finger over her lips. She couldn't help herself as I lifted my shoe. She burst out laughing, leaning against the house for support.

"I thought we were supposed to be quiet," I said through clenched teeth as I rubbed my shoes across the browning grass.

"What's," she laughed more hysterically, "the point, they'll smell us if they don't hear us!" She broke up again.

"It's not that funny!" I smiled in spite of myself. "Okay, a little funny. Like I said, I was never that good at this stuff."

She caught her breath. "We'll wash it off at the beach. Your shoe might get wet, but you aren't coming in my car with that."

That's when we heard it. A faint knocking sound. Three small wooden sheds that looked like large outhouses sat in the far corner, about fifty yards from the main residence.

"Slave quarters," Dana muttered.

We waited for the sound to come again. A louder bang came from the farthest outhouse. We went over and tried to peer through the slats, but despite its dilapidated look, the inside was snugly covered with wood, making viewing impossible. A small moan and another thump seeped through.

We located a spot where a door used to be, but it had been boarded shut. A tall ladder leaned against the back side. I climbed up. A rolled-up drop ladder was secured against the outside of a trap door in the roof. The door had a large wooden plank that secured it from the outside. I removed the plank and dropped it to the ground with a hollow plunk.

I wrenched the door open. Mostly darkness, but my eyes adjusted. Enough sunlight angled in through the flamboyant tree overhead for me to make out two hollow, terrified eyes brimming with fear. A feminine moan drifted up and in a beam I caught a glimpse of long blond hair and a slender frame.

"There's someone in there. She's gagged and bound from what I can see. Young too." I heard nothing, then turned just as I felt Dana tugging on my shorts. I almost fell into the opening.

Dana had climbed up next to me. She put her hand over my mouth. One of the dogs, a Rottweiler, sniffed at the grass where I had stepped in its feces. She handed me the plank.

"We can't leave her," I whispered.

"Let's go," she said.

"I'm coming for you, I promise," I whispered into the darkness. I left the trapdoor open and we slid down the ladder. Edging my face around the corner, I saw the German Shepherd had joined his buddy. We stood under the ladder surveying the back of the property. Ten-foot metal fencing laced with sharp pointed arrows on top looked decorative, but served a more sinister purpose, surrounded us. A giant "stay away" message if ever there was one.

"Watch the dogs," I told Dana.

"What are you going to do?"

Hauling the ladder to the back fence, then gently leaning it against the iron, I climbed on top and slipped my foot between the arrowheads. As I crawled over, my shirt caught and there was a loud *riiiip*! Dana ran toward the ladder as the dogs heard the rip too.

"Throw your bag over!" I said. It sailed over my head as I held to the top of the fence waiting to aid her escape.

She climbed the ladder. The dogs charged over, barking. Sounds erupted from the front of the house, but I didn't bother to look. As I pulled Dana up and over, an arrowhead tore a wide gash in her thigh.

"AHHHH," she screamed. All pretense of stealth disappeared. She dropped to the hillside and tumbled.

"Dana!"

I jumped down as Mr. Make-America-Great rounded the shack, shotgun in hand. He pumped the action and raised it as I hit the ground. Our eyes met, but I dropped and rolled, grabbing the shoulder strap of Dana's bag as the blast hit the fence with sharp tings.

When I got up, my whole body ached, but aside from the bruises, I seemed unhurt. Dana moaned and gripped her leg. I ripped the torn fabric of her pants aside and wrapped my already shredded shirt around the wound to staunch the flow of blood.

"Can you walk?" I said.

She grimaced, holding my shoulder as she pushed to a standing position. The barking dogs were coming now. The owner had let them out the main gate. We moved off to the north through the slicing blades of grass.

"Get my cell," Dana gasped.

I pulled it out of her bag. "No reception," I panted. The dogs were coming. To the right of us, I spotted smoke. The sweet smell of roasting Red Snapper filled the air. Barbecue.

Unfortunately, that house was at least five hundred yards away, uphill. We moved too slowly. Panic kicked at the inside of my chest. Three deep breaths and the panic subsided.

The main road had to be much closer. We were better off getting there and hoping for a car or going to that house on the corner. Dana's leg dragged, acting as an anchor.

"Come on, I need you to be strong right now," I said. "We're gonna to get out of this."

She looked at me, her thinning red hair plastered to her face. For the first time in my experience, she looked truly tired. Despite her labored breathing, she pursed her lips with determination.

We shuffled toward the road. The dogs closed in followed by a heavier sound. Human footsteps crushed the foliage with boot-hard force.

"You interlopers are dog food!" our pursuer shouted.

Another voice came from right behind us. "Who dere? Wha' you want on my prop-a-tee?"

"Oh gam. Dis woman hurt," I said to a hard-faced West Indian man with humongous hands.

"Wha' happen?" he said. He held a machete in his right hand and a plastic bottle of water in his left.

"We need your help," I said.

"Wha' t'ose dogs from?"

"Da white man wid red hat up dere," I pointed. "He tryin' kill us."

Barks grew closer each second. "Please," I said. "He might kill you too."

The man dropped his water bottle and reached behind his back, producing a gun. "No, he no kill I."

He released the safety and grinned, his teeth brown and yellow with chewing tobacco. He spit some on the ground, then waved the gun for us to follow.

Twenty yards ahead, we arrived in a clearing surrounded by trees. On the ground beneath the trees, a bed of palm fronds was laid out. The shade made the location cool and inviting.

"Stay down. I be back."

Dana collapsed. Blood, dirt, and leaves splattered my green shirt. I propped Dana's leg up on my bent knee then checked my cell as I gently stroked her cheek. It had reception. I called the only person besides Dana whose phone number I had on hand.

"West Indian Manna, can I help you?"

"Lucy! Hey Lucy, it's Boise."

"Who dis? You breakin' up," Lucy said, sounding annoyed.

"It's Boise, Lucy. Boise."

"Oh, hello Boise. Wha' you wan' now? You know you forget to lock your door again today? Someone gonna rob you, boy," she scolded.

"Lucy, I need you to come out Hull Bay and get me. My friend's hurt."

A heavily calloused bare foot kicked my phone into the bushes. I howled as the kick grazed my ear.

"Who da fuck you callin'?" a deep voice rumbled. The guy with the pistol. "Mi'son, I don' want no more people out here, you hear?"

He leaned in so close I could see the jaundice in his eyes. "I tell dat crazy white man to go, but now you have to go too."

"He's got someone hostage up in that place up dere," I said.

He stopped and stared at me, raised his gun, and clocked me across the head. I plummeted into a black crater.

CHAPTER 14

"Yeah boss, he on da phone when I come back." "Fuck!" It was the bald guy who owned the dogs. "I'm gonna have to interrogate dem. Maybe have ta kill 'em."

Rolling over, I tried to reach up and rub my face, but my hands wouldn't come out from behind my back. My feet were stuck together. My temple throbbed. To my right, just coming into focus, lay Dana--bound, gagged, and unmoving.

We were in one of the shacks in the backyard. People talked outside, but I couldn't make out what they said.

At least Dana and I were going to die together. I always had a fear of dying alone. My hands were tightly bound with what I guessed was clothesline with half-a-dozen square knots.

Shifting to my left, my fingers were able to wiggle. The knots held fast. The rope ran down my arm, but fortunately they'd left a little play in my wrists.

After ten exhausting minutes, sweat dripping from my brow, I'd released two of the knots. Footsteps approached. I returned to my original position and closed my eyes.

The trapdoor in the ceiling creaked open. I saw red on the back of my eyelids and felt warm sun on my face. The door shut again. Climbing out would be difficult, but it was also time consuming for them to climb down and check on us. I continued my escape efforts.

My hands were free after another hour or so. Dana's pulse was weak but steady. After freeing my feet, I found no obvious method of getting out as the room seemed empty and darkness made searching for some hand-hold challenging.

The tiny room trapped heat, but it was bearable thanks to shade cast by the large trees outside. I knew Dana was hurt badly and at least one other hostage suffered in an adjacent hut. Even if I got out of this mess, what would I do about them? I couldn't possibly get Dana's dead weight up through that ceiling door, so that meant going and coming back.

Then another more dangerous plan surfaced as I realized why we were still alive. They didn't know what I'd passed along in my phone conversation. There must be someone else in charge who they had to consult because the more I thought about it, the more it seemed like the best course would be to dispose of us immediately in case anyone came snooping.

Murder, while neater, was also a bigger risk if they got caught. They needed some back-up on that decision. Someone with the balls to make the calls. We might run out of time when that call came. Maybe it already had and they were only waiting for nightfall to finish the job.

Dana's shallow breath rasped. Rubbing my hands over her face, then pulling the gag off her mouth, I whispered, "Dana?" Nothing. I unbound her arms and legs, raising her injured leg and leaning it against the wall. Dried rivulets of blood dotted her leg. Might as well let her remain oblivious to our predicament until I reasoned an escape. I squinted up where I thought the trapdoor was, but the malevolent blackness revealed nothing.

I moved on to my next sense: touch. Bending down, I felt for the rope I'd tossed aside. Picturing the bottom of the trapdoor on the other shed, I remembered a small metal ring. If I could get the rope into that ring, I had a chance to pull myself up.

"What's the point? The door is board-locked from the outside," I muttered to myself. Then I heard Evelyn in my mind, always the rational thinker.

"When solving a problem, take it one step at a time. Don't worry about the other problems down the line. Stick to the issue at hand."

She was right. The walls felt smooth as linen. Pawing the floor, I found a bucket reeking of urine. I suddenly had to pee very badly. I urinated in the bucket. Another bucket covered by a lid smelled even worse. This I could work with.

They clanked as I stacked them. I stopped moving and listened. Nothing. Pushing the bucket-tower into the corner, I climbed, balancing and willing my one-hundred sixty-five pounds to become lighter.

Once on top, I held the wall for support, then got to my feet, positioning them on the rim of the upper bucket where there was more support. Swinging my hand in an arc over my head, I caught nothing but air.

I pulled the rope out of my pocket and swung it about. It hit something. Judging the distance, I tied the rope into a loop, then threw it out, over and over to no avail. In a frustrated effort, I tried to throw the rope higher, pushing from my feet. The buckets tumbled away and I fell, cart-wheeling. "Ooph!" escaped my lips as my elbow struck Dana's breast.

"Hey, watch it! Boise?"

"It's me. Sorry," I said. "Welcome back."

"My fucking leg is killing me," she said. "I feel like throwing up."

"You're fine, but we need to get outta here. Can you stand? I need your help."

Something softly scraped against the outside of the house.

"Lay still," I whispered.

Laying back on the floor, I hid the rope under my body. The hatch popped moments later. Soft moonlight streamed in. I heard the rope ladder drop down and the strain of the knots against the descending party's heft. I opened my eye a sliver to see the West Indian man who'd knocked me unconscious. I tensed, ready to attack.

His feet hit the floor. Was it my imagination or was he being very quiet? He put his hand on my shoulder. I lay as still as stone, wanting to buy time and ambush him if he turned away.

"Da man? Wake up," he spoke softly right into my ear. I brought my head up with all my might, cracking him in the cheek. He fell back, landing on top of Dana, who squealed.

Leaping to my feet, I dropped my knee into his crotch. He folded up, holding his cheek with one hand and his balls with the other as he rocked in the fetal position.

"Get off me," Dana moaned. "Get the fuck off me!"

I got to my feet and shoved him off Dana. He rolled away, whimpering like a puppy. I could see a folding knife sticking out of his back pocket. I snatched it away and stuffed it into my pants.

"Now you have to move. I know it's painful, but this is our chance."

Dana winced and started up the ladder. "Kick him one more time."

"Why?"

"Because I can't," she said.

I kicked him in the upper back, but my heart wasn't in it. He'd be stuck in here. Good enough for me. We climbed up the ladder, me pushing her from behind. Her wheezing continued.

"Come on, Dana, you can do this," I said.

The West Indian stood and had started climbing the ladder. He moved slowly, but Dana moved slower.

"Keep going, I'm right behind you," I panted.

She wheezed in acknowledgement. I relaxed my grip and slid down the ropes. My hands burned. At the last second, I brought my feet together. They hit him squarely in the chest. He tumbled back, striking the floor with a *thump*. Snagging the bottom of the ladder, I climbed up a few rungs, then shoved the bottom rung into the back of my pants and continued ascending. I looked back once, like Lot's wife. He lay sprawled in obvious pain. He held up a hand and stuck out his thumb.

We got to the front gate. The lock was in place, but not latched. The dogs must have been inside. We slipped out and down the road. Luckily, the journey back to Hull Bay was all downhill. Halfway back, Dana collapsed. We hid in the bushes as a lonely Volkswagen puttered by.

"Stay here, I'll run down and get the car."

"No," she said, then nodded realizing that was the only logical solution. I started away, then heard, "Boise."

"What? I gotta go!"

She held up the keys. She gave me a look which said, "Do I have to do all the thinking?"

My back protested, aching from all the shenanigans of the afternoon. The car was still there, but the beach was deserted except for one couple sitting behind a mangrove tree smoking a bong. They waved to me, and I waved back before racing off.

CHAPTER 15

We arrived at the emergency room. They cleaned Dana's wound and stitched her up. A thin West Indian doctor in green scrubs wearing thick horn-rimmed glasses pulled me aside.

"What is this?" the doctor asked, sipping from a silver Diet Coke can.

"Not sure; she showed up at my place. We work together. Guess I was the closest person," I said.

He set the Coke down, removed his spectacles, and began cleaning them with the edge of his smock. "Okay. What's your name again?"

"Boise."

Dana and I had talked about keeping answers minimal, so there'd be no need to lie any more than absolutely necessary. I had called the cops on one of Dana's burner phones she kept in the car. We dropped it out the window not far from Hull Bay.

As he mounted his glasses back on his nose, he said, "You saved her. She needs blood, so we're going to keep her overnight. I'm not sure how she's even conscious." He paused, then said, "Isn't she Dana Goode, the reporter?"

We had given a fake name, but it was clear he knew the answer already.

"I like her stuff, but lately not very investigative, is it?"

I remained stoic, so he continued. "I think this was in the service of investigative journalism. It looks like someone dragged a blade over her leg."

"Basically," I said.

"I blog. I have a site where I talk about Saint Thomian history and current events."

"Why don't you tell this to her?"

"Doesn't seem like the right time--not to mention she's asleep. I figure you can pass it on for me. Ease her into it, so to speak. I have a decent number of followers, over seven hundred, so it could be a viable forum where she can reach readers and tell stories the paper won't print." He handed me a card, with the website domain name and a phone number. "I'm Earl DeVere. I have to get back to work."

"Can I see her?" I asked.

"I'll take you down so you can look in on her, but she needs to sleep."

Lucy was waiting up. She ran out from behind the counter and stopped me.

"Wha' happen?" She said, looking me up and down. I limped and my body ached everywhere from being abused all day.

"Just a long day," I said.

"No, no, you don't get to do me dat. I call da police after your phone hang up, but dey say call back when I have somet'ing. I t'ought you was dead or somet'ing. W'at happen?"

I explained that a reporter had roped me into helping her find this place out toward Hull Bay and the property owners didn't like us on their land. They were up to something. "I better leave it at that," I concluded. "In the movies, if you tell people too much the bad guys might come torture them for information, so the less you know detail-wise, you know, the better. Irie?" I hoped the movie part would relax her, but her eyes widened. "Also, not so sure I can trust the police around here."

She nodded. "Fa true."

CHAPTER 16

Noise from the planes taking off made me feel like we were having an earthquake. They roared over a gradually shrinking hill that the government had been dynamiting into oblivion since I was a kid, after a plane failed to climb over it fast enough on takeoff. I had a garbage bag slung over my shoulder and some rubber gloves I'd pilfered from the emergency room.

After checking in on Dana earlier that morning, I'd made my way over to Lindberg Bay in her car, which she didn't need. After her release from the hospital later in the afternoon, I'd pick her up. That gave me six hours to complete my environmental community service.

I leaned over to retrieve a cigarette butt. It was a pet peeve of mine. The way smokers didn't seem to think cigarette butts being tossed on the beach or the pavement constituted littering.

I picked a couple purple sea grapes and ate them after washing my hands in the ocean. In the shade of the circular leaves I pondered what the fuck I was doing here.

No real job. No real friends. Had I made up this whole mission to feel better about my dead wife? Hell, was all this shit made up? Why was I following some crazy, redheaded reporter into the clutches of a fraternal cult of white boys who hated everyone who didn't look and think like them. Without even getting paid, I'd already been kidnapped and almost murdered.

Roger didn't care. He'd chosen to be a fucking drug dealer and he got killed. Was anything shocking about that scenario? The rest of his family seemed uninterested. Hell, the rest of the fucking world seemed uninterested. So what was I doing?

The Guinness I pulled from my backpack had already started to get warm. It still tasted good. Why not just get a bartending job, start surfing again, and sit in the sand with a brew and a book the rest of the time? After dropping the empty beer bottle into my trash bag, I continued down the beach, finding cans, paper towels, and even a condom.

Around four o'clock, the hospital clerk called and said I could come get Dana.

In a wheelchair outside her room, Dana was dressed and ready for the world. They helped her into the car. We drove in silence for a minute before she shook her head in irritation, "Where were you all day?"

I adjusted the rearview mirror. "I had that thing to take care of."

"Your wife?"

I nodded.

"Makes you not so talkative, huh?"

I pulled over. "Dana, you didn't fully appraise me of our situation yesterday. Being taken hostage is not something to be taken lightly."

I flicked the signal on and pulled back into traffic. She said, "Can I at least give you my address?"

"Just direct me," I mumbled.

"Okay, you missed the turn back there," she pointed back to the right.

"Great," I said, "Just fuckin' great. Just like yesterday. You know, for a reporter, you aren't great at reporting!"

Finally, we came to her house: a white, two-story job on Crown Mountain sporting a steep driveway. At fifteen-hundred feet, Crown Mountain was the highest point in the Virgin Islands and one of the nicer sections of the island. The car bottomed-out in the steep driveway as I pulled in.

"Boise, you have to enter at an angle."

I stepped over a pile of newspapers sitting on top of her welcome mat and helped her inside. Black and white framed news headlines announcing the deaths of famous people covered the walls of the foyer. The bold names of Bobby Kennedy, Gandhi, JFK, and Martin Luther King, Jr. assaulted us as I hustled her into the living room and laid her on the couch.

She had a cane they'd instructed her to use for three weeks. "I'm sorry you're cross. I know you're scared for me." She paused, then continued, "Pick me up tomorrow at ten?"

"I thought you were supposed to work out of your house this week," I said, dumping her antibiotics and pain meds on the kitchen counter. Dirty dishes and pots filled the sink. A vintage typewriter sat on her dining room table next to stacks of newspapers from all over the world.

Warm landscape paintings of St. Thomas' countryside and the surrounding ocean covered the walls of her living room.

Gathering up the mail and newspapers, I unloaded them on the glass coffee table in front of her. After placing a large glass of water and leaning her cane against the corner of the sofa, I headed for the door.

She yelled in a delayed response to my earlier question, "Yeah, no, that working from home shit ain't gonna fly. See you tomorrow at ten."

At the Greenhouse, the food went down like sandpaper and the beer tasted rancid. I forced myself to finish the burger, then left the rest. Willy, the Australian bartender I'd befriended over the last few weeks, asked what was wrong, but I said nothing.

Back at The Manner, Lucy handed me a note. "Someone drop dis off fa you," she said.

Marge clanked around in the kitchen.

"What time?"

"I don't know. Marge get it and give to me. I was cleanin' your mess. Don' forget, tomorrow rent due."

"Here," I said handing her money.

"I wish all you was all like dat." She pecked me on the cheek.

The only time a woman kissed me anymore was when I handed her money. I imagined that's how fathers with teenaged daughters felt. As I trudged up the infinite stairs, I rubbed the yellow legal page between my fingers.

I tried to anticipate who the note was from. Opening anonymous mail gave me chills. Almost no one knew I was here. The few acquaintances I had flashed through my mind, then my brilliant deductive reasoning flashed again on the most obvious clue: legal paper.

Miguela Salas had some information for me. It said I should meet at her office tomorrow at ten. My free-as-a-bird lifestyle had a scheduling conflict. Dana would have to wait.

CHAPTER 17

When I swung by Miguela's office the next morning, she handed over another file.

"What's this?" I asked.

"Yes. Someone who knew you. You should talk to her."

A picture of a cream-skinned black lady in her sixties stared up at me. Shoulder-length silver hair, wire-framed glasses, and eyes that smiled. Roger's grandmother, Glor. "Jesus, I didn't know she was still alive. Where is she?"

"Out near Bolongo Bay in one of those condos they finished last year. She got tired of the crime down here," Miguela said.

"It's hard to admit your home's gone."

"Her home is not gone, it's for sale," said Miguela.

"That's a house, not a home."

"Do you want a water, Mr. Montague?"

"Sure. Please just call me Boise, Miguela," I said.

"Here you go, Mr. Montague," she handed me a cold, plastic bottle. "May I say something personal?"

I downed half the water in a swig. Do all the women on this island have to make some observation about my psychology?

"Sure," I mumbled half-heartedly.

"You need a bath. Personal hygiene is vital to civilized social interaction amongst humans."

"I stay at the Manner, well, you knew that, and yeah, the bathroom was busy this morning. It's a shared one. When women are around, you know," I laughed.

"No, what about women being around, Mr. Montague?"

"It's a unisex bathroom and shower, so you know," I shrugged.

Her expression remained blank. I rubbed my hands together, glancing around and noticing her lack of law books again as well as an absence of anything on the walls, not even her law diploma, which most lawyers loved to display.

"What law school did you attend?" I asked, still trying to manufacture a connection.

"Nova Law School."

"Nova. Huh. Where's that?"

"Florida," she said.

The silence descended like an anvil. I patted the brown file folder sitting in my lap.

"Well, thanks for this. Guess I'll get out of your hair. I'm sure you've got lots of work to do," I said, scooting my chair away from her desk.

"Good-bye, Mr. Montague. Good luck."

"Thanks. You too."

I breathed a sigh of relief once out of the awkward dimension that was Miguela's office. She was probably too much of a social outcast to practice law anywhere but St. Thomas.

On my way to pick up Dana, I passed an accountant office with a chalkboard in front that read, "TAXES DUE! SUPPORT YOUR GOVERNOR!"

Taking a sniff of my armpit, I realized Miguela's awkward honesty could benefit me if I heeded her admonition about personal hygiene. On the way, I zipped into A.H. Riise, a famous cologne shop downtown. A cute salesgirl spritzed my wrist repeatedly until I selected a cologne endorsed by Johnny Depp in the two-ounce size, figuring I'd be ready for a change by then.

Right before Dana got into the car I splashed some on my neck and torso. Another sniff. I was good to go.

"You're late," Dana greeted me, followed by fluttering eyelashes and a wrinkled nose. "Smells like A.H. Riise opened a branch in my car."

I started to explain about Miguela Salas, but she waved me off. "We need to stop at the store on the way back here. I'm stuck without a car, so you've got to help me."

"All right, but you do live here. You have other friends, right?" I said.

"None of them are driving my car. Take me to the office, then let's head back out Hull Bay way."

Although I thought it was crazy, Dana was right--we had to confirm that something had been done for that poor girl trapped in the other shack. Dana didn't trust the cops. If nothing had been done, we'd have to try again, and soon, if it wasn't too late already.

We made a quick stop at her office and I told her about Miguela giving me Glor's address. Depending on what happened out at Hull Bay, I'd go see her late today or tomorrow.

On the drive out, I told her about Dr. DeVere. "This guy wants me to submit to his blog? I'm a professional. I don't blog."

"Wow, that's the first time I've really thought you were a snob," I countered.

After a moment she said, "We're coming up on the place. Park here."

The tiny side road had several more tire marks than before. Many vehicles had been out here since our excursion. We limped up, acting like we belonged. A burly West Indian police officer sporting a crew cut and blackout Oakley sunglasses stood at the entrance, hands on hips and his chest puffed out. Dana held up her credential.

"So, what happened here?"

"I can't talk 'bout on-goin' investigation." His voice rumbled like a v-6 engine.

"What's your name, officer?" Dana smiled, turning on her charm. "I'm Dana and this is Boise, my assistant."

I held out my hand. He stared at it, then finally shook. "Officer Cheevers."

"Did you find anyone in the sheds out back?" I threw the question at him before he could think much.

"No. Wait, what?" Cheevers withdrew his hand, then stammered on, "What shed? What you talkin' about? Dis a crime scene. You gotta leave."

"Did you book anyone?" Dana smiled again. "Come on Cheevers, you can tell us. Don't you want to be a source for a worthwhile story just once?" She waved her hands in a circle. "No one's watching."

He looked behind him, then up and down the road.

"Is someone else here we should know about?" Dana asked.

"No, we alone. How you know about da sheds?"

"An anonymous source, just like you," she said.

I started to walk past him, but Cheevers put his hand on my shoulder, gentle but firm. "You can't go in t'ere. We still investigating."

"So are we. This here's a territory of the United States. Freedom of the press, buddy," I said, attempting to sound like Dana.

"No, you cannot go in t'ere. Me boss won't allow it. He say everyone stay out, especially da news. You check?"

He put his hand across his body and gripped the handle of his baton. Backing up, I nearly tripped over a loose stone. "Yeah, yeah, I check da man."

Dana smiled again and exaggerated her limp as she moved closer to him. "Please, just tell us if you found anyone in the shed on the northwest corner in the back. We're worried about someone."

His Adam's apple bobbed up and down as he tried to remember what the police manual said to do in this situation.

"No, dey ain' foun' nobody in t'ere. Nobody. Okay? I ain' sayin' not'ing else. Go away. Okay? Go a-w-w-way." He stuttered the last word, clenching his jaw with the effort.

"I'm going to share something we know with you. If you share it with your police buddies, please don't say who told you. Understand?" I said.

"Tell me," he said.

Dana gave me a tiny nod.

"There was a girl trapped in that shed. We need to find her before she gets killed."

Disbelief flooded his face.

"It's also true, so if you care about saving people, you'll tell someone about this." I thought a moment, then looked into his young face. "Do you want to be a detective?"

He nodded.

"Then say you found something in the shed that suggests they had a prisoner in there, or better yet, let's you and I go look. Maybe we'll find some evidence that convinces you our story is true and you can use it to convince your superiors to open a missing person case." His sunglasses had fogged up. He slipped them off as he pulled a soft cloth out of his breast pocket. He wiped the moisture clean.

Dana moved in closer, sliding up on her cane. "In the future, we can help each other with these cases and stories. You know, I scratch your back, you scratch mine?"

He put his sunglasses back on. "All right, let's go." He pointed at Dana, "You keep watch. I'll be back."

We trudged off toward the northwest corner of the property.

"We didn't know how to get in. We gettin' a warrant to cut t'rough because we don't like damaging property. Too many people suin' us all da time," he said.

I took the ladder from against the back fence and leaned it against the shed. "The trapdoor is up there. Inside there's a ladder so you can climb down."

"I ain't climbin' down in no dark shed where dey keep prisoners."

He climbed up. The wood plank clanked down beside me. He poked his head in after turning on his flashlight. After a minute, he waved his index finger back at me, then climbed back down.

"Empty. No visible evidence dat anyone was dere."

We returned to Dana. She cursed. "What about the house?"

Cheevers rubbed his forehead. "I already listen to you too much. Da house look empty, but if we find anyt'ing, I call you." He winked at Dana and she handed him her card. "Now, go before da others get back."

"I think he likes you," I said as we returned to the car.

"So what next?" Dana asked. I didn't get the feeling she was really asking as much as she was seeing where my head was.

"I need to go see Auntie Glor," I said.

"Roger's aunt? Boise, you agreed to help me on this. This is urgent and we lost time already."

An ache rose in my trapezius at the base of my neck. I reached up and rubbed it, digging into the firm flesh. Again I considered my obligations: Dana or Roger. Dana was alive, breathing, busting my ass. Roger was dead, a rotting corpse west of downtown, his soul suffering eternal torment for ruining people's lives with drugs.

Dana kept pushing me. Her constant desperate need to control me and use me for her selfish ends was starting to fray my nerves. Did I owe her any more than I owed Roger? More importantly, Auntie Glor was alive. She was a damned good person. I doubted that had changed. What if she felt cheated by the system that didn't care about her grandson? Hell, maybe Roger wasn't so bad. Perhaps he made a wrong move and died trying to get out of that life. All I had was the word of Iris Adams at the historical society that Roger was a bad guy who deserved what came to him.

"Yeah, well, we're gonna lose a lot more time if we're dead or in solitary confinement. Last night wasn't my idea of a good time. I need another day to regroup," I said, getting into the car. I tried to close the door. She blocked it using her cane.

"Come on, Boise. There's a scared girl out there who not only needs our assistance but can probably answer a lot of questions about these guys."

Leaning forward, head in hand, I accidentally honked the horn. A small dog yelped from somewhere on the hillside. I fucking hated it when she was right. I'd abandoned Roger by leaving all those years ago, now I was going to abandon him and his grandmother again. "Can we get out of here before his buddies get back and see us near the crime scene? I think we got lucky with Cheevers, the others won't be so polite."

"Here's the deal, Boise. If you want to keep driving my car, 'cause don't think I won't let it sit, then you are going to help me with this before you go tackling ancient history."

I stopped the car, pulled the emergency brake, and got out.

"Hey, Boise!" Dana yelled after me. "Boise! You can't leave me here. We have to go find that hostage."

I kept walking down the hill. At Main Street a shrill screeching behind me spun me around, as Dana's car moved in a jerky fashion, like a teenager driving a stick-shift for the first time.

When I got next to her, I yelled, "Are you crazy?" She was using the cane for gas and her good foot for the brake.

"Unless you want me to kill someone driving like this, you need to take me home."

"Fine," I grumbled. "Tell me what's next."

"A guy named Biff is next. He spends a lot of time talking to people about what's happening."

"Are we also gonna chat with Chet and Aunt Trudy over a hearty breakfast?"

"Biff knows things and usually steers me in the right direction when I get desperate. He says the cops are sitting on a missing person who fits what you saw, a blonde in her teens or early twenties, lily-white skin. They came to him days ago looking for any angle he had, but he had nothing. Now, he knows a few things. A rich girl from an important family was taken from down in Frenchtown on March twenty-seventh."

"How old is this girl?"

"Fifteen."

"The girl in that shack looked at least twenty."

"It's her. Trust me. She's a mature looking girl who attracts the attention of older men."

"But…"

"Boise, let me finish." Dana pursed her lips. "We need to move. Start driving to Frenchtown. The fastest way is to head down the right after you pass Mafolie."

I had no idea what would happen next.

CHAPTER 18

Dusk closed in, making it difficult to see. I ground the gears to slow the car's descent. A moped buzzed past mounted by a grinning boy wearing sunglasses too large for his face. He drove right in the middle of the road, and I swerved to avoid him. After nudging some foliage on the edge of the road, Dana gave a bark as a leaf popped into her lap.

She directed me to pull up next to the Frenchtown ballpark. Cops and postal workers played games there between January and June. The lights were on when we arrived. Players dressed in yellow shuffled through the grass and dirt heading off the field, shoulders slumped.

"I remember coming here to watch games as a kid," I said. "I used to space out and stare over at the seaplanes taking off." I pointed to the small section at the western end of the harbor that housed the seaplane ramp.

"She was taken right here if Biff's right," Dana said.

I glanced around and spotted police caution tape around one of the parking spots abutting the road.

Dana's gray eyes sparkled in the lights, watching the police tape as well. Her eyes were watering.

"You okay?" I asked.

"You mean my eyes?" She pointed at her face. "I have allergies that sometimes act up in the evening. I've never really been able to put my finger on what causes it."

She took a tissue out of her bag and dabbed her eyes. This girl's plight was weighing on her. Had she lost someone to similar circumstances? Dana seemed softer, more vulnerable than I'd ever seen her in our brief acquaintance.

I killed the engine and stepped out onto a huge crack in the concrete. My ankle rolled into the seam, but I let my weight fall on the car, preventing any great strain.

"Boise, I don't need you on a cane too," she laughed.

"Don't worry, I'm out of shape but still sure-footed." Circling around to her, I shook my sore foot, "walking it off" as coaches liked to say.

I leaned on the car, bringing myself to her eye level. Dana always wore running shoes, I guessed because in her line of work, she had to get physical to get a story, as we'd done out at Hull Bay. With her shoes on, she stood at no more than five feet two inches.

"We're going to have to ask around to figure where exactly she got abducted," Dana said.

"What's your story? You mostly seem like a hardened reporter who's seen it all. Why is this rich girl's plight so special?" I asked as she gazed at the field.

She pushed herself back and sat on the hood. "You see these guys?" She pointed at the winning team. A group of athletic, well-built men and one woman. "They all have a family, right?"

"Presumably."

"You have a family?"

"My mom. Sister in jail and a brother," I said.

She giggled, then said, "Sister in jail. Wow. Okay, but still, you have a family." I waited, then she said, "I'm adopted. My mother or father, who knows, left me on the steps of a church. They put me in an orphanage. My parents adopted me when I was four."

I nodded, not sure what to say. It didn't seem the right time for some platitude about how she was special because she'd been chosen by her adoptive parents.

She continued to gaze at the field, her mind envisioning another time and place as she spoke. "I was scared, alone in that orphanage. Without a net. No mom or dad looking out just for me. And that place was pretty good compared to where this girl is, right?"

"Maybe," I reluctantly agreed.

She wiped her cheek with the back of her hand. "Yeah, well, I don't like it when girls wind up out there with wolves, all alone." She leaned back and laughed, like she had when we first met. It struck me as a forced laugh this time, lacking the giddy freedom she'd had in the newsroom. "Besides, I bet it'll make one hell of a story, and finding her myself guarantees an exclusive, right?"

I didn't know what to say, so I followed her line of sight as she continued to stare at the men milling about on the field.

"Isn't that the cop softball squad that's leaving?" I asked.

Her expression grew hard and serious as she said, "Let's wait till they're gone. They aren't gonna help."

"Jesus, Dana. How do any crimes get solved if the police and this governor spend all their time hiding every criminal event? Don't answer that, just sayin,'" I petered out, looking up at the first stars of the evening.

"The weight of the world is weary," she replied. "Look, they're taking off."

***

We moved over to the parking spot with the yellow police tape, surveying the likely abduction site for clues.

"So, someone just drove up, yanked her away and stuffed her into another vehicle then dashed out of here." I looked off down the road. "Sounds like this girl needed protection. Who was with her?"

"We don't know if anyone was with her, but if they were, they're keeping quiet." Dana turned around in a tight circle. "Who would have seen this?"

"How'd Biff know she's rich?"

"He's private about sources. He claims someone could tell by her outfit and her purse. Designer stuff."

I followed her gaze across the street. There were shops, but cars lined the street in front of them, mostly obscuring the view. Many of the windows were tinted and had writing on them announcing sales for whatever wares they sold. We walked over and questioned the clerks, but everyone said they'd told the police everything and had no real information. I checked the line of sight to the Normandie Bistro, a bar my father used to frequent. It was poor. Someone in the far western corner of the patio could have seen something. Otherwise, no good angles.

CHAPTER 19

Lucy pounded on my door from the inside.

"Boise, you got someone downstairs wantin' to talk wid you."

"Don't speak so loud. Why'd you pound on my door so hard? You in my room?"

"Because you won't wake up. Take a shower, den come down. He'll wait."

"Who?"

"Someone lookin' for you. He white and tall." She turned away, then came back. "I'm not secretary. Dis ain't your place of business."

"No, no, nothing like that, Lucy. I don't know who this is, but I'll be down in five."

I hit the showers and headed downstairs. Like she said, a tall, white guy sat at the bar drinking something clear.

"Boise Montague?"

"Yes. You are?"

He held out his hand. "Attorney Patrick Roberts. I'm here because I represent a party who wants to know why you are looking into the death of Roger Black."

"Okay, Mr. Roberts, that's fairly vague. What party is that?"

"I'm not at liberty to say. My client has asked to remain anonymous. Suffice to say, I just want to know why you are, I don't know, I suppose *investigating* would be the proper term, Mr. Black's death. This case was closed by the police two years ago."

"Well, Mister, what was it again?"

"Roberts. Patrick's fine."

"Well, Mr. Roberts, I'm just seeing that all the kinks in the line are straightened out before I put the hose away."

I ordered some food and a drink from Lucy, who was behind the bar acting busy, but really just listening to our exchange.

"Sure, I understand, but what I don't understand is why?" Roberts said.

"I'm not sure I have to explain that to you."

He stared at me, then took a sip of his soda. I wanted to stop talking but his silence had the desired effect. "I'm his friend."

"You," he looked me up and down, "were friends with a drug dealer?"

I laughed. "Don't let my boyish good looks fool you, I'm a dangerous man." Not even the hint of a smile from Roberts' chiseled face, so I cleared my throat and continued. "Childhood friends. I don't think Roger's death was fully investigated because it was written off as a drug killing." I looked down the bar, watching Lucy pour my drink. "Things are rarely that simple in my experience, so I'm checking things out on my own."

"And?"

"Nothing. Just checking." I stared back at him as Lucy plopped my drink down with some peanuts. I popped a handful into my mouth. "They're fresh. Planters. Have some." I slid the bowl toward him.

"No thanks. Who else have you talked to about this?" he asked.

"You know what, Mr. Roberts, I believe I'm done giving you information until you tell me what this is about. Hey, Lucy, could you turn on ESPN? I think there's a dart competition I'd like to see." I actually had no idea what would be on ESPN at this hour.

Lucy handed me the remote. I turned it on. I watched an overweight guy roll a ball down the lane, pointedly turning my attention away from Roberts. Bowling, almost as stimulating as darts. He continued to stare at me, then broke off his gaze and drank. He sat there another couple minutes, then stood up.

"It was nice meeting you." He held out his hand.

I shook it and grunted. After he walked out I called Dana. "Hey, can you get me anything on an attorney named Patrick Roberts?"

***

Dana and I rode in silence as she tapped away on her iPad.

"Anything yet?" I asked.

"Nothing. I need to access the database at the paper, it's much more complete and secure. The only thing I did was Google the guy, but you could've and should've done that yourself."

"What'd you find?"

She read from her notes. "A lawyer who does a lot of work for the university. He often helps students from there at a discount, mostly with family law matters. Who is he?"

"He stopped by to see me, but said his client was confidential. I want to weed out who his client is."

"Ah, busting open da source. Irie."

"Does he have an address?"

"Yeah, he does. Drop me at the paper and go stake it," she handed me a slip of paper with Patrick Roberts' address on it. As I tried to snatch it from her fingers, she pulled her hand away. "But on one condition: after three, we gotta work on finding that girl. Remember, Roger's dead, Boise. She's alive, but I gotta do some paperwork before we can do more legwork." She dropped the address into my lap as she got out in front of *The Daily News*. She hobbled inside, as rain drops began pelting the windshield.

The address was on the west end near the university. To my left, I passed a deserted soccer field. To my right, some people strutted down the side of the road.

The women wore giant orange scarves in their hair and the men dressed in traditional ice, gold, and green Rastafarian tam-o'-shanters, the colors of many African nations, and the Rastafarian religion. The group looked happy and free, walking along with the typical broad smiles and animated speech of many locals.

I drove on, a smile cracking my face for the first time that day. I was a free man living in paradise after all. A block from Roberts' office, I parked.

His office looked like a house sporting a sign thrown up outside to denote it was now a law office. It read: "Patrick Roberts, Esquire." No parking lot, just street parking and a two-car driveway. The university perched on a hill about half-a-mile away.

I waited, a trickle of sweat working its way down my back. The rain had stopped, but puddles hung about in the ubiquitous potholes. Other than the center of town where tourists frequented, and the Havensight area where the cruise ships docked, the roads sucked. The difference between the "real" island and the "theme park" sections of St. Thomas had grown more pronounced over the years.

After twenty minutes, a college kid rode up on an old mountain bike. He maneuvered up Roberts' driveway and locked the bike. I slunk down in my seat and watched him go inside. He was a good-looking guy, with a slender eighteen-year-old body and a baby-face.

Dana buzzed.

"Yes," I answered, never taking my eyes off the bike.

"I need you back, now," Dana said with blatant urgency. "I need the car."

"I'm in the middle of something here. Can it wait an hour?"

"Do I sound like I can wait? I need to follow a lead and I needed to leave five minutes ago. Come pick me up." She hesitated, then said, "Please." She hung up before I could protest further.

My personal phone rang as I eyed the office. I picked it up without looking at the caller I.D. "Yes." Forgetting Dana wouldn't be calling me on this line, I mumbled, "I'm leaving, just give me…"

"Hello, Boise. It's your mother."

CHAPTER 20

I held the phone away from my face. Her usual half-smile stared up at me from the display. It said "Mother," which was how she always referred to herself. Not "Mom" or "Mommy" or "Mamma" like the other kids' moms, but "Mother." Always "Mother."

"Hello, Mother. I'm in the car, so let me put my ear piece in."

I fumbled with the tangled ear-buds and finally got them in. "What's happening?" I asked as I stared the engine. I waited a moment. The boy came out as I put the car in gear.

"Boise, are you there?"

"Let me call you back." I hung up. The boy faced in my direction, unlocking his bicycle. Zooming in using my phone's camera, I snapped four quick photos. None were spectacular from this distance, but good enough to build an identification. He pedaled away and I followed. Sure enough, as we reached the soccer field at the bottom of the road, he turned left toward the white buildings of the

University of the Virgin Islands' main campus. I drove on to town, cursing Dana's timing, but grateful for what I'd gotten.

"Who's this?" I asked Dana, holding up the photo I'd shot of the kid.

She studied the picture of a short-haired boy of about eighteen looking up as he unlocked his bike. "Where is this?"

"Roberts' office."

"It looks like a house," she said squinting at the building behind the biker.

"Seems zoning's another optional thing around here. There's probably a crack house operating in that residential neighborhood when we all know crack dens are zoned industrial." I waited while Dana continued to stare at the photo. "Do you know him?"

She studied his face another long five seconds, then came out of her spell. "Nope, never seen him. Looks like some college kid. Maybe an intern or he's doing something for the kid on student loans. Who knows?" She handed back my phone. "We have to move on this now." She handed over a sheet of paper.

"Whose birth certificate?" I asked.

"The missing girl's. I got bored waiting for a page to load, so I went on the good doctor DeVere's website as he requested. He recognized the girl and posted her name. Not sure how." I must have had a blank look on my face, so she continued, "Remember that doctor, Earl DeVere?" I nodded and waited for more. "Do you see the father's name?"

I scanned down the page, finally falling on the box titled "father's name." Cecil Jarl. Dana hobbled away toward the door. I followed her. Once outside, she pulled a cigarette. "Will sweat for smokes." She leaned her cane and her shoulder against the wall, lighting up.

"Cecil Jarl. Ever heard of him?" she asked.

"No," I replied, coughing lightly.

"This is big. He's the president of Payne & Wedgefield." She raised her eyebrows and dropped her chin slightly into her chest.

"Aren't they the assholes who are putting up all these hideous buildings everywhere?"

"He's got his own island, but he's set his sights on St. Thomas. Rumor has it, he has everyone's ear from the governor on down. Supposedly he's of Danish descent, so he feels he has some rights here."

"I thought the governor ran things."

"He does, but maybe he takes suggestions from Jarl. The bigger question is, why did it take an independent blogger slash doctor to reveal that this chick is Jarl's daughter?"

"Jarl doesn't want to appear weak or vulnerable. He wouldn't be the first man of power to keep his family affairs confidential. Probably has a private security detail," I said.

"Yes, he has that, as does all his nuclear family. This means the people who took her found a way around or through. Furthermore, it happened right there in Frenchtown, less than a mile from the Payne and Wedgefield offices." She grinned. "Makes him look bad. He might also want to send a message to these guys. A message that's not so legal."

"Yeah, well, that doesn't seem to matter much here," I added. "So, are we still on the prowl for," I paused and read the birth certificate, "Celia Jarl?"

"Are you kidding? This just became the biggest kidnapping since the Lindberg baby."

"You said he has a private island. How much time does he spend here?"

"Lately, on and off, but I don't watch his movements closely. I bet he's here now, but not sure."

"Are you going to run the story?"

"It's already out on DeVere's blog, so he'd have to get credit. It'd be a better story as an exclusive with us getting her back or helping the police."

"This Jarl doesn't sound like my kind of guy," I said.

Dana took a drag and exhaled slowly. "Based on what I just told you? You saying you're getting out of my taxi?"

"I'm just not sure I should spend my human capital on this rich guy and his rich daughter. They have a bunch of security and the police. Meanwhile, my friend's rotting in obscurity. You know, solving a cold case would also be a good story," I argued.

She nodded, then dropped her cigarette. After crushing it she returned inside.

"Boise, I need you to see this through with me. I'll help you with Roger after we make headway here, I promise."

"What about the next big thing? When this one's done, Pickering could move you on to another hot commodity. How're you going to convince him, or yourself for that matter, that the next kidnapping isn't more urgent than my cold case?"

Dana sighed. "Look Boise, it's not every day that we're captured, thrown into a shack at a compound, and discover that another person's also imprisoned there. Yes, there'll be other cases, but this one's a bit more personal. For me, it's like Roger is for you. The question really is, why don't you want these guys found? They could've killed us."

"I don't know. Yeah, they're bad, but you must have been in these situations before at some point." I paused, debating whether to push the issue, then pressed on with my hunch. "Does it have something to do with the photo in your drawer?"

Dana said nothing. Her red hair frizzed out more than usual today, matching her harried mood. I could tell she was steeling herself.

"All right, Boise. I know about Evelyn and we've built trust. I suppose I owe you."

I wanted to scoff and tell her friendship shouldn't be so calculated, but I sensed if I did, I'd lose her. Like a fish nibbling at the hook, if I tugged too hard, she'd dart away. The soft tick of the clock echoed like a hammer. In the far corner, another reporter shuffled papers. Although he wasn't paying attention to us, Dana leaned closer. She placed the small photo of the young girl that she'd hid in her desk drawer the first day we met in front of me.

"That's my dead daughter, Mila. She died because I couldn't protect her from my husband. I want to protect this Jarl girl. Can we do that?"

It seemed like she'd been thinking about, maybe even rehearsing, this explanation for some time.

I leaned back in Givens' chair. "Does this woman ever come to work?"

Dana stared at me waiting. I pushed out of the chair and declared, "All right, let's go see DeVere."

CHAPTER 21

I asked to see Dr. DeVere. The receptionist told me he was stitching someone up and would be out in twenty minutes. I leafed through the latest issue of *Where*. It was all about Carnival, the island celebration with Calypso music and parades leading up to Easter. During Carnival, juvé, an all-night dance-fest in the streets, also took place. Photos of moko jumbies, men who pranced around in stilts wearing scary costumes, littered the magazine. They represented spirits. Throughout my childhood they had towered above the crowd like giants.

"Hey Boise," DeVere said as he marched towards me patting his hands with a paper towel. He tossed it into the nearest waste bin. "What brings you and Ms. Goode over my way?" He looked at Dana and nodded. She stuck out her hand. He laughed awkwardly, "Sorry, but doctors don't shake. We know too much about germs."

Dana cut right in, "We need to know where you got that stuff on your site."

"You'll have to be more specific."

"How do you know about Celia Jarl being the victim of this kidnapping?"

He wagged his finger at her playfully, "Ms. Goode, you should know better. Is there anything else?"

"I, er, we need to know because we are trying to find her," Dana continued. "We need to speak with your lead so we can find her before it's too late."

DeVere's humorous demeanor vanished. "Ms. Goode, I expect to be taken seriously."

"And you are, as a doctor. It's very respectable."

"Um, Dana? Eric? Can we just cool off a minute?"

He removed his glasses and vigorously rubbed them using his coat.

"Eric, we respect your integrity as an amateur journalist. We do. Right, Dana?"

"My name's Earl," he said.

"I meant Earl. So sorry," I said.

Dana rolled her eyes at me, then muttered something indecipherable. I whispered into her ear, "Be nice."

"I respect your integrity," she said in a hushed voice, like a child who'd been scolded and told to say sorry by her mother.

"Okay, now, Earl," I turned back to the doctor. "Can you help us in any way with moving further down the road on this? We think it's a racial thing."

Dana erupted, "Boise! Quid pro quo! He hasn't told us anything, so why are we sharing? Listen, you, you, blogger. You better just come clean. I want to find this girl. Time's running out. I don't have a dick, so I can't participate in a pissing contest. You want to trade jobs? By all means, give me your doctor salary and I'll give you mine. Sound good?"

DeVere spun on his heel and charged back through the double doors into the operating area.

"Eric, I mean Earl, wait!" I yelled. The receptionist shushed me, holding a finger to her lips. Directing a screaming Shakespearean whisper at Dana, I said, "What the fuck was that?"

I stormed out of the hospital. Dana limped after me, banging the cane with extra force on each step.

"You have got to calm down and let me be the diplomat. You suck at this," I said, getting into the car without helping her. She struggled into the passenger seat and slammed the door.

"Let's go back out to Hull Bay," she said. "I want to look at that site again."

We drove in silence. Cutting through downtown, we got stuck in a parade route. Tall as trees, five moko jumbies tromped through the crowds, looking down and smiling through make-up as peacock feathers waved atop their headdresses.

"Let's go back toward the hospital and up over Mafolie," Dana said, impatience welling up again.

I turned the car around, riding up onto the curb to make a u-turn. The roads out to Hull Bay were deserted as many people had the days of carnival off. Many would be at the parades and would participate in juvé, which was to take place in two nights.

We arrived on the road where we'd been abducted and I pulled to an abrupt stop. Our dark incarceration in the shacks flashed through my mind and I had to force myself to breathe. Dana rested her hand on my shoulder.

"You okay?"

I waved her out of the car and sat catching my breath while rubbing my forearms. Counted to ten. Soon my heart-rate slowed. Dana leaned in and looked me up and down. "You better park further away."

After pulling the car a few hundred yards down the main road, I trudged back. Dana sat in front waiting. Police tape was still wrapped around the gate, but it wasn't locked. Dana pushed it open, snapping the tape.

We found an open window. I pulled out the screen and climbed in, then let her in the front door. An ashtray overflowing with white roaches and tweezers sat on a small round table by the front window. The lookout tower.

The louvers were shut keeping us safe from being seen if the cops showed up. I picked a hiding spot Dana could scurry into quickly and made a mental note.

"Find anything?" I asked to break the silence.

"If I do, you'll be first to know," she said.

I opened the pantry and the fridge. There was something, 'cause people had to eat and cops were stupid. A pizza box had been crammed into the bottom shelf, a receipt taped to the lid. "Backstreet Pizza: Thickest Crust in the Indies."

"Look," I held up the box as Dana leaned over the desk drawer.

She shot me a dismissive glance and went back to searching. "Pizza?"

Ripping the receipt off the box, I dangled it in front of her. A smile spread across her face like a stain.

"Keep looking," she said.

Everything else in the kitchen was generic stuff. Dana shuffled out of the bedroom waving one sheet of paper.

"It's a Payne and Wedgefield letterhead," she said.

Dear Sir,

We are happy to be doing business with you. You are getting top dollar from our firm for your property. Please do not make us take legal action.

Sincerely,

Cecil Jarl, President (signed)

"Impressive; a letter from the man himself," I said.

"Why this stuff is still in here is the bigger question," she said, taking the paper back. "Aren't the cops following up?"

That's when we heard a car outside. I pried the louvers apart ever so slightly. A police car stopped in front.

"Did you wrap the police tape back around the gate?" she said.

"Sort of. We ripped it, so that was difficult."

The cop got out and swaggered toward the gate, his gun belt twisting on his hips like a tight hula-hoop. He reached for the tape. I inhaled and held my breath. Then his radio chirped. He clicked the receiver and turned around, slogging back to his cruiser.

"He's leaving," I gasped.

CHAPTER 22

The sign said, "Backstreet, we like 'em thick since 1972." It was true, Backstreet Pizza made the thickest crust I'd ever had. We ordered a large. Dana ate one slice and I ate four.

My sweat-soaked arms finally started to feel cooler as I waited inside. Unlike most pizza joints, the owner had opted to invest in air conditioning. This was done for one reason: to capture more than just the locals. I'd come here as a kid and the place was as hot as every cheap pizza place around the world, but each slice had felt like a bit of heaven when my father would bring it home, which was only on very special occasions--like him getting a paycheck. Sobriety would have also qualified, but that occasion was so special it never happened until I was grown up.

Dana stood up and looked at the photos on the walls. She asked for the bathroom. The girl behind the counter pointed her back through some red and white curtains. What were we hoping to find?

I sat there taking the place in: scuffed white walls, black and white framed photos of various famous Italians, and a single wall covered by color photos of a West Indian man posing with people who were definitely not Italian.

"Hey, who's this in all the photos here?"

The counter girl reached behind her head and tightened the red bandana that held back her thick locks. I admired her wide nose and full lips that made African women so sensuous.

"Tommy."

"Does he have a last name?"

"Scarpetti. Why you don't ask him yourself? He in back." She pointed through the curtains where Dana had gone to use the bathroom.

"Is that cool? I mean, doesn't he want privacy or something back there?"

"If you goin' back, take this."

She dropped a large pepperoni pizza onto a wooden tray and sliced it into eight large pieces in three rapid cuts, then held out the tray.

Grabbing the round board, I headed back. Upon parting the curtains, I saw a man wearing sunglasses in the far corner of a cooler, dark room. Italian flag suspenders ran up over his chest and shoulders. His big white teeth glistened in the candlelight from the round table where he sat facing Dana. He wore a cowboy hat, which contrasted nicely with the suspenders.

"You bringin' my slices?" he said as I ambled up. I set the board down on a stand in the middle of the table. "Where da plates?"

Dana gripped my arm as I started to sit. "Could you get plates for all of us?"

I looked at her. Her eyes remained locked on Tommy.

I got the plates and came back. "My Amici! I'm-a Tommy Scarpetti. You named what now?"

"Boise." I shook his oily hand. I wiped my hand on a napkin.

"Pleased to make you. Dana asking me questions. You interested in answers too? She says you are okay."

"If it's okay with you, Tommy, I'd like to hear what you have to say."

"Here's what I have to say about this white guy and this black guy who order pizza from this place. I don't know 'em. Let's ask Gina." He whistled, then yelled, "Yo, Gina!"

"Hold on, Tommy! I got someone up here," Gina yelled back.

"Where's Little Nicky?" Tommy yelled back.

In another dark corner a large figure rose up like a fat muka jumbi. "I'm here, Tommy," came the deep-throated reply.

"Shit, Nicky!" Tommy grabbed his chest. "You almost stopped my heart. How long you been there?"

"I take a power nap around this time, Tommy. When I heard you yell to Gina, it woke me out of it. What you needing?"

"You know this white guy and his West Indian friend who always order from here out by Hull Bay?"

"Yeah, I ran a pie or two out that way before. I know dem."

"Dey ordered lately?" Tommy asked.

"Yeah, but not out to Hull anymore. They was over toward Sub Base last time."

"When was that?" Dana blurted.

Little Nicky didn't look at her. He stood there, his arms at his sides, his face stoic as Zeno.

Tommy laughed after a moment, then said, "Hey Nicky, you can answer da lady. When?"

"I think it was dis week, maybe on Monday or Tuesday, not on da weekend," Nicky said.

"How do you remember that?" Dana said.

"I just know," Nicky replied.

Right then, Gina came through the curtains. "Tommy, what the hell's the idea of callin' to me when I have people payin' da bills up front? We ain't got enough business you know!"

Tommy laughed. "You right dear, you right. I find Nicky. It's all good."

Tommy took another bite of pizza. Gina made a face and went back up front. I followed her.

"Hey, Gina, I left my pizza here, but don't think we're gonna eat any more. Can I get a box?" I said.

She grabbed a small box and I dropped the remaining three slices into it. I handed her the empty tray. She was looking at the register again.

"Everything okay with your register?" I said.

"Yeah, just some reconciliation thing from last night. You want something?"

"I'm Boise." I held out my hand.

"So."

I dropped my hand. In my youth I recalled people here had been friendlier, but everything seemed to have changed in the last fifteen years. Even small places had big-city attitude.

"Did I do something to offend you?"

"I don't like people who never came here before callin' me Gina like we old friends."

"I meant no disrespect. How can I get to know you if I don't introduce myself?"

"Slowly, by coming in and being friendly over time. After a long, slow while, we be friends." She waved her fingers through the air. Her dozen or so bangles made dings as they banged together. "Dat how it done."

"What if I told you a girl's life depends on us being friends now? What if I said she might be dead tomorrow if we don't become friends today? That's why we're here. To make friends and get answers quick."

Her eyebrows lifted in attention. "Who girl?" A customer walked up and stood behind me. I stepped aside. He paid, she handed him a box of pizza and he left.

"She's the daughter of some hotshot real estate tycoon. She was kidnapped a few days ago and time's running out. We need to find the guys who bought pizza here for delivery out to Hull Bay. We think they have her or at least know something."

"Oh shit, you mean those two assholes out on that little road? We don't get too many Hull Bay deliveries because we never used to deliver out dat far, but we need da dollars. I send Nicky out dat way."

"Well, those guys gone from Hull, so we tryin' to find where dey went," I said.

Dana limped through the curtain. "Where'd you go?"

"I'm talking to Gina about it," I said.

"We need to go, they're down Sub Base. Nicky said we could follow him down."

The phone behind the counter rang. Gina answered it.

I whispered to Dana, "Can we trust these guys? What if they take us there and Nicky hands us over or shoots us. Sub Base is industrial. If they get us in one of those warehouses, we're gone."

"Tommy's not like that. He worships Italian gangsters, but he's a baby when it comes to the real thing. He hates blood," she said.

"All the more reason he'd have someone else take care of matters," I shot back. "It's starting to get dark." I pointed out the glass door at the fading light.

"You afraid of the dark?" It was Tommy. He'd slid up beside us.

"It's just that they'll be no one down there at this hour," I said, "You know, to give us cover. We'll stick out like *papagayos*."

"We're in luck, they just ordered a pizza, so us coming won't be surprising," Gina said, holding up an order slip. "The usual meat mash-up with extra sausage."

"What's da name?"

"Dey always say da name is Julian, but I t'ink dats afta Julian Jackson, as dey is into boxing," Gina said.

I started to ask her another question, but she cut me off. "No credit card. Dey use dollas."

I sighed and sat down, waiting for them to prepare the first pizza I'd ever delivered.

CHAPTER 23

We piled into Tommy's maroon Cadillac. He dropped Dana and me off a block away, then pulled up in front of the place. Little Nicky carried the pizza to the door as Tommy slumped in the front seat. Another car's headlights lit up the road. Nicky hid his face and held back from knocking until the car was out of sight. It was unusual to see traffic down here at night, so I looked at the back for the license plate. The light over the plate was out. A late-model black Mercedes.

In the flickering streetlight Little Nicky had something dark in his hand under the box. I tapped Dana and pointed. She waved me off, but I wanted nothing to do with guns, although practically speaking, I hadn't come up with another way to deal with these goons other than fisticuffs.

I'd had a modicum of martial arts training that ended when I was fourteen and I'd only used it once on Murray Kohn in the seventh grade to push him off me when he decided he hated me for beating him in a foot race. He hit the dirt and I hit the principal's office.

"We're gonna wind up in jail," I whispered to Dana.

"Shhhh," she hissed.

Nicky knocked. The door opened and I heard an electrical zap. The guy who'd opened the door tumbled to the ground. Nicky waved us forward as he shoved the body aside and strapped zip ties over the guy's legs and arms. Nicky glided like a huge ballerina after checking the downed man's pulse, then nodded to Tommy that he was still alive. I recognized the prone figure as the Caucasian kidnapper who had bossed the West Indian around that day in the country.

It was a small industrial space, full of rolls of fiberglass, a couple boats under repair, and the nauseating stench of resin. In one corner, an outboard engine lay disassembled in a puddle of dirty oil. A single oleaginous sneaker print marked the floor next to the puddle.

A crack in the door provided a peek into a small office at the back of the room. A light was on inside and what sounded like a boxing match. I heard the roar of the crowd as an announcer raved about the power of someone's right hook.

Dana nudged me. I popped out of my reverie and sidled up beside them, poorly imitating Nicky's twinkle-toes, but confident they wouldn't hear me over the television. Tommy glanced inside, darting his head in and out rapidly. He waved us in.

The same girl from the dark shed--her straight, blonde hair matted down with sweat and dirt--lay on a couch, sleeping despite being bound and gagged. She looked emaciated and exhausted. Black and yellow bruises covered her visible skin.

Tommy shook her awake gently. He put his finger over his lips. She nodded in wide-eyed recognition; terror, the only emotion she had likely known for so long, was replaced by cautious hope.

Nicky hoisted her onto his shoulder like a sack of potatoes. She moaned. I pulled out my Swiss Army knife and freed her feet from the silver duct tape. He put her down once her limbs were freed. She walked with support from Nicky and me. Tommy acted as a lookout.

Dana had remained by the nearest boat. The guy by the front door twitched, perhaps coming out of his electrical unconsciousness. Then, a wiry man wearing a stained baseball cap over clumpy black hair stood up on the boat deck above Dana. His pock-marked face reminded me of Nelson Mandela.

"Hey, mon, where da pizza?" He faced the door and spotted the body. "Rudy!" he yelled.

This guy was going to be a problem, so I darted under the boat with the girl still holding my shoulder. I removed her gag. She moaned--a soft, cat-like sound. I gently put my hand over her mouth and whispered soft shushes in her ear.

A shot rang out as Tommy dove behind the outboard engine's housing. Rudy's partner had a gun. Nicky had his Taser out, but to use it, he needed to get closer. I lost Dana in the commotion. Freeing the girl's hands, I told her to stay put. Her chapped lips stretched and cracked as she coughed.

"Daddy," she croaked.

"Are you Celia Jarl?"

She nodded.

I whispered, "You're okay, Celia. We'll get you back to your daddy."

At this she shook her head back and forth violently. "Okay, it's okay, we'll do whatever you need."

Nicky took refuge in the office and I pointed adamantly up at the boat indicating I needed to do something about the lunatic before he shot someone. I headed toward the hanging ladder on the north side of the boat. As I got under the ladder, the gunman started descending, so I stopped. His gun pointed toward Tommy and Little Nicky's position. Two shots ricocheted off the ground, forcing them to remain under cover. I plunged my tiny knife into the meat of the goon's inner thigh.

Warm blood bathed my hand. He tumbled off the ladder with a howl. I leapt on top of him, but he shoved me off. I tumbled away, then spun around to find him pointing the gun at me with one hand as he tried to staunch the bleeding from his leg with the other.

"Drop da knife," he hissed. He rubbed his knuckles across his eyes, smearing blood across his face.

Dana crept up behind him. She cracked her cane down on his hand. The gun flew loose, but not before a bullet discharged. My left shoulder exploded.

Screaming, I tumbled to the floor, dropping the knife. Dana hit him again, this time across the head, but lost her balance with the second swing. A hulking figure loomed over me. The smell of lightening invaded my nose, before all went black.

CHAPTER 24

White ceiling like a silky sky. Six incandescent bulbs shined down at me. I felt rested for the first time in years. Dana leaned in. Pain shot through my arm as I tried to reach up. I cringed as Dana's face blocked out the blinding lights.

"Lights," I croaked.

The lights blinked out.

"You're in the hospital, Boise. Dr. DeVere was in the ER. He removed the bullet and stitched you up. Sounds good, right? We got that girl out of there. She's okay."

I heard the door open. "Oh good, you're up." It was DeVere. "Now, he needs rest. You all can stay but let him sleep."

The pain from trying to lift my arm subsided to a dull throb. I thought of beaches. On the beach, I saw my wife, pacing up and down, barefoot through hot sand. She wore nothing.

Her breasts had dots of sand on them. They glistened. Then, out of the bush at the edge of the beach, my mother came, carrying a white robe. She put it over my wife, who stared out at me across the bay where I stood on the water wearing a suit. My mother turned as she tied the terrycloth belt around Evelyn and the two stared at me; at first with love, then with melding defiance.

My eyes popped open. No one was there. I reached over with my right arm, grasped a cup on the table, and took a long drink of room-temperature water. Dana hobbled in on crutches.

I stared at the crutches. "Yup, I twisted the other ankle, so a cane won't cover it anymore, at least for a few days. It's better than a gunshot."

I laughed, then cringed as pain swelled in my torso. "Laughing's good for healing, except when the physical movement causes ripping in your stitches," she said.

This time I smiled. I could smell myself. "I need a bath," I said, wrinkling my nose.

"No argument here." She turned back into the hallway and yelled. "Nurse!"

A moment later, a petite young lady came into the room, shushing Dana. "You can't yell down dis hall. Just come get me."

"Mr. Boise needs a bath."

She took me to the showers and I managed to bathe myself with the nurse's assistance. It was difficult to keep still even when doing simple tasks, especially using one hand. I came back almost one hour later to find Dana typing away.

"Hot story?" I said.

I read over her shoulder about the rescue and our investigation leading to the events of last night. "It sounds more exciting when you write it. Also, the aftermath sucks," I said, lowering myself back into bed.

CHAPTER 25

After signing many pieces of paper to release the hospital from any liability for my future condition, I left. At The Manner, I climbed the stairs gingerly. I slipped by reception to avoid explanation to Lucy or Marge and slumped into my increasingly familiar bed.

The room had been cleaned and my scattered things piled neatly on the desk or on my dresser. I watched a soap opera and dozed off within minutes. Searing pain woke me. It was forty minutes past when I was supposed to take my next dose of pain medication. After downing two pills, I found an old bag of chips and ate a handful since I wasn't to take the pills on an empty stomach.

Sweat dripped from my armpits, rolling into the middle of my back. As soon as the pain dulled to a tolerable level, I hobbled down the hall and took a sponge bath and brushed my teeth. As I took my cell phone out to get into the bath, I noticed the ringer was silenced and I'd missed seven calls from Dana along with three texts demanding I call her.

Fewer than forty-eight hours after being shot, she demanded to meet. I thought we had rescued the girl and the urgency was over, but I supposed urgency never ended for Dana. Despite my guilt, I ignored her calls. Back in my room, I air dried under the ceiling fan in all my glory.

Half dry and just having flipped over, a knock came. I wrapped a towel and opened the door to greet Dana.

"Sorry, I'm indecent," I muttered.

"You're also not dressed," she said and entered. She sat down at my tiny desk.

"To what do I owe the pleasure?"

She picked up my phone. "You did see that I called eight times and left three texts?"

"I'm really tired and it seems the job's done, so I thought I'd lay here and watch soap operas while I dozed and sipped a Guinness."

"Okay, where's the Guinness?"

"That's the problem. Getting a Guinness would involve calling down to Lucy or Marge and I don't want any company," I said, laying back on my bed and putting my good arm over my eyes.

"Celia was at the hospital too you know," she said. She slapped a file onto my knee. "Care to read about it?"

"Isn't this...never mind. What's it say?"

"She was pregnant."

That made me lift my arm off my face. I grimaced with the sudden movement.

"The story will be published tomorrow, but I'm debating whether to include that information in this first edition."

"You're going to sit on it?"

"If it leads to a bigger story, yes."

I picked up the phone and asked Lucy to bring us each a beer, then stared at Dana. She was a poker player. Not unreadable, just letting you see what she wanted.

"What's this mean?" I asked.

"She's underage. Sixteen years old and three months pregnant. Lost the kid at the hospital yesterday," Dana said, finally showing some compassion as she dipped her face into her chest. "Sad to see a young girl pregnant. Even sadder to see her kidnapped and the stress possibly leading to her miscarriage."

Celia must have been pregnant before the kidnapping a couple weeks ago. Were they related or was it a coincidence? Regardless, the pregnancy was a separate event.

"Hey, look Dana, I'm sorry. Really." Dana was tearing up and waving her hand at me like a beauty queen.

"You tell anyone about this..." she trailed off. The hum of the ceiling fan filled in the empty air. A knock at the door.

I pulled on a t-shirt completing the towel-t-shirt ensemble. Marge handed me two Guinnesses.

We drank and looked through the louvers at the tips of coconut trees in the yard below and the town that led away from the bottom of the Danish brick steps. A lizard scuttled across the window screen. It stopped, looked, and listened before moving along and out of sight.

"So what does this mean?" I asked again. "She's underage. Do you think it's statutory rape?"

Dana met my gaze, some kind of hatred in her eyes. "Rape-rape I think. Yeah, at least statutory."

"Wait, what are you basing that on?"

"A feeling," she yelped, defiance in her voice.

"Dana, I know you feel sure about this, I can see that, but where are you getting this hunch? Is it in this file?"

"There are pages missing," she said. "Missing. That means something someone doesn't want others to know. That's my job. In my experience, when pages are missing it means someone with access wanted to hide something."

I considered what she was implying. The pregnancy could have come from a single incident of rape or an ongoing sexual relationship.

"So what's that mean for us?"

"I don't know, but it seems our work here isn't done."

CHAPTER 26

"Hey Dana, you promised that we were moving on once we saved her." I shut the file and handed it back. "How do you know that this wasn't consensual and she just wasn't careful?" I paused, measuring my next words. "She's a wealthy, mature young woman whose rich parents probably don't keep a close eye on what she does."

"I think it's something like that, but not exactly," she said.

"Dana, I need to get back to figuring out what happened to Roger. I feel for the girl, but that doesn't make her an automatic rape victim."

Dana took a sip of her beer. "Do you have a pencil?"

I found one in the top drawer next to the Holy Bible, then sucked my teeth.

"Sorry, tip's broken."

"No, I'll take it."

She dug into the boot around her ankle, breathing deeply with relief. "Damn thing itches so much, I'm about to pop a vein," she said as she offered the pencil back to me.

I crinkled my nose. "Keep it for next time," I said.

She hesitated, then put it in her bag. "Thanks. Look, I know this isn't important to you, but…"

"Not true," I said, cutting her off. "But, I have to prioritize helping Roger. Dana, there'll always be another case, another story, whatever. I'm a firm believer we have to make time to do what's important to us. By ignoring this case, I'm saying that Roger isn't as important to me as this rich asshole's daughter. My actions say those words and I can't keep saying that to my dead friend."

"But he's dead," she said, a sad smile playing across her face.

"What does that mean to you?" I countered.

"He doesn't know whether you care or not."

"Maybe he does and maybe he doesn't, but either way, I know." I paused. "Do you get it?" I jabbed my finger into my chest, then repeated, "I know."

"Sounds like you have to do this, but will you be around if something urgent comes up on this?" She shook the file like it was a bottle of orange juice. I conceded I would.

"One more thing," she held the file open. "Did you read the signature on the bottom of page five of this medical report?"

"No. I doubt I'd know her personal physician," I said.

"You know this one."

I peered above her index finger at the signature. Earl DeVere.

CHAPTER 27

Celia Jarl was on my mind. Dr. Earl DeVere had more to do with this than it seemed at first. He was both Celia and Cecil's personal physician. In addition to working in the ER at the hospital three days a week, he had a private practice over in the old medical building in Estate Thomas as an on-call physician. He'd failed to disclose this to us. I wanted to believe he was just protecting his patients' confidentiality.

Dana would dig and give me some freedom to work on my Roger angle before coming back in to help her. She had her friend, Annie, who'd finally returned from a trip to Denmark three days earlier. Annie would shuttle Dana around since she could get someone else to work in the family's store, Little Switzerland, for a few more days.

Roger's grandmother, Glor, would be my next visit, even though Dana had asked that I go canvas some more people in Frenchtown. Leafing through the papers Miguela had given me, I located a brochure for the new condos out in Bolongo Bay where Auntie Glor had moved. On the front of the brochure was written "#8977." I headed out to Bolongo Bay.

At the gate the guard twisted his mustache, staring at the number.

"Her name's Glor. I think it's short for Gloria."

He twisted his mustache until I thought the hairs would tear out of his skin. He held them in a tight bunch, then let go. It untwisted while he pointed at me.

"Oh yeah! You mean the old woman from downtown who come out last year?"

"Sure," I said, "that sounds like her."

"Lemme see." He started to twist again. He ran his index finger down a sheet of paper on a clipboard hanging from the window. "Yeah, right here. She in number eight-nine-seven-seven."

"That's the number I just showed you."

"All right, you just follow this yellow line dat way," he pointed back over some trimmed hedges. "When da road split," he made a v-shape with his hands, "follow da white line all the way back. She back against the hill in a cul-de-sac. You dig?"

No one answered when I knocked. A red Ford sat in front, shining in the heat. Rust bubbled at the base of the antenna and some Bond-o colored the driver's door a hazy pink. Several terra-cotta pots occupied the walk with hibiscus and lilies blooming.

I mopped my brow and sat on the curb after digging out an old bottle of water I'd heard banging around Dana's trunk. The water was hot, but I was thirsty.

A short older woman with glasses and a surprisingly light gait glided toward me. She slowed upon seeing me stand. I was wearing my straw hat and one of my nicer t-shirts.

"Yes," she said, "can I help you?"

"Auntie Glor?"

"Yes, the kids called me that. Who are…" Recognition trailed across her face. "Boise? Is that you?"

I nodded. Tears welled in my eyes and she matched my sentiment. We embraced, while thoughts of her peanut butter and jelly sandwiches and the glass of milk she'd offer every time I yelled in the front louvers for Roger to come out and play streamed through my mind. This woman, more than my own, was my grandmother.

We pulled away and she wiped a tear from my cheek. "What are you doing here?"

"I came to see you."

"It's been," she paused trying to count the years, then giving up, "so long. Where do you live?"

"Here. I moved back."

"Why? Why would you come back? It's not the place you knew as a child. It's all for show now, for the tourists. No soul."

"Well, Auntie Glor, you're a cheerful one to come home to."

"Oh, Boise, I just tell it like it is. Why don't you come inside? I'll make you a sandwich and some milk. How's that sound?"

"It sounds like the first taste of home."

I followed her inside.

"Sit, sit."

She went into the kitchen and rummaged in the refrigerator. I caught a glimpse of myself in the glass table-top. My stubble grew in ragged patches. I liked to think I had some tough-guy thing going with that look, but to someone like Glor I probably looked unkempt. Should have cleaned up more for my visit. She probably hoped someone had gotten out and made something of themselves, but I had nothing special to tell her about the last twenty years.

She padded over carrying the sandwich and a glass of milk. I took a bite and drank. She poured herself water from the tap.

"Did you go by the old place?"

"Yes," I croaked through sticky peanut butter. After sipping some more milk, I continued, "Jesus, it's hot here today."

"All right, that's enough about Jesus," she shot back. "You don't have to like him, but you better respect his name in this house."

"Of course. Won't happen again."

Sliding a bowl of peanuts between us, she popped a can of Sprite and took a drink. She mumbled something to herself. She got up and came back with a photo album that had a dirty blue cover. Wiping it off with a napkin, she opened it: Roger as a baby sitting in front of a piece of elk-horn coral filled the first page.

"He started out so beautiful. Even when you knew him, he was somewhat aggressive and worried about being a man, but he had a good heart."

I agreed; Roger had been a good kid.

"When did that change?" I asked.

"It seemed right about when you left. You were his closest friend. He got lost without you. I think he felt deserted."

"Thanks for not making me feel guilty," I said.

"Oh no, it's not your fault. Please don't think I mean that. It's just what he felt. Irrational, but then again, we all feel a lot of irrational things. That's why you need Christ."

"So what then? I left at twelve to live in St. Croix and he was still here with you guys to care for him. I mean, friends are nice, but family's what keeps it going, right?"

"Sure, he had us, but we weren't enough. I believe not having his no-good father around was a blessing and a curse. That guy was a bad man, and he was no father, that's bad too," she said.

I crunched on some peanuts. They were unsalted and tasted terrible.

"So what happened?"

She slowly rotated her Sprite can around in a circle on the counter, then said, "He got involved with a father-figure, who also happened to be a drug dealer."

I knew Roger lived with his grandparents and at the time I viewed it as a normal state of affairs. Many of my friends growing up lacked a positive male presence in the home, myself included. The men that were around often kept to themselves.

Guillermo, Roger's grandfather, shuffled around in black socks and brown criss-cross slippers. He never paid Roger much mind. Providing a roof was the beginning and end of his duties.

My father spent a lot of his hours drinking in Frenchtown, far from our home. He probably wanted to drink at a distance, that way he could be the person he was when my mother and I weren't close by. I'd never know that man. I took another swig of beer, but it tasted like milk. I spat it out on the counter.

"Boise! What in God's eye was that about?" Glor asked as she rushed to the sink for the paper towels.

Grabbing them from her, I sopped up my mess. "Sorry. So sorry, just, uh, felt a cough coming on and couldn't stop."

"As I was saying, Roger got into being a big man after you left. Maybe it was being alone without any real men to model himself after or maybe it's just what teenaged boys do."

"I suspect a little of both," I agreed.

"He met this girl at school. You remember he went to the Seventh Day Adventist downtown? I think her name was Becky. He started doing things with her and being gone all the time. She was a year older. He always looked older and he was tall. You remember, right?"

I nodded. I could see the memories taking their toll on her, but I had to hear what she needed to say, even if it was painful.

"He wanted money for a car, but we didn't have it. Even if we did, I told him he had to earn his own money. I suggested he get a job and for once, Guillermo agreed with me," she sighed. Removing her glasses, she rubbed her knuckles into her eyes, like she could squeeze the pain out with enough pressure. She sniffed, put her glasses back on, and continued.

"He said he didn't have time for a job. He wanted something different. Said something about freedom from oppression to the man. I said he didn't have to get a job, but if he wanted something besides his bike, then that was the only way. I guess he found another."

"Drugs?"

"My grandson became a drug dealer," she said, finally breaking down and sobbing.

I hugged her as she let the years flow out. As she blubbered and wept on my shoulder, I could feel the pain of her loss in every breath she took. She shuddered, then pulled away, wiping away tears.

"It's so stupid, but I always feel I should have done something differently. I feel guilty about my son every day."

"Roger's father? I never met him."

"Good for you. Lucky. I still don't know what I did for god to give me a boy like that. Made me turn my back on the lord for a long time. Now I know it was to test my faith. I failed. I spend every day trying to make up for that failure." She paused and stared at me with renewed compassion. "Do you have children, Boise?"

"No."

"You never got married. It's because of that unkempt facial hair and those awful clothes you wear." She shook her head disapprovingly. "Patrice did not raise you like that."

After I said nothing, she dropped her head and put her hand on my shoulder. "Everyone needs a family, Boise. I just want you to have the best."

"I know, Auntie Glor. I was married, we just never got a chance to have children. She passed."

"Oh goodness, Roger, I mean, Boise! She was young?"

"Yes. Very. Did Roger's father come around?"

"He was an altar-boy. You know that? Our family's been in the Catholic church since the beginning of colonization. We're St. Thomian originals, brought over by the Danish West India Company to work the plantations before this became a trading port. Back in the seventeenth century. For slaves, we have a long lineage; longer than most Europeans here in the New World."

The tears finally subsided and her voice returned to normal. Now she had an edge again, her guard back up.

Reminiscing over family history brought up a lot of painful memories, but if I wanted to continue to see my way clear to Roger's killer, I had to be tenacious.

"What was your son's name?"

"Don't call that man my son. I made my peace with that long ago. He's not my son. He was a disturbed man. I hate to say this, but he's probably better off dead."

"What should I call him?" I said.

She sighed, got up, and went to the pantry. She pulled out a box of tea and set it on the counter then filled a small silver kettle with water.

"Do you drink tea?"

"Sure, I can drink tea."

The gas stove *foomped* to life when she held a match near the burner. She turned her back to me as she continued.

"Jonathan was his name. Where's your wife?"

"In Los Angeles, at a cemetery in Redondo Beach. It's next to an ugly mall, but the cemetery itself is nice. Convenient." I wanted to stop, but for some reason I kept speaking. "She died just before her twenty-eighth birthday. She liked to watch baseball. She liked the Dodgers," I trailed off.

The kettle whistled. Glor gazed at me and crossed herself, then kissed her hand. She reached toward me, then pulled her hand back.

"What else do you want to know about Roger?"

"Who would want to kill him?" I said, as she poured hot water into a cup and set it in front of me with a pomegranate tea bag.

"You look like an herbal tea drinker," she said, cracking a smile.

"Obviously."

At this, we both let out a relieved sort of laughter. After sipping the horrible tea, I asked for sugar. She gave me honey. "I stopped keeping sugar in the house. Honey helps my allergies. Did you know that?"

I spooned a lot into my cup to drown the taste of the fruity, hot concoction. The ceiling fan whirred lazily above the dining room table, keeping it barely cool enough for me to avoid sweating.

"Roger had a surplus of people who didn't like him. I believe it was who they said, a rival dealer from out in Tutu who didn't want Roger coming for his territory. These men engage in war, and mostly the causalities are everyone else." She stopped and took a long gulp of tea. "Who cares? Roger's not worth your time, Boise. I been going to mass on both Sundays and Wednesdays to make up for raising that boy."

"What about his personal life?"

She sighed again. "You mean to persist. Very well. His personal life. I don't know anything much after high school."

"What about high school?" I said.

"He acted the fool. He had some notion of being a ladies' man. Wanted a car very badly. I think that's what started him down the road. Avarice leads only one place."

"It's one of the deadly sins."

"Amen. You remember Sunday school. Yes, when I wouldn't buy him a car or let him use mine, he found another way."

I sipped my tea and found the taste with two tablespoons of honey pleasant. My stomach groaned. I asked to use the bathroom.

It had been too long since my last pill. I pulled one out of my pocket and popped it into my mouth, chasing it with water from the bathroom sink.

"You okay?" Glor said as I emerged five minutes later, a little flushed.

"Yeah, it'll be fine in twenty minutes." I took another sip of tea, hoping the hot liquid would dissolve the pill faster.

"He wanted a car, so he must have had a girl to drive around in it with him, right?" I said, forcing a grin despite Glor's morose expression.

"Boise, this is not a smiling matter."

With a more somber look on my face, I waited. After ripping a paper towel off the roll and wiping up unseen crumbs from the kitchen counter, she continued.

"I suppose there was a girl. He liked these, these, Muslim-looking girls with bushy eyebrows and big lips. Their hair's so black. You know, they come from somewhere in the Middle East where Anderson Cooper always reports there's bombings and such."

"You mean she was Lebanese?" I asked, knowing St. Thomas was a haven for Lebanese immigrants.

"Yes, that sounds right. Is that Muslim?"

"Well, I believe that's the predominant religion in Lebanon, although I think many of the ones here are Christian. That may even be why they came over," I said.

"This girl, Becky or something, had a father who owned one of those shops selling t-shirts and all sorts of other garments in Drake's or Palm Passage."

Many of the Lebanese immigrants on the island had gotten into the jewelry or garment business in the more touristy sections of town.

Glor hesitated, taking another sip of her tea. "I'm pretty sure it's in Drake's. You remember where that is?"

"Drake's is in the middle section of the archway malls by the waterfront."

"Around where Cardow's is," she said, nodding. "She was trouble from the start."

"Was she a bad person?" I asked.

"Well, judge not lest ye be judged." She held her hands up like a person being held at gunpoint. "But I think she had designs on Roger beyond a few dates. She wasn't good for him. She made him do things," she finished, falling into a humming rendition of "Amazing Grace."

I let her hum for a full minute. She wandered away, returning with a four-by-six photo. In it Roger and I sat on the dock in front of my grandparents' beach house at Lindberg Bay.

Our hair and clothing whipped in the wind. We each held a fishing line wrapped around a stick. Roger's hair blew against his face as it was a bit long and his curls loose. Like me, he had a mixed heritage. Guillermo was Puerto Rican and Glor had some African heritage although her skin was light brown. My loose, kinky hair also blew around in my face. We were so young.

"I need to go in the garden. Clear my head." She pointed at the door. "Please, take your time and finish your tea. Let yourself out. No need to lock up."

With that, she patted me on the shoulder and glided into her bedroom on those light, dancer feet. A few minutes later she came out wearing white tennis shoes, a large

Chinese straw hat that looked like a pyramid, cloth gloves, and bulbous sunglasses. She walked out into the front yard, shutting the door.

I had work to do.

CHAPTER 28

I could have asked Glor, but something told me she would say no. So, I just went. When I got to the base of Bluebeard's Hill, I picked my way up the rutty road and through the rusty gates of Roger's childhood home. My surrogate home. In the evening darkness, I circled the deserted house as cars hummed in the distance, drivers finding their way to small destinations in the looming darkness of the tropical spring.

After a while, I sat down on the steps leading to the front door. The heat of the day clung to the concrete and creeped up my back. A street lamp hummed near the bottom of the drive, black insects buzzing around it. Another street light was mounted directly across from the house, but it was burned out.

The white metal louvers on the ground floor held fast, but one window around back inexplicably had frosted glass louvers. Using a fist-sized stone, I was about to shatter the panes when I realized prying the metal fixtures back and removing the louvers would be quieter. Inching closer so I could use my injured arm as well as my good one, I pulled the brackets apart and slid the glass out. Repeating the task five more times, I kicked in the filthy screen and entered.

The air inside smelled of mildew. Ambient light from outside didn't penetrate the bottom floor, which resembled a built-out basement. I cursed, thinking I'd have to return to The Manner to borrow a flashlight before I remembered my phone.

After sliding my finger down and up three times, the menu with the flashlight icon appeared. The room burst into view.

Scuffed white linoleum, a twin bed, a desk, and an uncomfortable-looking plastic chair comprised the furnishings. Disheveled sheets swathed the bed, as if someone had slept there the night before. A charcoal drawing in a minimalist frame hung over the bed. In it, a boy smiled out at me. I remembered the drawing--it had been in the house forever--moving from room to room whenever Glor redecorated.

I crept into the hallway, poking my head into the laundry room and another bedroom. They were as silent and nondescript as the first. At the end of the hall I reached a small foyer with an old bike sporting a flowered banana seat. I couldn't resist squeezing the horn bulb. It shrieked loudly in the enclosed space. To my left, stairs led up to the main living area on the second floor.

The living room was naked without a couch or television. Otherwise, it looked very much as I remembered it. A black piano tinged with dust dominated one corner.

After inspecting the house, I snapped some photos, wary of the extreme brightness of the flash to any outside onlooker, even through drawn drapes. I made my way down the narrow hall, stopping to peruse two more bedrooms, including one where I'd spent dozens of nights after Roger and I begged our parents for a sleepover and promised, with fingers crossed, to get to sleep early. The large four-poster bed still dominated the room and a portrait of some long-dead relative from the 1920's hung on the wall.

The bed in this room was made with a flower-print spread covering the sheets and pillows, as neat as a hotel room awaiting a new guest. The bathrooms had little to offer other than unused rolls of toilet paper and nearly full tubes of toothpaste in the medicine cabinets.

The last room in the rear of the house was the kitchen. As I turned right into the cooking area, my light hit upon a large portrait above the sink. It was a painting of the boy I'd followed from the Law Offices of Patrick Roberts to the university days before.

My blood congealed around my heart as the first genuine connection in my quest slammed into place. A bottle of Malta India balanced precariously on the ledge between the two basins of the sink below the portrait. A loud pounding echoed through the house.

I flashed a photo of the portrait and the sink, then stepped back for a larger photo of the entire kitchen. Racing out the back sliding-glass door and down the stairs, my breath shot out in rasping fits.

A police cruiser was parked in front of the house, an officer standing in the street reading something on his cell. Spying the pile of Styrofoam and cardboard boxes near the downstairs door, I buried myself in the rubbish, leaving an opening so I could watch the yard and street. He finally looked up from his phone, and using a Maglite, made a cursory survey of the house and yard from outside the fence.

A second officer pounded on the front door. A few minutes later, he marched down the stairs and past my hiding spot before barking into his radio that he'd found nothing.

They produced a notebook computer and took turns typing into it before climbing back into the cruiser and driving away, silent and menacing as a shark scanning the ocean for prey.

CHAPTER 29

After a day of doing absolutely nothing but feeling lonely, I woke up too early. Everything would be closed for at least another hour. I headed out, trying to slip by the lobby/bar area unseen. Halfway down the steps Lucy yelled to me.

"Boise, where you off to so early?"

"Got work to do. See you lata," I waved, trying to be nonchalant.

"Tonight I need your rent again. You supposed to pay in advance. If you don't pay tonight, den you need to get steppin,'" she said, making her fingers walk through the air.

I flashed a thumbs up over my shoulder as I trotted down the brick steps toward the nearly vertical climb up Government Hill. Hugging the gutter on the north side, I huffed and puffed as a steady stream of cars flowed down the hill, many of them pulling into angled spaces that lined the other side.

I gazed up at the stately Government House, towering above the town of Charlotte Amalie and tried to imagine the strange sort of power this governor wielded over his fiefdom. A guard stood at the entrance, casually chewing gum, while chatting on his cell phone. People wandered in. The greetings casual and familiar. The guard seemed to recognize all the folks entering that morning.

I bought a couple doughnuts and a small carton of milk to wash it down. Glor had given me a taste for milk again.

My phone buzzed. It amazed me that it had taken her this long to give in to calling me. I let it go to voicemail as I pulled my second doughnut out of the bag and took a hearty bite.

Charlotte Amalie's center ran between the Waterfront and Dronningens Gade, also known as Main Street. The Danish mark remained, although their influence was ultimately minor in terms of the actual culture that pervaded the island. Guinea and the United States wielded a stronger hold on the natives and the economics, even when Denmark officially owned the Virgins.

Proceeding down Nye Gade, then turning right, I dodged people already crowding the dirty sidewalk as they pointed at different shops and failed to watch where they were going. I plowed through, feeling the blast of air-conditioning from the jewelry and liquor shops along the north side of the street. I passed Hibiscus Alley, then came to Drake's Passage.

Glor had been sure the shop where the Lebanese girl worked resided in Drake's, but I wanted to explore the other passage she'd mentioned, Palm. I hesitated, then continued west, past the Royal Dane Mall, which housed three interconnected alleys, then arrived at Palm Passage. It was just before nine. The cruise ships had let their passengers out early, so I hoped all the shops inside would already be open for business.

I donned a pair of shorts and a tank top along with socks and tennis shoes. A camera dangled around my neck. In the first gift shop I entered, they sold various Caribbean souvenirs, including palm tree salt and pepper shakers and spoons in plastic cases that said St. Thomas, USVI on the handles. I always wondered if anyone ever ate with those spoons.

Three customers browsed. The proprietor's eyes drooped and he yawned. This didn't feel right, but I was unsure how to find the right place. I started to ask the guy behind the counter something, then fell silent. He wouldn't have known Roger and I had no names or even a description of any worth.

He looked Lebanese, but what was I going to say, "Hey buddy, you know a Lebanese woman who used to date a West Indian drug dealer named Roger?" I was at an impasse and couldn't think of how to make use of the information Glor had provided.

I continued toward the waterfront going in and out of each store. Nothing in Palm Passage felt right, so I sauntered over to Drake's and made my way through that mall.

At the north end of the alley, I found myself in a clothing store dominated by t-shirts, tablecloths, and loose-fitting island clothing for women. The sign said, Del Rio Gift Shop. A short fellow with a comb-over sat behind the counter on a bar stool. Reading glasses clung to the end of his large nose as he sipped from a tiny gold espresso cup and read the paper.

He looked up and favored me with an easy smile. "Can I help you, my friend?" he asked in a heavy Middle Eastern accent. "You look like you could use a new t-shirt. Please look about."

"Thanks," I said, using an unplanned Southern drawl.

"Are you from Texas?" he asked.

"Uh, no. Louisiana," I lied. The false declaration made my drawl more severe.

"Oh. I don't know anyone there, but my nephew lives in Houston," he said. "Well, you let me know." He went back to the paper after delicately pouring a splash of coffee from a thermos into his cup.

"Hey, I was wondering, what do you know about a cute girl that worked in one of these shops a few years ago when I last came 'round."

"A cute girl?" He lowered his glasses even further. "I have two daughters. They work here in the afternoons. Are you looking for a wife?" He looked me up and down then sneered, clearly not interested in having me for a son-in-law.

"No, just thought I remembered someone from this shop," I sputtered. I had no idea where I was going with this, but at least I had a Lebanese guy with daughters in a conversation. St. Thomas wasn't that big a place and the Lebanese population could not have been more than a few thousand.

"Oh, because you say my daughters are 'cute' could be bad for you if intents are not good. You understand? Besides, they only date Lebanese. You not Lebanese."

"I meant no disrespect. I just met, might have met, someone here my friend knew," I said. "Never mind, I'm just gonna keep looking 'round."

I walked the store, leafing through humorous t-shirts and trying to come up with a way back into this man's good graces. He watched me over the rim of his glasses. The daughters might be more cooperative, so I decided to make myself scarce until after two.

CHAPTER 30

Island Ice Cream, a tiny shop that had been there my whole life, had the best on the island. I didn't recognize the owner, but it could have been his son, or someone else who wanted a taste of paradise might have bought the location. The sign hadn't changed, literally. I had to squint to make out the fading twenty-eight flavors pronouncement.

I took a big lick of my green pistachio ice cream with almond chunks as I wandered through the blast of cool air into Del Rio. I wasn't sure why, but that little man and his strong reaction to me compounded my feeling that I was on to something there. This time I entered in the back, from an exterior alley that abutted Drake's.

The little guy was gone. A dark-haired woman with sparkling eyes and tastefully-applied rouge sat behind the pygmy counter. A beauty mark dotted her face above the right side of her upturned mouth. The little guy's tiny gold cup and newspaper was still on the counter.

A girl of eight with the same jet-black hair, but poutier lips, lounged on the wooden steps behind the counter which led up into what must have been a storage attic. She gripped a Gameboy console. Light from the screen illuminated her features as she mashed buttons in rapid, repeated patterns.

"Hey, how you doing?" I said, cheerful as I could muster.

"Fine, thanks. Welcome. Are you looking for anything in particular? A new t-shirt perhaps?"

She pointed at my shirt using a slender painted fingernail. No wedding band. The girl had to be her daughter which meant either she appeared younger than she was or she'd given birth around age twenty.

I looked down at my shirt and saw a splotch of green on it.

"Shoot! Man, I always melt ice cream on my shirt." Pathetic, but this was what I'd come up with for round two.

"It's okay, we have inexpensive t-shirts on this rack and this wall. They're six each or two for ten."

The daughter rolled her eyes, but never took her attention from the Gameboy.

"Mom, can I use your phone yet?"

"No, not until you apologize like you mean it."

We walked over to the t-shirts.

"Wha'd she do?" I asked as she helped me find my size.

"She said the s-word earlier when I told her she'd have to help cook dinner tonight with her aunt."

"The s-word? Wow, where'd she learn that?" I asked.

"School or her cousin," she said.

"How old's her cousin?"

"Eighteen. No, maybe he turned nineteen. I can't keep up. You have kids?" she said, looking at me like she knew the answer.

160

"Nope. But after this conversation, it's my top priority," I said.

"You're wearing a wedding band, so what, you just put your wife off because you don't want the responsibility?"

"I, um, well, since you asked, my wife passed," I said.

"Oh, oh gam. Sarry, so sarry," she fell silent for a moment. "So, the t-shirts you would fit into are here," she ran her hand across the hangers like Vanna White.

"Is she your only daughter?" I said.

"Yes, my only..." She made a clucking sound at the girl. "Audrey! I told you not to use my phone!"

Audrey stood up, stuck out her tongue, and darted out the door to the alley.

"Shit! she yelled, "not again." She darted out the back door after her daughter. "Look after the store, mister. Be right back, promise."

She was gone before I could answer. I stood inspecting the shirts and wondering what to do next. Of course, at that moment, a corn-fed guy wearing an Ohio State baseball cap and his short, brunette wife entered the store followed by three giggling teenaged American girls sipping Cokes.

"S-word," I muttered as I went over to assist the couple. They asked about trying things on and I located the dressing room. Luckily, they came out and didn't want anything.

I checked the clock on the cash register. Almost ten minutes had passed. How far did my responsibility extend to this unknown woman who'd just entrusted her business to me? The giggling girls crowded around a wrap-around skirt with bright colors and flowers.

"Hey, like, do you know how much this is?" the prettiest and oldest looking one said as she batted her heavily mascaraed eyelashes at me.

"Let me see," I said pretending I knew, but couldn't remember exactly at this moment. "I think we just lowered the prices on these outfits." I found the price tag. "Yup, they were," I stared at the price tag and quickly added twenty percent, "forty-nine ninety-five, but now are thirty-nine ninety-five," I said, handing back the outfit.

I turned and there she was, holding her daughter's hand. "You're a natural," she said, beaming at me and the girls. "I wish I didn't need to still work here or I'd let you take my place."

"Uh, excuse me. Would you two just get a room or better yet, give us a room to try these hot outies on?"

I pointed to the dressing rooms and all three girls piled into one, six outfits in tow.

"You can only, oh forget it," she said, as the girls were engrossed in their phones and trying on clothes. Audrey was wriggling to free her hand from her mother's talon without success. "Stop it!" she yelled at Audrey, then bent down and whispered in her ear. She stood up and pointed her open palm at me. "Go on."

The little girl stared up at me, showing fear for the first time. "Mister, I'm…" she buried her face in her mother's pant leg.

"Take your face out of my leg and talk to," she looked at me, "what's your name?"

"Boise." I decided to be truthful.

"Tell it to Boise. Look at his face."

She tried to pull her leg away, but Audrey held fast, moving with her mother's slide. I bent down to her level.

"Is there something you want to tell me, Audrey?" I asked in a high-pitched tone. "It's okay, you can tell me."

"Sorry," she whispered, peeking one eye out.

"Say it like a big girl," her mother instructed from above.

Audrey let go of her mother's leg and threw her arms straight back, then yelled, "Sorry! Sorry! Sorry! Okay?"

I stood, startled. Audrey zipped behind the counter, cowering behind the register.

"It's a start, but until you say a more formal sorry to Mr. Boise, no phone," she said, smiling at me like we'd done well under the circumstances.

"Now things are unequal," I said. "You know my name, but I don't know yours."

"Noa. My father owns this palace," she gestured again like Vanna White.

At that moment, the girls stormed out of the dressing room, each wearing an outfit. They pranced over and twirled in unison like a dance trio.

The tallest one eyed me after completing her spin. "What do you think?" she said grinning. The others waited expectantly.

I looked at Noa, who gave me the "sell my stuff" shrug, so I said, "Yeah, I think this one would look great on you and this one matches your eyes better." To the tallest one with the mascara, I said, "And the one you're wearing is perfect."

She gave a curtsy and they all filed back into the dressing room.

My cell phone buzzed. Dana again. I killed the call.

"You don't look very interested in your phone call," Noa said.

"I'm not a great fan of being bothered when talking to a beautiful woman," I said.

She blushed. "Is there something I can help you with, before more customers or more likely, my daughter, interrupts us again?"

"Yes, there is. I saw your father earlier and he mentioned that he has two daughters."

She hesitated, then said, "I have a sister. There's two of us." She squinted at me. "What's this about?"

I made a quick decision to take the direct route with her.

"Please don't be alarmed, but I wondered if any of you knew a boy named Roger Black growing up?" I paused momentarily deciding how much to divulge. "He was a very close friend of mine until I was twelve and I'm trying to find out what happened to him."

"What happened when you were twelve?" she asked.

The girls piled out and dramatically dropped three outfits on the counter. They also picked out three colorful matching visors. Audrey popped out from behind the counter, and one of the girls put her hand over her mouth.

"Oh! Hey, there's, like, a kid running the register?"

"Audrey, how many times have I asked you not to startle the customers?" Noa said, as she slipped back to ring up the items.

The girls giggled, paid, and left. The store fell quiet except for the oscillating fan and the *whoosh* of the air-conditioner as it powered on again.

"He doesn't look familiar to me," she said coming back and examining the photo of Roger from Miguela's file. "First off, he's black." She held out her hand, "No offense.

I just don't date black guys even though there's lots of 'em around. Not my type. Second, my father would kill me."

"I don't mean that, just look again."

This time she took it in her hand, examining it more closely. My cop buddy Henry had mentioned this technique when he had trained me to be an investigator for a law firm in Los Angeles. The first time you show most people a photo of the person you're looking for, most people won't touch it. A quick glance, then they say they don't know anything and never saw them. You wait and get them relaxed about why you want to know, then show it again. You try to get them to handle the photo, this makes the connection more intimate and brings them into the cause.

"This is a friend of yours?" she asked.

"We grew up over there right next to each other until I moved away in middle school," I said, pointing to the east. "Look, I'm not trying to get anyone in trouble, it's just he was a good friend, and I have to help his family."

"What happened?"

"He passed away, but he left some unresolved stuff in his estate. I want to be sure there's no one out there who should know. You know what I mean?" The truth only took you so far.

"Not really."

"Well, it's kinda confidential," I said gently.

She nodded.

"There could be some inheritance family members are entitled to, but I can't talk about that further." I hesitated again, weighing my options. "I think he has a kid out there and that kid would be entitled to a lot of money. He died intestate."

"You had me at money and lost me at intestate," she said. "Also, a kid implies that you do think there was more to us than friends, right?"

"Not you, but someone you might know."

"Why? Why me?"

"Because, Roger had a thing for Lebanese girls. Audrey's your only kid, right?"

Audrey was behind the counter on her mother's phone. Noa started to say something then her mouth dropped closed. She looked at me and I could see the drapes were drawn now.

"Thanks for helping me make a sale and for watching the store. Good-bye, Boise," she said.

She went behind the counter, took the phone from Audrey, and handed her daughter a small book. Audrey glanced at me, then buried her face in the book.

Hiking back to The Manner, my mind was awash in possibilities. I'd struck a nerve. Noa knew something, or at least worried there was a possibility she knew something. It might even have been a long-shot, but it was there and I needed to witness her next move. I dropped off my tourist camera, changed outfits, and made a one-eighty, heading back to Drake's Passage to see what she'd do next.

People wandered in and out of the shop for the rest of the afternoon. At ten after five a car pulled up. Noa walked into the alley and slid in after strapping Audrey into the back seat. Using my phone, I snapped photos of the license plate and the female driver, who looked to be in her early twenties. She was short like the father, but with softer features than Noa.

Their mother must have been a tall woman, because Noa didn't get her height from her dad. I'd have to find out more about them, but one thing was sure: my best bet right now for getting info on Roger was Noa. She appeared only a couple years younger and must know something to shut me out like an atheist slamming the door on a missionary.

***

My financial reserves were holding, but beginning to worry me. I ducked into the bar. Marge stood at the ready while two customers drank in silence. A Johnny Horton song hummed through the speakers.

"Marge, I owe you money," I threw up my hands in surrender.

She pointed toward the kitchen. I found Lucy cooking a pasta dish.

"Hey Lucy, I came to pay you."

"Ha! You don't know? You paid," she said. "Till next Wednesday, you paid."

I stared at her a long moment. In lieu of pinching myself, I scratched my head, then she continued, "Da lady wid red hair and she limp. She pay. You gave her good time?"

CHAPTER 31

"Yeah, I comin,' I comin,'" I shouted. I stumbled over my sneakers and cursed before finding the light. The sun had taken the morning off.

Dana stood there, using a dripping umbrella as a cane. "Shit, it takes a long time to get up here in the goddamn rain," she said as she pushed her way past me and sunk into my only chair.

"Please, come on in," I muttered.

"Have you listened to my messages or read my texts?"

"No, I just woke up," I retorted. "In fact, I hadn't woken up yet, you woke me."

"I have more leads for us to follow. DeVere has something to do with all this, you believe that?" she said.

"Sure, whatever. I mean everyone's in on it probably, right? What are there, five hundred people on this rock?"

"We need to go talk to that doctor and find out what's really going on. They published the story on our rescue. You're gonna get business out of it. Did you see it yet?"

"No, I haven't had time to read the paper," I rubbed the sleep out of my eyes. "Why didn't you leave me out of it?"

She sighed. "I'm doing you a favor. It'll be good for some paying business."

"By the way, I don't want you paying for my room. I'm not your kept man," I said.

She held her hands high. "Can we just get going?"

I brushed, flossed, and slathered some Speed Stick in my armpits. We huddled under the umbrella as I supported Dana down the stairs and into the car. We got to the hospital at nine.

***

"Hello, Earl," Dana said as DeVere walked up with his coat streaming behind.

"Dana, I'm extremely busy with my rounds." He looked down at a clipboard he carried. "Is there something you need help with immediately? Is your leg okay? Oh, hi, Mister?"

"Boise, just Boise."

"Right," he said, "nice seeing you both again. What's the matter?"

"We have some questions about your involvement with the Jarls, Cecil and Celia," Dana said, hitting him with the goods. I liked it.

"Not this again!" DeVere turned and headed back down the hall.

As we got in the car Dana slapped the dash. "Irie, irie, brodda! We got him. I love hitting people like that and getting the whole truth in a nano-second."

"You can't print a look," I said.

"No, but you can run 'em into a corner they have to talk themselves out of. That's when they go on record.

More powerful than money: the need to save your own ass," she laughed.

Back at *The Daily News*, Dana flew into Pickering's office like her hair was on fire. She barely limped and was soaked because I couldn't keep her under the umbrella.

She charged out and powered up her laptop.

After a minute, I waved my hand in front of her face. "Well?"

She didn't look up, the glow of the screen making her eyes look even crazier than usual as she typed.

"If you don't need me," I started to get up, at which point she grabbed my wrist.

"Let's just stay out of the rain and gather ourselves for a few," she said. "Give me some more key strokes. You'll thank me."

I rolled my eyes and settled back into Givens' chair. "I need to eat," I complained.

She threw a take-out menu at me. A ruckus sounded from the back entrance where Dana and I had first met. We looked at each other, then I grumbled, "It couldn't be."

Dana shrugged. "Yeah, probably. He said he'd come around for a meal on...oh gam...yup, the last Thursday in April. I guess take him out for a morning dinner?"

Sure enough, Professor Tyfoe was banging on the door of the basement using the handle of a hairbrush. He wore a threadbare tweed jacket, a white dress shirt, and dilapidated loafers.

Twirling the hairbrush, he bowed. "So good to see you, my boy! Shall we sojourn to Victor's?"

"Professor, so good to see you. Victor's isn't open yet. Might I suggest we go to Island Bakery?"

His face contorted into a grimace, but immediately snapped back to a chipper demeanor. "Yes, I love the ox stew at Island Bakery. We can walk."

The professor and I ate while he told me about a student who had two left hands but was smart as a whip. We made another dinner appointment for the last Thursday of May. When I returned to *The Daily News*, Dana was still hard at work.

I propped my feet up and pondered the situation while studying the ceiling. For the first time I noticed lime green swirled into the white paint. It looked like different types of paint had been poorly mixed, probably by hand to save money. Typical island incompetence.

From Pickering's office I could hear Dana and the editor bickering about where to go with the story next. Pickering barked at her like a sergeant--a very well-manicured sergeant. He stood board-straight, his suit had not a stray hair or lint on it.

Through the half-closed blinds of Pickering's big glass window, Dana waved her arms and winced once, grabbing her leg where her wound was still healing. She pointed at her leg and said something like, "I did this for this story, but it's not over yet. I'm not stopping."

Dana stormed out of his office and over to me. "We gotta go see Tommy and squeeze juice out of DeVere."

Tommy lounged in the back of the pizzeria, wearing a wild carnival hat and a mask of feathers. A teenaged girl sprawled next to him wearing ice, the Caribbean word for red, gold, and green face paint. She sat up straighter when we entered. A television, that hadn't been on last time played one of *The Godfather* films at a low volume. It captured my attention.

"I like the visuals and I already know all the dialogue by heart," Tommy said, lowering the volume with a remote. "So, greetings, man and woman of mystery. You going to this afternoon's parade?"

"It's wet out; no parades," Dana said. "Besides, we all have work to do."

"What's it you require of me today? What evils are we righting that cannot wait until after our celebration of debauchery prior to Lent? You know Dana, you really should live in New York."

"Well, if *The Times* calls, I'll go. This story could put me on their radar, so could we get serious for a moment?"

Tommy eyed me, then shrugged. "Okay, what?"

"What do you know about this doctor over at the hospital? Earl DeVere."

Tommy pulled a notebook from beneath the baggy shirt he wore and leafed through it. "Here we go, DeVere. Went to Johns Hopkins and did his residency in Atlanta. Fell off the radar for two years, then applied and got the job as head of emergency medicine here in 2012. No island ties that I'm aware of." He shut the notebook.

"How does a guy with a two-year gap in experience get that position?" I asked.

Dana chimed in, "In case you hadn't noticed, we don't have the most cosmopolitan locale here for highly trained professionals. The Danish found it extraordinarily difficult to get doctors to move here in the seventeenth century. They jacked doctor's pay way up by requiring merchants who anchored in our harbor to be examined at exorbitant rates." Dana paused and looked at Tommy before she settled her gaze back on me. I felt like I was back in Sunday school. "As soon as the doctors had their fortune, they returned to Denmark. As wonderful as the tropics are to visit, the heat and isolation gets to people."

Tommy's eyes glinted through the slits in his festival mask. We sat, watching *The Godfather* until a server came in carrying a cheese pizza.

"Eat," was all Tommy said.

CHAPTER 32

I looked sideways at Dana as we slopped through the rain,
her limping with her arm over my wet shoulders as I held
the umbrella over her red head.

The rain slowed and steam rose from the hot asphalt
of Back Street. Cars crowded the area between the stone
and plaster buildings. It felt confined, especially without any
sunlight to open things up. I couldn't tell where my sweat
began and the rain ended, but the soft deluge felt good.
Most of the walls were painted bright island colors: yellows,
whites, greens, and baby blues.

"Is everyone here a shade of gray?" I asked.

Dana didn't seem to hear me.

Once in the car, I followed her directions like a
somnambulist. We were in Sub Base again, outside the
kidnapping warehouse. In daylight, it looked benign. Metal
I-beams held up galvanized roofing over a concrete slab and
a bedraggled yard. Two old cars with rotting tires and years
of rust occupied the only off-street parking. We navigated
through a hole in the fence.

The sun broke through the clouds. I pointed out a partial rainbow to Dana who showed little interest. The door was shut, but the padlock remained unlatched. It was simply turned in to look like it was locked. Apparently this was a popular tactic.

"You'd never know only a few nights ago real things happened here," I said.

Once inside Dana said, "I need to check one thing, okay? You search that side, I'll manage over here in that office where she was being held."

"What are we going to find? You think they left a business card?"

"Just let me know any kind of identifying things you find. Anything. There's no stupid questions."

"Where do babies come from?" I asked.

She tried the office door. It didn't budge. She picked up a wrench from a work bench and smashed the window to the right of the door. Once I cleared the glass away, I climbed through to let her in.

Dana marched to the file cabinet and I began to wander through the warehouse proper. In the far corner I found a grungy shower. A metal operating table was behind the curtain.

"Hey, Dana. Got something over here."

"Bring it over, I'm busy," she yelled over her shoulder. She'd shut off her cell phone flashlight and turned on the desk lamp. In her hand she examined a gray file folder.

"I can't. Just come over," I said.

She froze at the sight of the table. It was clean, very clean, but also very out of place. I flicked on the overhead lights.

Dana flashed several photos and took a video to prove where we were. As we walked out she got a shot of the address in one continuous take.

"This'll get us some leverage."

I threw up my hands. "What have we got?"

She held up the file folder. "I'm pretty sure this holding company belongs to Payne and Wedgefield, although I don't bet we'll be able to prove it without a forensic analysis of the shell corporations between it and Payne. Either way, Jarl owns this place, which makes you wonder why his daughter was being held in a warehouse owned by her father."

Back at the hospital, we found DeVere in the cafeteria eating what looked like day-old chicken-fried steak.

"I thought they fed doctors better than patients," Dana said as we pulled out plastic chairs and joined him.

"No, everyone in the hospital eats the same food. What is it now, Ms. Goode?"

"Wondering how the blog's going?" Dana asked.

"Fine. If there's nothing else, I like to eat alone." He leaned over his tray like a prisoner.

Dana slid her phone across the table. "Ever seen that table?"

He peered at the phone, then up at Dana. "I like to eat alone. Thanks for stopping by to say thanks for saving your lives."

"Oh, we're grateful for what you did for both of us. Aren't we Boise?" I nodded like an obedient dog. "I just did some digging. You know, I never knew that you were originally from New York, like Cecil Jarl."

His face remained as placid as Magens Bay.

"New York's a very big place," he said.

"It is," she agreed. "But, what are the odds both of you also attended Columbia for grad school? The internet's amazing. I checked and there are currently only thirty-four-hundred graduate students at Columbia. That looks a lot less like a coincidence."

I picked up her thread, just like we'd discussed. "You graduated from med school one year after he completed his MBA. The odds go way up that you two knew each other. Like way up." I floated my hand up like a rising helium balloon.

"I've got nothing." Before he could go further, Dana showed him the photo of the operating table again. His eyes faded like the sun behind a thin cloud.

Dana grinned. "Nice operating table, huh?"

DeVere shoved his plate away. A bit of food splattered on the table. He stood and headed back through the double doors that said "Hospital Staff Only Beyond This Point" in large red letters.

CHAPTER 33

The dock down at Lindberg Bay: the wood felt damp from all the rain. Dana had dropped me off on Airport Road at my request. I walked the last half-mile. This was my private spot.

One ragged dock and the noise from the airplanes discouraged most tourists from venturing into the area. Before being taken by the government and torn down, my grandparents' house had been less than one-hundred yards from where I sat. By facing the ocean, I blocked out the mechanical sounds to focus on the ever-shifting sand, tumbling shells, and lapping waves.

Roger kept creeping into my thoughts. Cecil Jarl and his no-doubt-spoiled-brat daughter intruded, fighting for my attention. Roger was no prince, but at least I had a personal connection to the guy.

I possessed a photo of a kid, some interest from a lawyer who must know something, and the kid's picture hung in Auntie Glor's house. The only person I'd shown the photo to was Dana.

To detect, you're supposed to use the information at your disposal to ferret out specifics which would lead you closer to the truth. But instead, I kept trying to build details out of air. At an early age, I'd developed this need to do everything myself. As usual, it wasn't working.

It was five o'clock and in the distance I could hear traffic growing busier on the four-lane "highway." Since I was already down here, why not take a walk over to Patrick Roberts' law offices and confront the son-of-a-bitch? He'd popped in at The Manner unannounced. Why should I sneak around and let him have the upper hand? I wasn't a fan of the cloak-and-dagger stuff anyway, I preferred a straightforward encounter.

A splinter jabbed into the heel of my hand as I pushed up from the dock. I sucked it out as best I could, cursing as I tasted blood. My left shoulder throbbed from the gunshot.

When I reached the main road, I bought a Coke. I popped a colitis pill and chased it with the prescription painkiller they'd given me at the hospital. The sun dipped behind a stand of brush to the west as I knocked on Roberts' door. That's when I saw the bike, locked in the same spot in front as before.

The boy I'd photographed days ago opened the door. "Hi, can I help you?" he asked, but didn't offer to let me enter.

"Yes, I wanted to speak with Mr. Roberts about a matter. Is he here?" I said.

"He's a little busy preparing for a deposition. Do you have an appointment?"

"No. Could I come in and make one?"

A shadow of distrust crossed his face, but he stepped aside, bidding me to enter. The place really was a house and we were in the living room, which doubled as Roberts' reception area. In the corner, beneath a generic print of some abstract art, a spate of trashy magazines like *Us* and *People* were fanned out on a round faux wooden table.

"I'm Boise," I said, holding out my hand before the young man could sit down. "Boise Montague."

He shook with a firm grip. "Elias. Mr. Roberts' secretary."

"You are very young to be a legal secretary," I said. I pushed my chin down, pursed my lips, and in my best Darth Vader voice said, "Most impressive."

"I'm not a legal secretary per se, but I take care of his appointments. Probably more like a receptionist," he said giving a forced laugh.

"Still pretty good," I said as I sat down. "So, when can I see him?"

He opened an appointment book. "He has an opening tomorrow at three. Does that work for you?"

"Yes," I said. "Do you have a business card in case I'm running late or need to reschedule?"

He picked one out of a cardholder on the edge of his desk and handed it over. "Can I say what the matter is regarding?"

"It's personal and confidential. I'd rather discuss it with Mr. Roberts in private."

"Very good, Mr. Boise. I won't see you tomorrow, but Mr. Roberts'll let you in."

"Oh, where will you be?"

"Got class. I'm a student at the university and although I try to schedule most of my classes around the work day, it doesn't always work out. He's understanding."

"He sounds like a great guy," I said.

"Oh he is. He's done a lot for me and my family," he said as I opened the door. "Not your typical attorney."

CHAPTER 34

A voice message from Dana said, "Meet me over by the Greenhouse at noon." Just enough time to stop by the Del Rio Gift Shop.

I poked my head around the corner from the alley. Both Noa and her father milled about in the shop. No Audrey. Presumably she went to school, at least part-time.

Mr. Hariri settled down on the edge of his stool, started reading the paper and sipping coffee from his tiny gold cup.

Noa folded shirts on a table toward the rear of the shop. After thirty seconds I got her attention and waved her out. She whispered something to her father then slipped into the alley. We walked towards the waterfront, away from the bustle of Main Street.

"How many ships today?" I asked. This was the first question everyone who owned a tourist-based shop in St. Thomas asked every morning. *The Daily News* listed it right next to the weather and U.S. stock prices.

"Five. Not a great day, but traffic's steady," she said.

A guy from a jewelry store poked his head out and nodded at Noa. She went over and spoke to him. I continued down to the waterfront; Noa caught up.

She frowned at me. "Next time, we have to walk out of the alley. Everyone here knows me and they'll talk about what you and I are doing."

"That's easy: nothing. Talking."

"Easy for you. You're unattached and unencumbered."

I was itching to show her the cell photo of the young man from Patrick Roberts' office but held off.

"So, what do you want besides getting me in hot oil?" she asked.

"I wondered if you'd asked around about my friend."

She stared at me blankly.

I pulled out Roger's photo. "You know, my friend Roger Black? The guy who had a thing for Lebanese girls."

"I remember. Is that all you want?" She shifted her weight onto one hip and crossed her arms.

"I stopped to say hello to you and see how things are going," I said.

"Do you always do that?"

I was at a loss. "Look, Noa, I'm trying to keep my life simple. That's why I'm back here. I'm trying to find someone who can help me with Roger."

"Right, heirs and inheritances. I remember," she said. "Well, I'm not in touch with all the Lebanese girls in St. Thomas, you know."

A bit of Middle Eastern pride was butting against my questions. There were a bunch of things happening around me that wouldn't gel. The lawyer, and this Lebanese connection, and then there was some missing ingredient.

"It's hot out here, Mr. Boise, so I'm going back to the store. You need me for more?"

"What's the story with Audrey's father? Is he a friendly sort?" I asked.

Ignoring me, she walked into the mouth of the alley. I'd have to handle Noa with kid gloves from now on.

When I got to the Greenhouse to meet Dana, I bellied up to the bar, ordered a Guinness.

I liked the anonymity of the Greenhouse. Only a handful of locals frequented the place, so besides the staff, the people coming and going were always alien. It kept the view fresh and the chances of running into unwanted company to a minimum.

Dana was late, an unusual event. Nothing on my phone. I walked to the edge of the stairs and looked out at the waterfront crowds. My breath quickened when instead of Dana, I spotted the kid from Patrick Roberts' office was humming along, almost jogging past. Abandoning my beer and Dana, I took off after him. Dana was in the parking lot and she waved as I ran off.

"Boise! Hey, Boise," she yelled. Luckily, the kid never looked back at the yelling woman or I would have been made.

I tried to remember his name. Elliot? Ebenezer? Something biblical. Elias!

He had a light brown complexion and loose curls. A laptop was slung diagonally across his chest, the contents bumping his right side as he walked. I had to work to keep up, but the running was over. My face burned. I felt a little lightheaded from my beer and the sudden exertion. He made a right into Drake's Passage and glanced back once, but never in my direction. Dozens of tourists camouflaged me.

He continued up the passage and the closer to Main Street we got, the thinner the crowd grew. He slowed as he passed the Del Rio Gift Shop and glanced into the store before moving on. He ignored the other shops. Pulling out my cell, I responded to Dana's all caps messages about standing her up by replying that something urgent had come up and we'd have to meet later. Tailing him would occupy the rest of my afternoon.

He continued walking towards Main Street, turned left, and halfway down the block stopped to unlock the bike I'd seen him riding days before to the university.

Not many people on the island used bikes because of the mountainous landscape. The area between the university and downtown was fairly level, so some people rode them in those areas. I hailed a cab and told him to follow the bike. The cabby frowned at this prospect but relented after some coaxing.

We wound up back at Patrick Roberts' offices after Elias grabbed a burger at a food truck near Brewer's Beach. Once he locked his bike up and went into the law office, we drove to the food truck. I bought the cabby lunch and paid him.

"I no like drive so slow, da man," he said, biting into a salt fish pattay, an empanada-like Caribbean staple of fried bread stuffed with meat. I ordered a beef and a potato pattay for myself along with a malt. We sat on the light gray concrete and watched the airport runway to the southeast. Under a tree on the beach, a group of men sat around on folding chairs surrounding a fold-up table with a faux wooden surface playing dominos and drinking cheap beer.

One of them slammed a domino onto the table so hard the other bone tiles leapt into the air.

"Domino, motha-fuckas!" he yelled.

I told the cabby to wait and I ambled over to the crew playing dominos. They all looked up, suspicious of someone they didn't recognize dropping into their circle.

A very dark-skinned man wearing a stained white shirt stood up, the same one who'd won the last game. He had the build of a bulldog, arms held away from his hips in a fighter's stance. He looked to be around fifty.

"Wha' you want da man?" he asked.

He smelled like rum. In fact, the whole area smelled like rum.

"Any you eva find a body on dis beach?" I asked.

"Yeah," said a squirrelly fella who'd been mixing the dominos face down in preparation for the next game. "Bu' why we talk wid you? Who you is?"

"I a friend of da dead," I said. "I trying to see what happen to my friend."

"You know dat man? Why we talk wid you?" the mixer took a drink from a plastic cup next to his right hand.

"Tell you what, I'll turn a domino and you turn a domino and if I get the higher number, you tell me. If not, well, let's discuss that later."

One of the other men chimed in, "If not, den you pay he twenty dollas."

The mixer nodded and grinned. "Yeah okay, like a bet. Come."

The bone-white tiles scattered across the table in a seemingly random order. I closed my eyes and selected one. A three. The mixer laughed and chose the one nearest his side. A five. All the men howled with laughter and slapped the mixer high fives all around.

"All right, twenty," the man said.

I handed over the bill. "Okay, spill," I muttered.

"I find he when I settin' up da table in da morning. All I rememba is he young and he wearin' a red shirt wid a big rip at da bottom of da shirt."

"Dat's it?" I asked, using my island dialect to emphasize my disappointment at this trivial bit of information. "Dat's worth twenty?"

"How I should know?" asked the mixer.

The bulldog got behind me and said, "You blockin' my seat." I moved out of the way as the men started selecting dominos for the next round.

***

The cabby brought me back to Roberts' office. The bike was gone. I really sucked at stalking. The cabby waited while I tried the entrance. The door was unlocked and the reception area deserted.

Very trusting.

A note addressed to Elias, asking him to call someone when he returned from his errand, lay on the desk. I opened the desk drawer and rummaged. A small framed photo was tucked in the back.

It looked like Elias, as a boy of eight or nine, sitting on the lap of a short, dark-haired woman with olive skin. She had that smoky, Middle-Eastern sexiness. I heard rustling inside Roberts' office, so I retreated back to the cab. I cursed at myself for being so startled by Roberts that I'd left the photo behind.

"Take me back to Drake's," I told the cabby, who was thrilled to weave through traffic and get back into Charlotte Amalie at the insane speed of fifty miles per hour.

CHAPTER 35

I perched myself outside the south entrance and strolled back and forth between the unnamed alley and the archway of Drake's Passage hoping I might get a glimpse of Elias. Upon my twentieth lap, I spotted him chaining his bike to a no parking sign up the block. He wore the same clothes and shouldered a backpack. He walked toward me, so I crossed through the slow-moving traffic and stood in front of a jewelry store across the street. Through the lines of pedestrians, I watched as he hoofed it into Drake's again.

I crossed back over and entered the passage behind him. He glanced into Del Rio, then entered.

I waited, window shopping momentarily, then peeked around into the store. Elias and Noa talked intently, while another younger woman sat behind the counter reading *US Weekly* and Audrey tapped the screen of her mom's cell phone. This was a moment when I wished I worked for the CIA and had a directional mic to pick up their conversation. Alas, I was but a poor local investigator with no James Bond gadgets at my disposal.

CHAPTER 36

Dana stopped by my place in her car; the doctor had cleared her to drive. Her guilt trips had convinced me to help her with Celia. Besides, I liked the girl.

Dana leaned her head out the car window. "So where're we headed?"

"St. Thomas Memorial, I called and asked for Earl DeVere. They said they'd page him if I wouldn't mind holding. I hung up."

As we drove, I told her what I'd been up to regarding Elias. "So, what do you think?"

"I think this idiot drives like Jabuti." The car in front of us crept along at fifteen miles per hour. Dana honked but got no satisfaction. "Can we go around?"

In St. Thomas, you drive on the left, but the steering wheels are on the left, like American cars, so the driver's on the edge of the road making passing a bitch.

Two cars were coming. "Nope, can't pass. Besides, it's a double-yellow here."

Dana banged her hand on the steering wheel and cursed. "Okay, getting back to Elias. Noa said she doesn't date black guys, right?" I nodded. "She's lying. Who needs to say shit like that? She likes black guys. Maybe she's dating Elias and he didn't go in there because her father would cut his dick off if he saw them together," she said. "Island men can be tribal about that shit. You said they're Lebanese? Shit, maybe more tribal than islanders."

She continued by spouting off about how fathers want to marry their own daughters, but they'll settle for them marrying someone in the same race, religion, etc. She concluded by saying Noa's father would probably kill Elias if he knew, so the guy's got to peek into the shop before showing up.

Dana's insights might prove useful, but Elias seemed a bit young for Noa. Then again, if men could date younger, why not women?

Maybe I was jealous.

Dana wanted to get back on Celia Jarl.

"I read they caught the kidnappers," I said.

Holding up her index finger and thumb about two inches apart, she winked at me through the gap. "That's only part of the story."

She pointed at her notebook at my feet. After skimming it, I whistled.

She nodded, then said, "Yeah, there's more to the story. I know it. That's why I want to revisit DeVere, so I'm excited you took matters into your own hands and set this up. I also called my friend Robin. She's a big-time gossip columnist here on the island. I told her about Celia Jarl's miscarriage."

I fumed. "You did what?" This was a grave breach of trust in my opinion. "Why drag an innocent sixteen-year-old girl into the gossip column?"

"Because I needed to give Robin something juicy in exchange for more information on Cecil or Celia down the road. Tit for tat. Besides, it could force Cecil into the open by making his private life public. Then we'll see if he made any missteps. Maybe Robin will find out who the father of Celia's baby is."

I rubbed my hand across my face a few times to get the film of guilty sweat off. "None of this is all right, but it wasn't my call, so it's off my conscience."

***

Dana decided to hang around in her own scrubs and the locker room trying to overhear information. She said she'd stay close to her phone in case I needed her to bail me out or start the car.

You'd be shocked how easy it is to blend in, especially in places where people wear uniforms of different types. We popped into a shop that sold scrubs, then drove to the hospital. I scouted where the doctors and nurses hung out to smoke and surmised that their locker area was nearby.

Wearing scrubs, I deposited a bag in an unoccupied locker. The only thing I didn't have was a name tag, but I had my excuse prepared. It never came up. I wandered around the hospital emergency room, making sure to always be carrying something somewhere so no one asked me to perform any duties that would expose my incompetence.

The whole place stunk of antiseptic. I obsessed about how bad hospitals were for your health. It made my skin itch. I ducked into a bathroom stall and counted to ten while breathing deeply. Donning a surgical mask from the countertop at reception made me feel safer and would disguise me if DeVere spotted me.

I rounded a corner as DeVere exited a room. Pulling off a pair of gloves, he dumped them into a wastebasket and strode up the hall to a bank of elevators. A heavyset woman wearing a muumuu also got into the elevator. It stopped on the fourth floor and the sixth floor before returning. My first stop would be the fourth floor.

Over a dozen offices were listed on the wall directory. Near the top was Earl DeVere, M.D., Room 402. To my left I heard a door shut. I ran down and rounded the corner. The office had a square window at eye level in the door. I glanced in then dodged away. DeVere stood in the corner, pouring something into a glass and gazing out at the parking lot. I leaned against the wall formulating a plan. This wasn't the right time. I needed to find some other way.

Just then, the knob began to turn. Hurrying down the hall, I kept my back to DeVere.

His footfalls echoed, becoming fainter. I doubled back. Locked. Through the door window I spied his cell phone on his desk. I needed to examine it.

Leaning on the door, I pushed and wiggled the knob, trying to move it away from the hole that held the latch in place. As with many things in St. Thomas, the doors at the hospital were not top of the line. The door frame had some give. With a firm pull on the doorknob away from the jam, the door slid open. Stunned elation flooded my veins. I crept inside and shut the door.

His old school flip phone wasn't locked. Glancing at the door repeatedly, I searched for Cecil and Celia's contacts. Cecil's information was easy to find and I jotted it down on a sheet of notepaper along with DeVere's cell and email. Celia's number wasn't there.

Someone was in the hall--nowhere to hide! The office was just that: an office, no closet, no bed. The only place to conceal myself was under the desk's leg housing. Dropping the phone back on the desk, I ducked under knowing I'd almost certainly be found if it was DeVere. Squeaking shoes stopped directly outside the door.

Keys jangled. A door opened. I waited for the inevitable footfalls inside the room, but a door shut and silence reigned. It must have been the office directly across the hall. Realizing I'd been holding my breath, I let out a whoosh of relief.

My hands trembled as I thought better and jotted Cecil's and DeVere's information on another sheet of paper so I had two copies in different locations. Didn't want all my eggs in one basket.

Continuing to scroll, I located Governor James' phone number and personal email. Perhaps that would be useful at some later date. I wrote it on the first sheet, the one I'd keep for myself.

Still not finding Celia, I tried variations. The only name that came close was Sexy Cece. Writing the number and email down under the governor's information, I stashed that paper in my wallet. The second sheet of paper went into my back pocket.

Looking through the glass in the door to see if anyone had entered the hall, I had no luck seeing very far to either side. I listened, held my breath, then pushed open the door. A nurse turned the corner right as I came out. Trying to look casual, I shut the door. She glowered at me. I forced a smile that remained hidden behind my surgical mask. She didn't reciprocate. She shuffled a little faster and so did I, in the opposite direction.

As I ran, I texted Dana to start the car and pull in front, ready to bolt.

I dove into the waiting car. Moments later, a security guard and the nurse who'd seen me come out of DeVere's office charged out the main entrance and scanned both directions.

Dana hit the gas and we tore away. I scrunched down in my seat and watched in the sideview mirror as the nurse gesticulated wildly and the guard tried to calm her down.

Had I returned the cell phone to the same spot on DeVere's desk? I couldn't recall, which meant probably not, since I would've had to make a point of doing so. Likely, that door would be more solid next time, although knowing St. Thomas, it could be ten years before anything got done.

CHAPTER 37

We rounded the corner out of sight of the hospital and I sat up in my seat.

A big grin spread across my face. "I got Cecil's contact info. The personal stuff. Maybe even on his private island. It's a New York area code," I said, holding up the sheet of paper from my back pocket. "I also got Earl DeVere's cell and email."

"What about Celia's?"

"No meat on that nut," I lied.

She snatched the sheet out of my hand with an annoyed sigh. "You said results. This isn't what I wanted."

"Are you kidding? I got firsthand data we needed. I risked my rass jus' now," I said and sucked my teeth at her. "Also, we now know dat DeVere know Cecil Jarl. We know it."

"All right, I see I got you riled. What do we do with this? I have other things starting to hit my desk."

"What about talking to the guys in jail?"

"They're out on bail. Till the next court date."

"Maybe we can find them," I said.

"One's a Jamaican citizen. I dug up some intel on him from a friend over there. Guy worked for Jarl as a handyman at his Jamaican estate, but always cash, no record of employment."

"What about the white guy?" I said.

"That's the white guy. The West Indian's a local. Jimbo Brigs. A pot farmer who's managed to keep under the radar. He bribes the cops with weed, like he's their personal supplier or something."

"The cops smoke weed?"

"How do you think cops cope with the stress of that job?" Dana asked. "You think this job ain't stressful? Maybe I'll go see Jimbo for personal reasons. He lives near that house in Hull Bay. His farm's out there from what I understand. I'll approach him on that tip. Will you come along? I'm bold, but he's Frankie's cousin."

"Frankie?" I asked.

"Francis Floyd Peterson." When I stared at her blankly, she muttered, "Wow, you really don't know much. You sure you ever lived here?" she said.

"Tell me about this Francis guy."

"First off, don't call him Francis. I'm not sure his mother even calls him that anymore. He dropped out in tenth grade and started running with some criminal from Red Hook," she said. "He helped me on a story once, but that's all I can say. We're, well, I'm not sure anyone's friends with Frankie, but we're friendly, I suppose.

"So he's not very bright," I said.

"Why, because he didn't attend college? Let me tell you something, you go into situations with people around here having that elitist attitude and you'll wind up next to your friend before long. Assume everyone you meet is smarter, stronger, and faster than you are. Always overestimate your opponent, just don't let him know. Make him think you think he's a moron, unless it's Frankie."

"What makes Frankie different?" I asked.

"He kills people who don't show respect," she said. "Respect him and you'll stay alive and maybe we'll even get some useful information."

Gritting my teeth, I took a deep breath. "What else?" We were driving too fast. I pulled my foot off the accelerator a little and the turns became smoother.

"He's second in command in Tutu."

"If he's so fierce, why isn't he the boss?"

"That's what makes him really dangerous. He's patient," she hissed. "He does things in a calculated manner, even when it looks emotional. He's trying to get you to behave irrationally."

I rolled up my window and made her repeat herself. A metallic oil smell filled the car once the window was closed.

"Okay, Francis, or Frankie, is tough, resourceful, confident, and patient. He's the Dalai Lama of crime. Got it," I paused while she gazed at me in the mildly illuminated car. Her eyes seemed to glow in the dashboard lighting.

"Stop staring at me." I shot back at her. "It's hard to drive. Look at the road or something."

She turned her head forward, but it wasn't natural for Dana to look away when dealing with someone. I liked that about her.

"What's that smell?" I asked.

"Gun oil."

I cringed. "Don't like guns much."

"I like being alive. You don't show up to a poker game with no money, Jabuti."

CHAPTER 38

The slot slid open. Cold, black eyes stared through us.

"We're here for Frankie," Dana said.

I nodded and waved awkwardly while the eyes examined us. The slot closed. Moments passed. My stomach churned. I popped a pill, gagging a little as it went down. Finally, the door opened. A man about six-foot-five with dreads and a large gun strapped across his chest stood aside as we entered.

We hustled down a long hallway with many closed doors or beads covering rooms on either side. Moaning seeped out of some of the unseen spaces. The smell of weed and sage permeated the air. We stopped outside a door where another henchman stood. Someone inside screamed. Our escort frisked us, taking Dana's gun.

"I'll need that back," she said.

He held his finger to his lips. The door opened and a man strutted out. Through the doorway I glimpsed another man hunched over in a chair, a long piece of red saliva hanging from his mouth to the floor. He groaned once, then fell silent. A spotlight made him nothing but a silhouette. Another guard from down the hall stepped inside and shut the door. A latch clicked home.

"Come," the man who exited the room said in a high-pitched voice.

We followed him and the giant who'd greeted us down the football-field-width hallway lit by flickering electric torches. It felt like a medieval castle. At the far end, we entered a red plush room.

Dana whispered, "Frankie calls this the Ites Room."

He went and sat on an ice, gold, and green throne that matched popular Rastafarian colors. The Rastas called the color red "ice" here in the islands, although I'd been told more than once the proper term from Africa was "ites." A carved lion—his teeth barred—leaned over the back of Frankie's throne, ready to pounce on anyone who stood in front of him. It was hard not to be intimidated.

"Wha' you want, Dana?"

Dana started to answer, then Frankie's gaze shifted to me. He had dead eyes. "Who dis?"

"I'm Boise." I held out my hand.

He made no move, so I withdrew.

"You from da states?"

"Hey Frankie, I need some help," Dana interrupted.

"Hey Dana, I gettin' to know my new friend here," he said, pointing at me and snapping his fingers.

"Boise," I said.

"Right. Boise. Right. Patience da hallmark of good negotiation."

Dana glared at Frankie and bit her lip as he turned back to me.

"So, Boise, what you bring to dis negotiation?"

"Just along for the ride," I said.

He leaned forward and reached under his throne. He pulled out a huge bag of weed and some Bamboo papers. He threw the bag and a pack of papers at me. I caught them.

"Roll," Frankie said.

I sat down in a red cushy chair, pulled a paper, and rolled a joint. Dana remained standing. Upon completion, Frankie snatched it from me and sniffed it. The henchman stood between Dana and me. His body odor stunk almost as strong as the weed.

"You ain't a weed smoker, man," Frankie said laughing. "I no trust people who no smoke. You religious?"

"No," I said.

"No? You believe in God." It wasn't a question.

"No," I said. "Don't believe in God."

"Jah. What about Jah?"

"Don't believe in Jah," I said.

The henchman reached over and lifted me off my seat by the neck. My muscles tensed in an effort to protect my spine and I wet my pants. My hands came together in a praying shape and I brought them up between his arms. I threw my hands apart and my knuckles hit his wrists. He released my neck as I sputtered for breath. Falling back into my chair, I tumbled to the carpet.

Spittle poured from my mouth making a wet spot in the carpet. Frankie threw a napkin on the floor. I started to blow my running nose into it and Frankie wailed.

"Not you, da rug! Dry da rug, da man!"

Through bloodshot tears I glared at him, then dabbed at the carpet till the wet spot disappeared. He threw another napkin. I cleaned myself up. Frankie stood and leaned over me, whispering in my ear.

"You believe in Jah now?"

I coughed again, then said, "No."

He roared laughter, then offered his hand. He hauled me into my seat and slapped me on the back.

"Damu, you can go. I want to talk wid my new friends alone."

Damu made a slight bow and exited. He came back a moment later and handed me a glass of water. I drank it, enjoying the cold wetness.

"Frankie, what's the meaning of this?" Dana said, trying to sound tough, but squeaking a little.

He stared at me, ignoring Dana. "You stand by dat crazy notion? No Jah? For real?"

I nodded. The room felt oppressive with the red, gold, and green everywhere and the deep shag carpet, like fibrous quicksand.

He paused, then turned to Dana. "You have somet'ing to ask?"

"I want to see Jimbo."

"Who Jimbo?"

"Your cousin."

"He in jail 'cause of you. Why I be telling you anyt'ing 'bout Jimbo?"

"We want to know who hired him to kidnap the girl," I blurted. They both turned and looked at me.

"Thanks, Boise, for not showing our hand too early," Dana snorted.

"Jimbo have not'ing do wid dat. Dis discussion ova," Frankie said.

Dropping my poorly rolled joint into an ashtray, Frankie pulled a huge joint out of a leather pouch on the side of his throne.

Lighting it, he puffed hard to bring the tip to life, then held the smoke in his mouth. He handed it to Dana. She tugged, then handed it to me. It had a very pungent smell. After one pull, my anxiety melted away a few moments later.

Frankie grinned. "Now dat's a joint." I nodded. He turned to Dana. "Wid Jimbo hiding, he don't get no work done. He scared. If you calm he mind, all right. Just do what he want. I arrange a meet."

Frankie handed me a shot of Cruzan Rum. We clinked our glasses and I downed the hot, clear liquid in one swallow.

CHAPTER 39

The taste of dry alcohol and smoke filled my mouth when I awoke the next day. After hitting Frankie's joint, it was all a blur. My head pounded as I dragged myself into the sweaty heat of the noon-day sun.

The Daily News building was a hazy blur and I stumbled twice going up the stairs. My phone buzzed as I reached the newsroom. Dana. Her desk was a cluttered mess. She held the phone to her ear, looking annoyed and excited all at once.

"Hello," I said as I approached her desk. Upon hearing my voice, she hung up.

"What the hell, Boise?"

"Well, good morning to you too, sunshine." I giggled like an eight-year-old.

"Jimbo called. He's agreed to meet with us out at Hull Bay today at two."

***

We threw a blanket down on the sand to the right of the algae-covered boat ramp. I stripped off my shirt and laid down, sucking on a bottle of water I'd snagged from the newsroom kitchen.

"God Boise, we're meeting with a source. Could you show some professionalism?"

Propping myself up on my elbows, I shielded my eyes using my hand. "Have I done something to offend you?"

"Just put your shirt on."

I squinted at her a moment longer then laid back. The warm sun felt good. It seemed like years since I'd last laid down shirtless on a beach. It was nice to do something new, something natural. Also, my gut had shrunk, forcing me to wear a belt that day with my shorts. All the walking and running for my life resulted in shedding a few pounds.

As I dozed off, a shadow sailed over my face. Jimbo Brigs. His dread locks swung about as he surveyed in all directions like a gazelle at a watering hole.

"Come," he pointed a dark hand toward a cluster of sea grape trees. "Ova here."

I started to pick up the blanket. "Leave dat," he growled, yellowed teeth like fangs jutting out of his wide mouth. "Just walk ova."

Following them to the sea grape trees, I yanked on my shirt as we walked. I picked a few purple grapes and popped them into my mouth. They were slightly sour, but good.

"Wha' you want?" Jimbo asked.

"I want to know what went down in that warehouse," Dana said.

"Why I should tell you? You why I-and-I in trouble."

"No, Jimbo. You are in trouble because you kidnapped a girl. The daughter of an important man. We just happened to walk into your life at that exact moment and things got crazy."

"I should…" his bottom lip quivered.

"Frankie told you my offer," Dana said.

"Yeah, he tell me," Jimbo said.

"So, tell me what I want to know."

"Wha' he doin' here?"

"My protection," she said. "He got me out the last time we tangled."

"As I recall, you save him from me. She your protection, right da man?"

"Just tell her the news so we can leave you alone," I said, trying to give him my toughest stare. He didn't look impressed.

"You t'ink I want wind up dead? Dis man. Dis man you want to know 'bout. He like t'ings his way. Ain't much room to hide in dis here island."

"Oh, I don't know, you seem to avoid getting your crops caught by the cops and they're a lot bigger than you are," Dana said. "Just let them protect you."

"Who?"

"The cops," Dana hissed.

"Okay, okay, you agree to forget what I look like at da trial, I tell you. Yeah?"

"Yeah, all right," I said. "If you can't give us some real info we can verify, deal's off."

"What he said." Dana added, "I think I'm rubbing off on you."

Jimbo's dark eyes searched in the blazing sun for answers. He plucked at a dead leaf, tearing out rounded edges and tossing them aside.

Dropping down in the sand, he muttered, "I want do me own way. You know I been workin' for Frankie long time. He my family. He help me, but sometime you gotta break away, be your own." His eyes kept darting around the beach and the overgrown brush on the access road.

Jimbo held his breath as a small, silver pick-up truck approached from the west end of the beach, branches scraping noisily across the spotted paint. A leathery fellow drove by grinning at us. Half his teeth were missing. A large fishing net filled up the bed of the truck.

"I jus' can't look around without jump out my skin," he said. "You can't mess dez people."

Jimbo pulled a joint out of his shirt pocket. He lit up, inhaling deeply and tilting his head back as he blew it into the trees.

"Jimbo, who are you talking about?" Dana asked impatiently.

I held up my hand. "Jimbo?" He still looked into the trees. "Jimbo, when you say dez people, who you talk about?" Talking to this man felt like coaxing a feral cat into my lap.

He pointed at my chest. "Lemme talk wid him alone. You take a walk on da beach."

Dana looked at me, then shrugged and limped toward the water, removing her shoes and hiking up her linen pants as she went.

"I-and-I no like reporters. You no reporter, right?"

"I no reporter," I said.

My innards groaned loud enough for Jimbo to hear. "You all right, da man?"

Standing up and clenching, I popped one of my pills.

"Wha' dat is?" he said.

"Pill from the doctor," I said. "It helps."

He held his joint toward me. "Dis help," he said. "Dis real medicine."

I stared at him a long moment, then took the joint and puffed. Smoking joints was getting to be a habit the last two days, but I hadn't smoked since college. I coughed.

"Keep it smooth, da man. Watch here."

He pulled in, then held the smoke before releasing it slowly and steadily. I tried again, imitating him. It worked better and I relaxed. I handed back the joint and leaned against the sea grape tree.

"Thanks," I said.

"You might need every day," he said. "Good for colitis."

"You a doctor?"

"I know medicine of ganga," he said. "I always tense, now I smoke ganga and no problem. I feel relax."

Dana watched us out of the corner of her eye. I could feel her impatience over the sound of the waves. A Boston Whaler motored slowly into the bay, heading for an anchoring spot next to a buoy about one-hundred feet offshore. I took another toke. He smiled at me.

"Feel betta, right?"

"Betta, right," I said.

"I can't let Frankie run me no more. Derek and me, we supposed to get out. One large shipment, den Frankie say I free."

"Free from what?"

"Slavery. My fadda's slavery."

"Your father enslaved you?"

"No, bu' it was 'cause he," Jimbo said, his eyes getting more glazed as the weed took effect. "Dis when I see Jah."

Jah was the Rastafarian word for God. Weed opened their mind to connect with God. A higher consciousness.

He rotated slowly. Sweat poured off his face, glistening in the sun.

"You best go now."

"I need something."

"I done give it. I done give it all. I do it to escape from dis here rock. I say I do anyt'ing. Anyt'ing."

"Did you do it for Jarl? Was it for Cecil Jarl? Did you take the girl for her father?" I begged.

"Yeah, a man from dat property place in Sub Base. Right. Payne and somet'ing. A man dere tell me he get me and Derek to Jamaica in style. Frankie won't know not'ing. Now, Frankie know. He say I his for good or he let me go rot."

"How will you rot?"

Dana walked back over, looking at her cell phone as she came. "Can we move this along?"

"We're not done. Wait over there."

"Shit's happening," she said, holding up the phone.

Jimbo took another toke on his smoke as he sat elbows to knees, head low. I said nothing. After a moment, Dana limped toward the water again.

"I don't know da man name. I know he from dem real estate place."

"Did you see him?"

"Yeah. He white. Tall."

"British accent?"

"Yeah, I t'ink so. English, yeah," he said.

"What will you do if you get out of this and I can make a deal with Frankie?"

"You? You ain't making no deal wid Frankie, da man. I done work for Frankie for good now. Dat's all dere is," he muttered. His head bobbed as he stared at the sand.

"Was there anyone else?"

"Nah, jus' me and Derek waiting wid da girl," he said. "I feel bad about I have to hit she."

"There wasn't a doctor?"

"I say I ain't meet no one else. Yeah, dere was doctor. He coming when you show up."

"You know his name?"

"I don' know and never see him."

"You know what he was going to do?" I asked. "This is important."

"Nah, somet'ing wid da girl."

Dana came back over. Jimbo stood after dousing the tip of his joint in the sand. He pulled out a dime bag and dropped the blackened roach in among some loose pieces of weed.

"Now, leave I alone," he said, ambling off up the beach toward the rocks. His thick shoulders rolled as he walked.

"So, what'd you get?"

Staring after Jimbo, I said, "British white dude from Payne and Wedgefield set up the kidnapping of Celia in exchange for guaranteeing safe passage for Jimbo and Derek to Jamaica without Frankie knowing."

Then Dana blurted, "What about DeVere?"

I shrugged. "No go. He said a doctor for Celia was on the way out to do something for her, but they never saw him or knew his name."

***

We passed the hospital, only a few minutes before we'd get back to the paper. I suggested we stop.

"Do you know where the doctors park?" I asked.

"No clue," said Dana. "We've come at DeVere over and over. This is a tired lead. Besides, what do we like

210

DeVere for? If anything, we should head for Payne and Wedgefield and see what we turn up there."

"I think he was there to get rid of the baby," I said.

"There's only one problem with that theory. Jarl's a staunch Catholic who thinks the Pope walks on water. He's donated millions to the church and has even had private meetings with the man himself. He's come out repeatedly saying he's pro-life in all circumstances, including rape."

"Humans are full of contradictions," I retorted. She said nothing, then I added, "I think DeVere's involved."

She sighed. "Me too."

The hospital had very little landscaping. Like most hospitals, the parking lot stretched on and on. After five minutes, we circled around the back of the main building and found parking spots with reserved signs. We got out and searched row by row, reading the signs with each doctor's name on them.

"It's here," I said.

Dana hobbled over and stared at the vacant space. We went inside to ask when DeVere would be on duty.

"He's on call now. I was about to page him for an emergency. He might not be available to talk for a while as it's a surgical procedure," the nurse added.

"Does Dr. DeVere perform abortions?" I asked.

"Dear me, no. We don't have an abortion clinic here anyway. Dr. DeVere does emergency medicine, mostly surgical procedures for triage. I suppose he might have done one or two to save a woman's life sometime, but none I'm aware of." She looked at Dana with a wan smile. "Does your daughter require an abortion? I can recommend a clinic."

"That's okay, we'll come back another time," Dana said.

We headed back out to watch for DeVere's arrival. He pulled up a half-hour later in a black, late model Mercedes.

"Do you think it's the same one?" she asked.

We watched him go inside then went to the car, inspecting it for anything that might jog my memory. The car was clean and appeared to be the same size and type I'd seen that night at the warehouse in Sub Base, but it had no scratches or dents.

"Not sure. There was nothing distinguishing about that car or this one," I said. As we looked at the doctors' cars in the lot, there must have been a half-dozen other black Mercedes.

"He remains on our radar then, but the coincidences keep mounting making his involvement harder and harder to ignore," she said as we returned to the car.

Dana's leg ached, so I drove her home. I crashed on her couch. As I lay in the darkness watching a square ray of moonlight on the floor, my eyes inched closed. I dreamt of a ship at sea in the night. A thin layer of magenta clouds masked the stars when I looked up. No land in sight.

CHAPTER 40

I stumbled to the bathroom and stuck my mouth under the faucet, guzzling my pill down. Dousing my greasy hair with water, I attempted in vain to get it under control. It'd been under my straw fedora for so long the roots ached. No hat today.

Dana had no mouthwash, floss or a spare toothbrush. I hated not brushing or flossing. I'd once read in a women's journal that if you ate an apple in when you woke up, it made morning kissing better because one bite eliminated bad breath. Dana had one in the fridge. Evelyn always hated morning breath.

I gobbled the apple, but felt a dark hollowness like my throat was a bottomless well. Assuming Dana was still in bed, I left without saying good-bye. Back at my room, the cell showed a missed call and shortly thereafter Dana texted: "Turn on Channel 2."

On my snazzy nineteen-inch television, I watched a press conference, palm trees blowing in the background and the sign for Payne and Wedgefield prominently displayed.

The caption said, "Tod Cavenaugh, Vice-President, Payne & Wedgefield."

Cavenaugh, a tall white man, spoke with an educated British accent.

"Mr. Jarl is elated by the bravery of the men and woman who rescued his dear Celia. The whole family is terribly saddened by the events and will pray that such a thing never happens to other families in St. Thomas. Mr. Jarl plans to donate one million dollars to the S.T.P.D. to create a kidnapping task force so that if such a thing ever happens again, the response time will be better, perhaps even preventing these crimes in the future." Cavenaugh folded the paper he'd read from and tucked it into his jacket pocket. He looked expectantly at the reporters.

"Mr. Cavenaugh, will we be hearing from Jarl or Celia?" asked a reporter in the front.

"As you know, Mr. Jarl likes to keep private, especially about family matters. He tries to keep his children out of the spotlight as much as possible. I am his appointed representative in this matter."

"Dana Goode, *Daily News*."

"Yes, Ms. Goode? Thank you for your heroism."

"I have a question as a reporter, not an involved party."

"All right."

"Did Mr. Jarl have anything to do with his daughter's kidnapping?"

"Pardon me?"

"Celia's kidnapping. Did Mr. Jarl have a hand in it? She was in a Payne and Wedgefield warehouse," Dana said. "I wondered how that came to be?"

Cavenaugh swallowed. My nose was almost touching the television screen. "I'm sorry, but Ms. Goode your information is incorrect. That is not a Payne property."

"Well, not directly, but a subsidiary," she retorted. "Are you suggesting it's a coincidence?"

"Honestly Ms. Goode, this is not the time, but I will address this now so this rumor stops. Payne and Wedgefield owns many properties throughout the island. We cannot possibly control what happens at every property that has a connection to us. Mr. Jarl had nothing to do with this and in fact reported that his daughter was missing as soon as he became aware."

"Why was there," Dana referred to her notes, "a delay in reporting it? I have here a two-day delay."

"Because she was supposed to be vacationing with a friend in the Bahamas. Believe me, Mr. Jarl reported it as soon as he realized she was not with this other family."

Dana started to ask another question, but Cavenaugh cut it off. "Thank you all for coming out."

He walked off into the Payne and Wedgefield building and the camera cut back to talking heads. I turned off the television and called Dana.

"How was I?" she asked.

"Making friends and ingratiating yourself to the rich and powerful as always," I said.

"Well, this ought to produce some action on their part if nothing else. What a thrill!" She sounded giddy. "Notice he was a Brit?"

"You live for this, don't you?"

"Yup. Meet me at the newsroom," she said and hung up.

***

Dana was typing furiously on her desktop when I entered the dark newsroom. Her laptop was also open and lit up.

"Why do you have a laptop and a desktop both open and running at your desk?" I asked.

"Edward Snowden and Julian Assange," she said. "The laptop never connects to the internet or anything else. It's really only a word processor. I don't use wireless internet, only a hard line. We're all in the surveillance business now."

"You do keep your texts and emails simple," I responded.

"So, what do we do today?"

Dana's phone buzzed. She read the text and stormed into Pickering's office, slamming the door behind her. The blinds banged around, providing me a glimpse of Dana and Pickering before settling back against the glass.

Dana charged out three minutes later. She hissed at me, "Let's go."

"What was that all about?" I asked when we got in her car.

"We need to go see Jimbo again."

With few cars on the road and Dana prodding me to drive faster we got to Hull Bay in a hurry. We charged into the little hut called The East End Bar and Grill at the base of the hill. Beaches and marinas in St. Thomas always seemed to have bars.

"You seen Jimbo?" Dana asked the bartender. He pointed to a tree outside near the patio. Jimbo lounged there holding a beer and smoking a cigarette.

He looked at us vacantly when we walked out. Dana hadn't filled me in on what we were doing.

"Jimbo, have you spoken to Derek today?" Dana asked.

"Nah, man, I don' speak wid he every day. Just on weekends mostly. What you want now, reporter?" he asked, grinning. "At least you can't touch he in Jamaica."

"Yeah, well, somebody did," Dana said. "Except it wasn't in Jamaica. I think something bad's happened to Derek in the Dominican Republic."

I'd been holding my breath this whole time, worried that something about this screamed cover-up and that the biggest loose ends were Jimbo and Derek. The people behind this must know they might talk.

"We've got to hide you," I said as I looked around the beach. Everyone looked local and casual, a typical beach scene of surfers, fishermen, and drunks.

Jimbo didn't move. He didn't seem to care except for a tiny tear running down his massive, passive face. I knew in an instant that Jimbo and Derek had at the very least been lovers.

"Jimbo, Boise's right. You need to come now. I know a place you can stay," Dana said as she started to turn.

"No," said Jimbo.

His body and face held still as granite. The single tear had dried, leaving a trail of salt.

"I'm tired of coming," he said. "I tell you what I know, now leave me be. I goin' for a swim. I-and-I need some peace and quiet."

Pushing himself up, he drank the remainder of his beer. He walked between us and patted me on the shoulder with his rough farmer's hand.

"You all right," he said. "Just keep lookin'."

His hair and clothes smelled of smoke. He stripped off his shirt near the water. His back humped. At the shoreline, he took another long tug on his cigarette, then dropped it on the pebbly sand. As he entered the water, he tried to dive in, but really collapsed.

"Shouldn't we stop him?" Dana said.

"No, let him swim," I said. "You want a beer?"

We looked again at the smooth water and could barely make out the ripples from his pumping arms now between the cresting waves and the boats anchored in the bay. An hour later he came back, suitably exhausted.

"You stab me. How do I know?"

"You want to field that one?" I asked Dana.

"I'll tell you what they teach in reporting school, or at least what I'm told they teach, since I never really studied journalism. You have to be there in person to really know anything, otherwise it's all hearsay, which is inadmissible in court for good reason."

"I know something else can help you. It's how we get dat girl to come ova da first time."

"What do you know, Jimbo?" I asked.

"Nah, you get me ova to D.R., den I tell you. Yeah?"

"What better place to hide a Jamaican than in the Dominican Republic," I said.

"I need to see if Derek dead for myself. He got no one else," he said, dropping his face down between his bent knees.

Dana's face contorted as she fought back tears.

When she recovered her composure, she asked, "How do you like boats?"

CHAPTER 41

"I better see if Pickering's in there," Dana said as we mounted the stairs to *The Daily News* offices.

"That's okay, I'm going to see what I can find out about Derek."

"You going to Santo Domingo too?" she asked sarcastically.

"Dana, I'm just trying to do what you asked and now I'm motivated. I thought you'd be happy."

"I don't do well with separation. I want us sticking together."

"Because you don't trust me?"

She shrugged. "Maybe. Maybe I don't trust me. I want your help, but don't want to lose anyone on my watch."

Evelyn crossed my mind. "I know what you mean."

She gave a satisfied smile. "Good, then let's stick together."

A large manila envelope rested on top of Dana's desk. She pulled a letter opener out of her desk drawer and slit it open carefully. I gazed up at the sign below the newsroom's clock. It really was true; the news never sleeps.

"I got something on Celia." Dana chimed, handing me a paper with a phone number on it.

"Is this her cell?" I asked. "Who gave you this?"

"Robin."

"You mean the gossip girl?"

"See, I told you it would be worth telling her about Celia, didn't I?" I reluctantly agreed. "According to her notes in this envelope, it goes right to the girl herself. She tried, but apparently Celia said she'd only talk to the crazy guy who stabbed that dude in the leg and saved her."

CHAPTER 42

My phone buzzed. A text from Dana read: "Dock east of the Normandie, where sea planes used to take off. Meet at News at 9am then go get him. Okay?"

I replied in the affirmative.

Outside *The Daily News*, Dana was waiting by her car.

"Let's go get him," she said, throwing the keys to me.

Jimbo wore Elvis sunglasses and a tam over his knotted dreads. All he had were the clothes on his back, a backpack, and a duffle bag. It occurred to me for the first time that we were helping a drug dealer and a kidnapper flee the jurisdiction.

"Da police ain't coming for me," he assured me. "Dey know I could get dem in a lot of trouble, all dem. If I-and-I testify 'bout all dem and their ganga," he said.

Dana yelled back from inside the car, "Yeah, I think the governor'd like this to be kept quiet. He might even help if he knew what was going on."

We drove out of Hull Bay and were halfway up the hill when a car going the other way swung around. Jimbo leaned forward between the seats.

"Dat's Frankie. He comin' for me!"

"Aren't you guys cousins or something?" I said, watching as the car in the rearview approached at high speed.

"I his servant. He can't having me leave. He need me grow da ganga."

"Why didn't you tell us Frankie was coming?" Dana said. "Shit, Boise, there's three of them in that car. We can't outrun 'em."

Slamming my foot onto the gas pedal, I hollered, "We're gonna try."

The car shot forward as the engine groaned, strained by its forty-thousand rough island miles. Hanging a sharp right, we swerved down the narrowest road off a five-way intersection. Frankie's car didn't lose distance, but on smaller roads, with hairpin turns, we had an advantage over his bigger sedan.

Each time we hit a straight-away, Frankie's headlights swelled into bright suns in my rearview, then we'd hit a turn and widen the distance, but not enough.

I spotted a dirt road to my left and hooked a hard turn. We charged over massive stones that clattered against the undercarriage. Half-a-mile up the road I slammed on the brakes and jerked to the side behind a tree. The deep growl of the Mercedes v12 motored by on the main drag.

Dana turned to Jimbo. "Did you speak to my man?"

"Yeah. He say he take me. You trust he?" Jimbo asked, his eyes narrowing. "I need a hit."

He pulled out a joint.

"No hits, Jimbo. You need to stay focused," I said pulling back onto the road.

"Boise's right," said Dana. "Besides, I abhor smoking."

Dana and I laughed.

Jimbo held out his hand to show us how nervous he was. It quivered like a wet cat.

"Stop here," Dana said, pointing at a little restaurant we were about to pass. She got out without a word.

"Where she go? We need get out of here!" Jimbo kept looking up and down the road.

"Relax Jimbo, Frankie's gone," I said, putting my hand on his shoulder. He jumped.

"Man, dat man don't want me gone. He want me here. He want me here bad."

Dana got back in the car holding a steaming paper cup. "Drink this."

"Wha' dis is?"

"Chamomile tea. It'll relax you. Sip it while we drive."

He stared at her like she had grown antennas. I backed out and started toward Frenchtown again.

"Me ain't no woman. Me don't drink tea."

Dana sighed. "Do you want your hands to stop shaking?"

Jimbo nodded almost imperceptibly.

"Just drink it."

She held it in front of his nose. The cup floated there between the seats, with Dana half-turned, her red hair whipping around her face. Jimbo relented. He took the tea, holding it in both hands to keep it steady. His eyes darted around at the open road as he drank.

"Why don't you slide down lower in the seat, then Frankie can't see you," I suggested.

His knees bumped my seat on the way down.

We arrived at the dock in Frenchtown without further incident. A film of rainbow-colored oil covered the water.

Discarded cigarette butts and litter dotted the concrete shoreline. Jimbo pulled his two bags out of the trunk.

"I told you one bag," Dana said.

Jimbo raised three fingers on both hands. An old man with a silver mullet standing on the deck of a twenty-three-foot sailboat a couple hundred yards out got into a dingy at the aft of the boat and motored in.

"Dat's not what he say," Jimbo lifted his chin toward the motoring sailor. Jimbo kept glancing behind us. I kept a lookout too.

The sailor climbed onto the dock. He grinned at Dana, a single gold tooth glinting in the sun. White stubble dotted his leathery face.

With a smoker's voice he croaked, "Hello, Dana."

"Dad," Dana said and gave the man a stiff hug. "Why's he got two bags?"

"I gotta get something for my trouble, honey. It's payment," Dad said.

"What's wrong with you?" Dana said.

"Honey, we live in a capitalist society. Even China's on board, so you should learn to…"

"I don't want to hear it. I asked you to do this as a favor to me."

"It is a favor, but the favor part don't keep food on the table. I know Frankie's stuff. It's very good quality." He paused and looked at Jimbo, who was still sipping from the cup and looking at the road. "Besides, what's Jimbo care, he's getting out of the business, right? Hey, Jimbo, can I have my merchandise?"

Using his sun-spotted hands, Dana's dad made a grabbing motion.

Jimbo kicked the black duffle bag at his feet over. Dana's father leaned down, examined the contents, then zipped it up and hoisted it onto his shoulder. Although wiry and frail-looking, he was clearly strong.

"Lookin' good. Okay, amigo, let's go," he waved Jimbo into the dingy. "Who's this?" he said to Dana while pointing at me.

"I'm Boise," I said holding out my hand. He took it, then pulled me into a hug.

I felt his whiskers rubbing on my cheek as he turned his mouth to my ear. "I like to hug. Brings people together faster. You got a good vibe goin', so you get a hug. Also, what's that you're wearing? Is that Dior Sauvage?"

"Not sure, sir. Is that the Johnny Depp cologne?" I asked.

"Ha!" he threw his head back. "Sir. Call me Sire while you're at it. Yeah, it's the Johnny Depp cologne. You smell marvelous!" I just stared at him.

Dana broke in, "No really, his name is Sire. Sire Goode."

From his crouched position in the boat behind Sire, Jimbo whispered, "We best be goin' before Frankie make his way ova here."

"Okay, we'll shove off. See you two love birds later," he said.

"Wait," I said. "Jimbo, you said you had another bit of info for us."

"Oh ho, I see, you all get paid to bring him here but I shouldn't be paid."

"It's not the same, Dad," Dana growled.

"Sure is. I told you to go to Wharton instead of literary school at what's-its-name college," Sire said, grinning like a lizard.

"I know da phone number for da girl. You could reach her."

He told us the number and I wrote it down. "You got an email?" I asked.

"Yeah," he said, and gave us that too.

As we got in the car, Dana said, "It's redundant but we can cross check the numbers."

I pulled out the number Dana had gotten from her gossip columnist friend.

"The numbers are different," I muttered.

"So, either she has two phones or one of them's wrong. Let's hope it's Robin who's wrong, otherwise we helped this drug dealer for nothing," Dana said, shaking her head. "This is why you need lots of sources."

"You know, Dana, helping him isn't so bad," I said.

Dana pointed her finger at me as she leaned into my face. "You forget that we got hurt because of this prick and his boyfriend. Don't let some fantasy about romantic reunited lovers cloud your judgment about these men. They're cruel."

"Then why'd you put him on a boat with your father?" I asked.

"Ha! Jimbo's the one who better watch himself on that trip."

"Sire's a dangerous man?"

She shook her head. "Sire Goode. What a fucking joke."

"You think your father's a joke?"

"No, but his latest name is. Ah forget it," she said waving her hand at me to drive. I started the car, but then turned it off.

"You know, it wouldn't hurt you to tell me something once in a while," I said.

She looked at me a long moment; mischief swimming around in her pupils.

"All right, I'll tell you. Sire's not his name, but what it is, I don't know."

"You expect me to believe you don't know your father's name?"

"Believe or don't, it's the truth. I've tried to find out, but nothin' doing. His name's as lost as the Carib Indians." Her breath hitched and she blew her nose. "The only person who might have known was my mother, but she passed two years ago and took that with her too."

"You know his last name. Can't you use that?"

"Goode? That's my mother's name. Only guy to ever take the woman's name in a marriage. In fact, he was only too glad to do it since he was already in trouble at the time. Fucker spent my whole childhood in trouble in one way or another."

"Did he straighten up?" I asked.

"You ever heard of a vegetarian tiger? He lives on trouble and scandal. Gambling, stealing, whatever. He just learned how not to get caught as he got older."

I watched the brush and the coconut trees zip by.

"We better call her," I said.

"You call. You're the hero," Dana said grinning.

"Yes, but you saved me in that warehouse. I'm not going to forget that," I said.

I pulled into the parking lot at Emancipation Park and took a spot that someone had just vacated. We wanted to make the call from the car because both of us were weary of others overhearing our conversation. Dana kept a lookout while I spoke to Celia. We rolled up the windows and sat a moment, then rolled them back down. Too hot.

"We'll keep the windows open unless someone comes near," she said. "What are you waiting for?"

"I'm nervous about what I'll find out," I said.

CHAPTER 43

The trees in Emancipation Park waved casually in the breeze. We'd found a spot with some shade, so I wasn't sweating too badly when I dialed the phone number Jimbo gave first. I wanted him to be the man I hoped he was underneath the desperation and misfortune. Being Frankie's cousin did not set you up for a life of middle-class bliss with a tidy job and a healthy dog.

It set you into the weeds of crime. Weeds that grew so tall and thick, you couldn't see the light of freedom. I wanted him to be a better man than circumstance allowed.

Celia answered on the third ring. I told her who I was. Dana hit a button on her voice recorder. The red light flashed on.

"I'm not supposed to talk to anyone about this," she said. "My father'd kill me if he knew about this phone. How'd you get this number?"

"Celia, we want to bring the people behind your kidnapping to justice," I said. "We need your help."

"Daddy took me out of there so I wouldn't have to deal with any of this. I don't know who those men were."

"You might know something that you don't even know will help us. Could you answer some questions? Please?" I said it as gently as I could.

Silence stretched away on the line.

"What?" she finally said.

"Do you know Dr. Earl DeVere?"

"Uncle Earl? Sure, he's my doctor."

"What do you see him for?"

"Everything." There was something in her voice. A guarded tone. "Is he okay?"

"He's the only doctor you see?" I asked.

"I have a dentist. Is she a doctor?"

"It's a different degree," I said. "But besides teeth stuff, you see Uncle Earl."

"Yes," she said. "Is that it?"

"Just a couple more questions. Did the men who kidnapped you say anything?"

"They just said for me to be quiet and not try to get away. They said everything would be fine if I behaved. They were, like, rough when moving me, but not really. They bruised me a bit, but no permanent damage, you know? I bruise easily."

"Okay," I said.

"I think daddy's coming back. I heard someone come in the house. I gotta go."

"Wait, Celia! Can I call you again?"

The line stayed open and I heard distant, indistinct noises, then the line went dead. Dana clicked the voice recorder again.

"Jimbo came through. He gave us the right number," she said. "What did she say at the end?"

"Nothing," I said. "Let's go eat."

CHAPTER 44

I laid there in bed, watching an early-season baseball game. The soft sounds and slow pace helped me think. She called him Uncle Earl, which sounded like a term of endearment for a close family friend.

Her father and Earl had attended Columbia together, but it sounded more personal than that. I stood and peered through the louvers down Dronningens Gade. Now that carnival was over, the streets gave off an eerie stillness.

The burner-phone Dana had given me rang. A blocked caller.

"Hello?"

"Hi, it's me," Celia's young voice. "I hope it's okay, your number came up on my phone. I need to talk to someone."

"Celia, what's wrong?"

"Daddy won't let me leave the island," she said.

"That's understandable. He's afraid for your safety."

"I wanted to come over for Carnival, but that got all messed up. I just want to see my friends and hang out on my own at some of the local clubs."

"Are you sure you should be doing that? How old are you?" I said.

"Does it matter?"

"Celia, it's not safe for you to be in crowds out in public just after what happened."

"Will you help me or not?"

"Help you? I'm not a pilot, I'm just a man who already helped you get away from kidnappers."

"So you are, like, the perfect man to help a damsel in distress again."

"I'm not because I agree with your father," I said.

"Then can you do something else for me?"

"I don't know."

"Please."

"Tell me."

"Ask Uncle Earl to call me," long pause. Then, "I have a medical problem."

"Have your father call."

"No! It's, like, a private thing. My father always has to stick his nose into my private business," she pleaded. "Please just ask Earl, I mean, Uncle Earl, to call. Okay?" She sounded much more desperate about this than Carnival.

"I'll see what I can do," I said. "Good night, Celia."

"Good night, Mr. Montague," she said.

"Call me Boise," I said, but she'd already hung up.

CHAPTER 45

I dipped my hand in the holy water and did a quick curtsey. Auntie Glor should be here since she'd said she went to mass on Wednesday as well as Sunday. She sat next to a rotund woman in her seventies in the third row and they were singing with the congregation. People filled almost every pew, but one row back from her I squeezed in next to a frowning man who mumbled the words with little conviction.

We stood up, sat down, and absolved ourselves of sin for another week. The Latin parts were lost on me as this was another difference in the Lutheran and Catholic mass. Lutherans mostly spoke in whatever language the place used. Catholics couldn't let go of making things complicated. Like lawyers they loved using Latin phrases to seem more scholarly than they actually were. It was a sin of pride in my opinion.

I waited on the steps outside for Glor. She spoke to the priest for a couple seconds, then turned. She looked at me and a smile broke across her face.

"Hello, dear," she said putting her arms around me. "So nice to see you here."

The rotund woman waddled out, hugged the priest, then paused next to Glor.

Glor gestured to me while speaking to her pew-mate. "This is Boise, Roger's closest childhood friend. We lived next door to one another."

"What a dashing young man. We talked about you last week. Glor tells me you're a lapsed Lutheran."

"Yes, I suppose that's accurate," I said.

"Well, you can come back to god anytime. No judgments, right Glor? I'm Claudine."

Glor pursed her lips and nodded. "I see you shaved. That's good. So, Boise, what brings you down here?"

"The calling of the Lord," I said, grinning at them. "Just that. And of course to see how you ladies are doing."

"Oh, isn't that sweet," Claudine said with a little giggle.

"Sweet," said Glor lifting her brows with sarcasm.

Claudine leaned over and whispered in Glor's ear, but Glor gave a shake of her head. Then, Claudine said, "Mr. Boise?"

I'd looked away, pretending not to see their disagreement. "Yes," I said, turning back. Sweat filled the fabric around my armpits. Stripping off my jacket, I slung it over my arm, and loosened my tie to keep from suffocating.

"Would you join us for a brunch over at The Greenhouse? They make a lovely omelet," she said, rubbing her palms together and almost jumping in anticipation.

"No!" Glor blurted. "I mean, I'm sure Boise has other engagements today. Lots of things to do, right?"

"Actually, I needed to take a break," I said. "I'm taking the day off from interrogating witnesses."

"Oh, that sounds so exciting!" Claudine said. "Can you talk about the case?"

"I can tell you a little bit, but I'll leave out the names," I nudged her playfully. "You know, to protect the innocent."

She laughed loud enough that the priest turned his head from the person he'd just greeted and gave us a fatherly stare of disapproval.

Claudine fiddled with her purse, then said, "Don't mind him, he just uptight."

"Claudine, watch that!" Glor said.

"Sorry. Glor has me working on speaking more properly, at least around the clergy and during mass. Well, mass be over, Glor."

"We're still on the church steps. Let's go already, before you make any more scenes."

We shuffled across the street and through the ice plant property. Ten sweaty minutes later we arrived at The Greenhouse. Locals packed the place, but there was a reserved table for Glor and Claudine and they squeezed another chair onto the table to accommodate me.

"'M' feet dem killin' me. I told you I want to drive," Claudine said.

"Claudine, behave yourself," Glor said.

"All right, all right. If I speak properly, can I talk to Mr. Boise about things?" Glor focused on her menu. "So, Mr. Boise, what are you working on? I love Sherlock Holmes stories and Sam Spade too."

"Those are great. I'm not as smart as those guys."

"Oh, he modest too," she said, giggling again. "I'm in this online mystery book group, so I love it. What's happening with Roger's case?"

"Yes, Boise, what is happening with the case?" It was Dana, she had appeared next to our table.

Everyone exchanged hellos, then Dana pulled me aside.

"What about the girl?"

I told her about the conversation the night before. Dana said we needed to go see DeVere. I promised to go the next day. She reluctantly agreed.

"Is this about Roger?"

"No, I went to church and they were there. We're not even discussing…" she raised her eyebrows, "…well, we weren't talking about him until this very moment. She brought it up."

"Remember, you have to keep this stuff quiet, especially in a small place like this," she waved her hand around. "Word spreads, we lose our edge. You got it?"

I stared at her. "Yeah, okay."

She tapped her man's watch with her finger, then headed for the exit. After a quick trip to wash my hands I returned to the table.

"What was that about?" asked Claudine.

"Nothing, she's just a friend who needs help sometimes," I muttered.

"Boise, you okay?" Glor said, putting her hand on my shoulder. Her gentle touch felt good.

"Yes, Auntie Glor. It's all good."

We ate and I managed to deflect the remainder of Claudine's questions, mostly by getting her to talk about herself. She'd grown up in St. Croix but moved here when she decided to attend the main campus of the University of the Virgin Islands.

I could tell that they were not going to let me pay, so I snuck up to the bar and told Willy, an Aussie bartender I'd befriended over the past month, I'd pay for the bill and to have the waiter say it was covered. They voiced the usual animosity people expressed when they felt taken care of without knowing the person well enough to feel safe about it.

"So, what've you found out about Roger?" Glor asked after we left Claudine at her car.

"I thought you already had your answers and I shouldn't waste time on the likes of him," I said.

"You gonna tell me?" Her hand lingered on the door handle of her rusty car. Her faded violet dress billowed in the wind, giving a glimpse of varicose veins through her stockings.

"Can you tell me who his surrogate father was?" I asked.

"Boise, why you got to go through these old pages looking for the worst?"

I sighed. "It would help me get to the truth. What I know so far leads me to believe there's more than a bad drug dealer relationship to blame. There's a passion that business, no matter how ugly, can't duplicate."

She eyed me a long time. I could see my reflection in her glasses. "His name's Phil."

"Anything else?"

"He lives in Fortuna. He did last I knew." She opened the door and settled into the driver's seat. "I need a new car."

CHAPTER 46

My burner rang. "Hello," I said, weary from the emotion of seeing Auntie Glor again.

"Did you talk to him?" It was Celia.

"No," I said.

"I asked for one thing," she said. I could hear her breathing hitch. "One thing."

"I already did one thing for you. It's your turn," I said, trying to sound hard.

"Please, I just have to see Uncle Earl. I need you to have him call me."

"You have his phone number, right? He's your doctor," I said.

"No, I lost that phone. I need him to call me. Please?"

"Listen Celia, I need to know what this is about," I said as I sat on the side of my bed. "I need more. What happened? Do you know why you were kidnapped?"

"Because Daddy's a powerful and influential man. People use me to hurt him."

"Is that a sound bite you rehearsed with your father's publicist?" I asked.

"No, it's just the life I live."

"Sounds lonely."

"Lonely? It's not. I'm surrounded by people. I go to an awesome school and I travel all over."

"Why do you keep calling me at night then? Shouldn't you be out with friends or with your boyfriend?"

"I don't have a boyfriend," she said. "Just tell Uncle Earl." She hung up.

CHAPTER 47

The next morning, I headed for the hospital to see Uncle Earl after I called and confirmed he was on duty. He hunched over papers on his desk. I knocked lightly on his open door.

"Come in," he said without looking up. Then he lifted his head and stood. "What do you want now? Where's your dragon?"

"Celia really wants you to call her."

His eyes narrowed to slits. "Celia Jarl?"

"You have other ladies in your life named Celia?"

He sat back down and hunched over his paperwork again. I cleared my throat. He looked up, then leaned back in his chair. "What is it? Do you have a message from my mother?"

"She really wants to talk to you," I repeated.

"I got the message. You can tell her that when next you speak. Now, I have to," he waved at the papers and hunched over again.

"Sure, sure. Hey, do you ever hang out in front of Saints Peter and Paul? I thought I saw you there a while back." I took one of his pens and wrote my phone number on a blank piece of paper on his desk. "If you decide to unburden yourself or if you want to tell your story, call me. I aim to find out what's behind Celia's kidnapping."

He pushed the sheet of paper off the side of the desk. It floated down into a gray wastebasket. He returned to his papers. I walked to the doorway, then turned back.

"You're hiding something. You have something to do with Celia."

"I'm her physician."

"It goes deeper than that," I said.

"There is nothing more sacred and confidential than the physician-patient relationship. Nothing." At this he stood and joined me in the hallway. After locking the door, he leaned close to me. I could smell ginger and peppermint on his breath. "You and Ms. Goode could show a little more gratitude since I'm also your physician. You wouldn't want me divulging your medical secrets, would you?"

"Thank you for helping us," I said as he slid by, clomping away down the tiled floor. "But helping some people doesn't give you the right to hurt others."

He entered the stairwell and the door shut with a clang. Moments later I followed, quietly opening the stairwell door. Two floors down he exited. I bolted down in time to see him turn a corner heading to the northwest wing. He used a key card to enter a locked door marked "laboratory – staff only."

Out in the parking lot, I glanced inside DeVere's Mercedes. On the front seat lay a pamphlet for space in an office building leasing medical spaces in Nisky Center, owned by Payne & Wedgefield. I looked back at the hospital. DeVere stood in a second-floor window, arms folded across his chest, staring down at me.

CHAPTER 48

My eyes wouldn't close. Evelyn's face smiled down at me from the ceiling. Outside, a gentle breeze whistled through the palm fronds as crickets chirped a symphony.

The crickets gave me a sense of isolation I enjoyed initially, but at the moment dreaded. I needed anonymity, but the level here was extreme. I thought more familiar faces and buildings without the history of Evelyn on them would be a salve for my wounds. Instead, without Roger to aid my transition back into island life, I stumbled into a profound loneliness.

The phone buzzed. "Blocked Caller." Celia was a spoiled child, but I was relieved she called because I still sensed she was in danger, even on her private island.

"Hello," I said.

"Can you meet me?" It wasn't Celia.

"DeVere?"

"Can you?" he repeated.

"I don't have a car," I said.

"I'll meet you."

I thought a moment, deciding whether I wanted a man mixed up in these matters to know where I lived.

"Please hurry, time is short," he said.

"Meet me at the downtown post office," I said, trying to find a place far enough away, but not too far. My legs were weary and I'd already showered. The evening heat was oppressive. I pulled on a shirt and huffed down the hill. Before I made it halfway there, sweat dotted my thin t-shirt.

Next to a gate swathed in bougainvillea blossoms, I waited. Two loiterers prowled Emancipation Park to my right, and I could see the outline of the great Fort Christian looming over the park. The blanket of night covered everything except for the small street lights, only some of which worked. One couple walked by, hand in hand, heading toward Wet Willy's.

An occasional car passed, then one stopped on the curb. DeVere's black Mercedes.

"Get in," DeVere commanded.

I hit a button on my phone sending Dana a text that I was meeting DeVere should she be unable to locate me the next day. We eased away from the curb. DeVere's appearance shocked me. His eyes were swollen and a bit of dried spittle stuck to the corner of his mouth in white flakes. He wore a wrinkled t-shirt with pajama bottoms featuring smiley faces on a blue field.

"I heard someone coming into my house, so I got the hell out of there and called you."

"Why not the police?"

He kept checking his rearview mirror, his eyes darting at every car we passed. "Yeah, they're helpful here. In fact, could be off-duty cops who're doing this."

"Is this about Celia and Jarl?" I questioned.

He slammed the accelerator and his body pressed against the back of his seat. His muscular arms bulged as he gripped the steering wheel, his brown skin turning white under the strain. I looked through the rear windshield and spotted a car with its headlights off gaining fast.

DeVere twisted the wheel and I slammed against the door. I realized I'd forgotten to buckle up. After a couple failed attempts, I clicked the seatbelt home.

"I made mistakes and he holds them over me."

"What's that? Who? Jarl?" I said.

"Just listen. Yes, Jarl. He's after me," he said, making an acute turn up into the hills. The car bounced over a deep pothole.

"Is he in that car?"

"Of course not! Jarl doesn't do things himself. He's the conductor. He has underlings who do his deeds. He maintains a safe distance and always has an alibi to cover his ass."

"So what'd you do to displease him?"

"Nothing. Well, nothing that should've mattered. I tried to do the right thing and it's coming back at me."

The mirrors in the car lit up, blinding me. My head rocked forward as something nudged us from behind.

"Will you stop being cryptic. What's he after?"

DeVere mashed harder on the gas pedal. We must have been ripping along at nearly one-hundred miles per hour. "A father's revenge. He and I were both arrested on allegations of sex with a minor many years ago in New York."

"You mean statutory rape," I said.

He looked at me through smudged glasses with red-rimmed eyes bulging. "They call it rape, but it's not. I'm not a deviant. Healthy men like teenaged girls. Girls, who a century ago got married. I see the sites for teens all over the net. The girls were consenting."

I didn't know what to say, so I let him continue. "The lawyer said the only way we were going to get out of it was to kill or bribe. Right before trial, the district attorney on our case disappeared. He was found in a quarry two years later. Jarl made it look like I did it. He's not a doctor, so the charge doesn't matter to him. He didn't want jail time. But for me, if the allegation of sex with a minor got out…if the board found out about it, I'd lose everything. And then, he'd produce evidence that I killed the D.A."

The car behind nudged us again. We started to spin. I grabbed the wheel and yanked to the left as brush on the edge of the road tore at the black metal. The car careened to the right, drifting sideways. My stomach rolled. DeVere's eyes bulged as the headlights from the pursuing sedan lit on his features before we flipped forward and shot around another bend.

"We have to go to the cops," I said in rapid breaths.

"Not an option. Jarl'll expose me or he'll kill me. I need you to get me outta here."

"Me? What makes you think I could do that?"

"You or the reporter. You seem to know how to do things like that," he said. His voice started shaking as the headlights bore down again from behind. "I know you were in my office. My phone wasn't where I put it one day. It was either you or Dana. I'm betting it was you."

I recalled not remembering if I'd put his cell phone back where I'd found it that day I broke into his office, but I wasn't going to admit anything.

"I'll give you everything on Jarl and on what happened with Celia," he said after a brief pause.

DeVere took another steep, upward turn leading further into the hills. Dark figures of brush and trees flashed by along with driveways of dirt and grass, broken down cars on blocks.

"Okay, we'll try. Talk." I punched the record button on my phone.

The headlights continued to follow, sometimes dropping back, then gaining, but DeVere managed to keep them from nudging us.

"Those are Cecil's goons following us," he said. "I think Cecil's decided we're not friends anymore. We never were, but as long as he held something over me and we shared a mutual hobby, he found me useful and trustworthy because I had a slave's choice, do my master's bidding or else."

A hobby. This guy disgusted me.

We eventually drove past a nightclub called For The Birds. The lot was full of cars, but there wasn't enough distance between us and Jarl's posse to get out of our car and into another. A couple standing outside the club pointed as we whipped past, the man shaking his head with disapproval.

Island roads weren't made for DeVere's Mercedes. Luckily, the bone-heads behind us drove a Caddie, which handled even worse. As long as the road kept winding, the distance remained constant.

"Why's Jarl so angry with you and what's this got to do with Celia?" As I asked the question, the whole thing came into sharp focus. I knew the problem and why this man deserved whatever was coming to him.

"Let me out," I said with alarming calmness.

"What? No, you're going to help me!"

"I'm not. You were having sex with Celia, weren't you?"

He didn't need to say anything. The swell of his cheek and the headlights in his eyes told me the answer. A man can hide who he is from everyone when things are calm and no one wants him dead.

He bellowed, "Cecil must have found out. I tried to break it off, but we were in love. I couldn't refuse her."

"The baby," I hissed, "was it yours?"

"Don't know," he whispered.

"You were going to abort your own child?" I felt sick. My chest hurt. "You told Cecil she was pregnant. Why?"

"She didn't want to give up the baby. She wanted to tell her father about us and get married. She didn't know what he's capable of."

We rounded a corner going downhill on the north side now. Up at the corner, in front of Sib's Bar, a drunk patron stumbled into the crosswalk, holding up her hand for us to stop. DeVere slowed, but the Caddie didn't. It plowed into us. DeVere swerved to the right, over an embankment into a small grassy field. Our car crumpled into the ground. My seatbelt caught me, crushing my chest. Airbags filled the cabin.

A pair of hands pulled DeVere out of the driver's seat. A face appeared wearing a colorful carnival mask. Feathers of red, yellow, and green covered the face. Deep-set eyes regarded me a moment. The eyes of a predator.

The mask floated away, leaving me staring at the whiteness of airbags and feeling a profound exhaustion. I heard the Caddie's engine rev, the murmur of a crowd.

For the second time since I'd been back, I wound up at the hospital. Bruises plastered my body, particularly my ribs and chest. My neck and lower back throbbed.

Doctors wrapped my torso, gave me prescription pain killers, and sent me home in a cab after the police interrogated me. I explained that the car behind us had forced us off the road after we attempted to stop for a pedestrian. I told them I was groggy after and was not sure what happened to the driver: Doctor Earl DeVere.

CHAPTER 49

I opened the door with a shaking hand.

"What?" I said rubbing my eyes.

Two cops. I'd seen one of them before. Perhaps on the baseball field when Dana and I were in Frenchtown investigating?

"We have some questions for you," the familiar-looking one said. His gut strained the buttons on his blue shirt. The second cop towered over his aggressive partner. Crooked white teeth cut a stark contrast against his dark ebony skin. He looked to be no more than twenty years old, while his partner looked forty or more.

Lucy stood next to him looking like Jack next to the giant. A white bar towel was slung over her shoulder. "I need a go. I leave Marge downstairs an' we have customers."

She headed off down the hall, the streetlights coming in off the boulevard obscuring her exit as I looked out from the open-air section at the top of the stairs.

"What time is it?" I said.

"We need to talk to you about Earl DeVere. You were the last person seen with him. Can we come in?"

The short one pushed past me into my room before I replied. The tall one followed, like a kid trailing his father.

I left the door ajar and pulled on a shirt. One of the other tenants ambled by in a wife-beater stained with sweat and tomato sauce. He grunted a greeting.

"I suspect the last person seen with him was whoever ran us off the road and grabbed him. Don't you have witnesses from up at Sib's?" I asked, trying to make out the name on his badge. "I was busy having my face crushed by an airbag. Couldn't see much, Officer Jenkins."

"So, you have nothing to add to the descriptions of the kidnappers?" he asked, his deep voice making me vibrate.

"No," I said, rubbing both temples in a circular motion.

The tall guy said, "You maybe have a concussion. You should go have your head examined."

"My mother told me that a lot," I said. Both men stared at me.

Music drifted up from the street. At first I thought nothing of it, then I remembered carnival was over. It sounded like a small steel drum band.

"Gentlemen, I really have to get some rest. Goodnight. My regards to your superiors."

I shut the door behind them with trembling fingers. Their shadows lingered outside my door. After I undressed and climbed into bed, they moved off, their footfalls dying on the carpeted stairs.

CHAPTER 50

If this was what fourteen hours of sleep could produce in me, I needed to do that more often. My head felt clear and when I looked into my bathroom mirror, my eyes gleamed with the mischief I intended to inflict upon the ruling class. My first stop: *The Daily News*.

As I stepped into the newsroom, I spotted Dana exactly where I expected to find her, at her desk, furiously typing. She looked up. A blend of annoyance and relief crossed her tired face.

"Look what fell out of the tree. Wow, is it tender?" she asked, pushing on my swollen cheek. "You look like a rat that just ate a mouse."

"It's good to see you too, Dana."

"I stopped by. Lucy let me peek into your room. I took your pulse," she grimaced. "I stepped loudly, but you didn't stir so I figured you needed the down time. You really with DeVere in that wreck?"

As I recounted the events of the night before, Dana asked thousands of questions and I answered as best I could. She added my information to her file and said she'd decide where it fit into the bigger story later.

"I got dirt on DeVere since he told you everything, but not sure anything'll stick to Jarl. I can't get a hold of our kidnappers. The phone's dead. My father said he dropped Jimbo off, but never saw where the guy shacked up in D.R.

"Dad tried but couldn't get him to open up further. That Jimbo doesn't trust easily, even when you save his hide. Dad's not much for surveillance, says it's too boring," she shook her head in daughterly disgust. "I have someone I'd like you to come talk to with me today."

"No," I said. She waited for more, but I had nothing more to add.

"Back to Roger then, huh?" she said.

"Yes," I said.

"I've got more urgent matters," she returned.

"I know. There was a time when I first arrived that you were as interested in Roger as I was."

"Yeah, well, things change."

"I'll see you when I'm done."

"Or if you need something," she said, leaning over the desk to cup my cheek. "I'm going out with Annie tonight. Want to come?"

"I wasn't even good at third-wheeling it with hetero couples," I said.

"Don't worry, we treat our third-wheels better. We know more about being awkward. Come on, it'll be fun."

"Nope, got a date with a jigsaw puzzle. It'll be less awkward," I smiled. "Back to the grind. One thing. You promised I'd get some payment for this. Can I collect?"

She looked thrown but recovered. "Sure. What you need?"

"As much as you can give right now," I said. "I'm eating into my money more than I'd like."

She unlocked the desk drawer on her left and brought out a manila envelope, then glanced over at Pickering's office. Pickering was looking at something on his desk.

"What is it?" I asked.

"Let's do this downstairs," she said.

We went down and got in her car. She pulled three hundreds out of the envelope. "Will this get you going?" she asked.

"Two more would be better." I felt uncomfortable but continued, "You've seen the price of pizza on this rock, right?"

"Okay," she pulled out three more hundreds.

"Is Pickering on your ass?"

"Boise, don't worry about it."

"Then can I get the other half in two weeks?" I said, feeling annoyed at having to continuously set the terms of our agreement. I felt like a beggar, something I despised about uncivilized places. I'd done a lot of negotiating lately and this felt like an unscheduled occurrence that could be avoided.

She looked around the street mobbed with tourists. "You know there are only four ships in today, but one of them's the largest in the Caribbean."

"Yeah, crowded," I agreed not knowing what to say. "Want help back up the stairs?"

"No, I'm going to sit a while," she said. "You go take care of your friend."

I headed off to the center of downtown and turned into Drake's Passage. If I wanted more on Roger, I'd have to talk to Noa again or return to the file and my looming meet with Roger's drug-dealing mentor, Phil Gardelin. Noa once again won out as the safer option.

This time I'd take a more direct route when I spoke to her. I planned to know something about who Elias was one way or the other and move along. As I entered the shopping arcade, Elias ran by me, bumping my shoulder. I winced as pain shot through my aching neck.

"Elias!" I yelled, turning to follow him. He never looked back, hitting the corner and rounding it apace. Everything still felt sore from the car accident and I didn't want to run, so I continued walking to the store.

Noa showed someone t-shirts and shorts. I leaned against the counter, the smell of coffee and sweet ice cream permeating the air. The customer took several items into the dressing room which Noa locked.

Approaching the counter, Noa asked, "What do you want?"

"Are you dating him behind your father's back?"

"Am I dating who?" she said. "Scratch that, I'm not dating. I'm busy raising a child. What do you care?"

"Because there is something going on here. I'm not a genius, but after watching and reading a lot of cop stories, I know that coincidences aren't," I said.

"Aren't?"

"I don't know, they aren't…" I searched for the word, "…I don't know, coincidences. They mean something. That kid, Elias. How do you know him?"

"Elias? What's he got to do with anything?"

"That's what I'm trying to figure. I met him at a law office down by the college and then I saw him come here. That's quite a coincidence don't you think?"

She blew a rush of air out her mouth, then pointed at the door. "I'm busy. I'm trying to make a living and I'm the only one in today. My father's busy ignoring everything and my sister has given up, so my hands are full. Elias is a family friend, but I have no idea what you want with him besides that."

"I'm not accusing you of anything, but I need to know more so I can figure this thing out," I said.

"And what's that?" she said.

"I think he's the key to finding out what happened to my friend, Roger. As I told you before, I gotta figure this out," I said.

She sneered at me, "How noble of you. You know what I think? I think this is about you trying to make up for leaving a friend behind. It's okay, some move on from this place, the rest of us are stuck here holding crumbling rocks together."

The sunburned American exited the dressing room. Noa asked her if she liked the outfit and they started talking about color patterns as another couple walked into the store. She brought the woman's purchases to the counter and told the couple she'd be happy to answer any questions they had when she was done. I waited.

I scuffed my foot along the store's threadbare carpet. In some spots where the racks stood, it had worn through to the fibers and in others the grey concrete shown through like eyes seeing from below. While I stood there, I thought about what she'd said, that I'd left my friends behind and they'd been lost without me.

Hot anger warmed my cheeks. It wasn't my responsibility to hold the world together for everyone else. When the customers left, I moved toward her, but her father walked in carrying a package. He squinted at the box, apparently trying to read the fine print on the label.

"Noa, I can no read this. Where my glasses?"

"Here, Papa, let me see," she said.

He looked up and spotted me standing in front of a row of folded t-shirts.

"Who this?" he said, pointing his chin in my direction.

"That's Boise, Papa." Then she whispered in his ear.

He located his glasses on the counter and read the name on the box, ignoring her introduction. I started to extend my hand when his face clouded over.

"What hell is this? Elias getting mail here?" He shook the box in his stubby hands. "What for? This our place of business, not his mailbox. I no want this boy around. He no good. He bad for you and me. I find another box or letter for him, trash. That's all. Like him, trash."

Calling the boy trash seemed extreme, but Noa had said earlier that her father disliked black people, so why would this boy even be involved with this family? Had he worked in the store at one time, then been fired? Her dad knew who he was, so a secret affair seemed unlikely.

Noa stuck the box under the counter. "Papa, let me see Boise out."

I whispered in Noa's ear, "I can take the box over to the lawyer's office for him."

Her father's face grew dark. "What you whisper in my daughter's ear, boy? What?" He looked at Noa. "Is he friend of Elias?"

"No, Papa, he's not."

"Get box out of here today or I throw away. Also, tell that boy his last name not Hariri. He cannot use my name or I kill him."

"Yes, Papa, I'll send it away now." She took the box from under the counter and handed it to me. We slipped into the alley. "I'm trusting you to deliver this to Elias."

I said I'd take it to Roberts' office.

"So, whose family is Elias friends with, 'cause it sure isn't yours."

She sighed, tilting her head to the right. "This isn't your concern."

"How is Elias related to you and why does your father say he can't use your last name? What is his last name?" I said, pressing the point.

She stared at me a long time, her eyes misting and then tearing. "I haven't seen my older sister in a long time. My parents disowned her. He's my nephew, their grandson."

I patted her shoulder, not knowing what else to do out there as tourists licked ice cream and enjoyed their day in paradise. A soft breeze rolled through, ruffling her black hair. I held my hat with one hand and squeezed the box against my hip with the other.

"They don't much like that Becca had a child out of wedlock. They're traditional," she said.

"Who's the father? Is it Roger?" I asked.

She shook her head, then went back inside the store. I didn't believe her. Standing on the dirty bricks, while bodies swirled around me muttering their concerns about where to go next and the amazing weather, I felt like I'd been transported back into my chaotic L.A. life.

Elias appeared to be a child raising by estranged parents: a drug dealer and a disowned Lebanese woman. Based on his age, they must've gotten together in high school and Roger had probably ignored the boy. Speaking to Elias seemed the best way to find out what his place in all of this really was. I also needed to talk to Noa's sister, Becca.

CHAPTER 51

After eating at the Greenhouse, I headed over to Patrick Roberts' office carrying the box. Feeling tired and achy, half-way there, I hailed a passing taxi. The Rastafarian driver dropped me at the bottom of a small hill leading into the residential area.

White university buildings loomed over the green slopes to the west. One fit man in a tank top jogged laps on the well-manicured soccer field behind me. Cut up telephone poles encircled the field as a border.

I seated myself on a rough pole. I turned to the west, so a car approaching from downtown wouldn't see my face. It allowed me to watch the runner on the field, which was more interesting than watching cars motor by. The location also afforded me a perfect vantage point to watch for Elias and Roberts to arrive.

After an hour, my mouth went dry and my head ached. It was nearly nine-thirty and I craved water. Roberts didn't keep regular office hours. Perhaps he'd gone to court today.

A car drove up the hill and turned toward the office. Roberts got out. He strutted to his office, holding a leather briefcase and examining a gold Rolex, a perfectly lawyerly pose.

I moved closer to the white Audi to snap a photo of his license plate and take various shots of his car. A bike charged up the road, the rider's head bowed with exertion. The rider raised his head. It was Elias, beaded with sweat. I ducked behind the passenger side of Roberts' Audi.

Elias stashed his bike around the side of the building then trotted down the dirt path leading to the door. I waited until he closed the door then counted to one-hundred before entering the office.

The reception area was deserted, but I could hear voices through the inner door. I found a water cooler in the corner and swallowed one of my horse pills.

Elias came out followed by Roberts.

"What are you doing here?" Roberts asked.

"Elias, I need to know something," I said, ignoring Roberts' question.

"Excuse me, I'm talking to you." Roberts raked his bony hand through thinning brown hair. "Elias, go in my office and shut the door," Roberts commanded.

"What's going on?" Elias asked, genuinely interested in what I had to say.

"I want to know about the woman in the photo in that desk drawer." I pointed at the drawer I'd looked through last time.

"What photo?" Roberts said.

"It's a woman I know," Elias said. "I'm not supposed to talk about her."

"Is she Noa's sister?"

"You know Aunt Noa? How?"

"You need to leave, Mr. Montague. You're trespassing." Roberts nudged me toward the door with a soft shove. I stood my ground and in reality, the frail man could do nothing to make me move. He pointed his finger at the ground like he was giving a summation at a murder trial. "You're not welcome here. You may not speak to my client any further."

"WAIT!" roared Elias. Roberts froze mid-push. "I want to talk to him."

Roberts stared at Elias, his eyes putting weight in his words. "Absolutely not. I forbid it."

"Oh yeah? Well, lucky for me, I don't need your permission! This man knows something about my family," Elias cried. "I want to know what it is."

"Your mother left me in charge," Roberts said. "It's for your safety."

"I know what it's for, but I'm a man now. I have things going right, Patrick. I appreciate you taking me in when I didn't want to go back wid my mother, but I have to be able to make some decisions at some point. You can't protect me forever," he said, resting his hand on Roberts' shoulder.

The attorney looked at Elias like a man who had no arguments left, then he found another. "Your mother wouldn't want you talking to a private investigator."

Elias smiled, pulling his hand away. "Then I'll let him do the talking. You can listen if you're okay with him trespassing. Otherwise, we'll go outside."

I could see Roberts probing for another way to arrest this discussion. Then I said, "Mr. Roberts, why can't we talk?"

Roberts closed the front door and locked it, then took a tiny cup of water from the cooler and threw it back like a shot of rum, crumpling the cup and dropping it in the wastebasket. He sat down behind the reception desk and pulled out the picture I mentioned from the drawer. He put it on the desk, propping it up against a book and rotating it toward us.

"Go ahead, Elias, find out what this man wants," Roberts said, leaning back and lacing his hands behind his head.

I pointed at the photo. "Is that your mother?"

"Yes," Elias said.

"Is her name Becca?"

"Yes," he said. "How'd you know that?"

"Because she dated my best friend after I left and I think they had you together," I said. "Did you know your father?"

He pulled out his wallet and took a ragged photo from behind his driver's license. I gazed at the adult version of Roger, a face I knew well when it had been innocent and still free of stubble.

"That's my friend," I said. "That's your father, right?"

He nodded. Roberts shook his head. "This is not good," he muttered. He stood up again. "Elias, I must renew my advice to stop talking to this man for your safety and your mother's."

Elias spun violently toward Roberts, but his voice remained stoic. "Do not interrupt this discussion again, Patrick, or we are leaving and you won't be invited."

The words shoved Roberts back into the chair like a hand against his chest.

Elias turned back to me. "Yeah, Roger Black. He's my pops. You knew him? How?"

I explained how we grew up next to each other and how I'd left when I was twelve.

"I came back hoping to see him and found out he was dead. I didn't even know. We lost touch," I trailed off lamely.

"Yeah, he died. Christmas Eve 2011," he said, reciting the date with hollow reverence. "Holidays aren't the same. I hate the decorations and cheer. Hate it." His eyes grew distant, then snapped back into focus. "So what? You wanted to meet the son of a drug dealer you knew before he was a drug dealer?"

"I'm here because I want to talk about his death," I said. "Rather, I want to talk about what you saw before he died."

At this, Elias looked at Roberts. "You knew this man was interested in my dad and you told him to do what?"

"I wanted to protect you from having all this dredged up, Elias. I told him to drop it and leave you alone," Roberts said. "I was being a friend."

I gave a breathy laugh at that. Elias spun on me. "You got something else to say, Mr. Boise?"

"I think you need to know what's really going on and what Roberts told you isn't it," I said.

Elias crossed his arms and waited.

"He represented himself as an attorney for you," I pointed at Elias' chest for emphasis. "Only he wouldn't tell me who you were. He wanted me to stop investigating."

"Investigating?" Elias said.

"Roger's, your father's, death," I said. Elias looked at Roberts, then back at me, then back at Roberts.

"What's he talking about, Patrick? I thought my father was killed by some drug dealer, but we couldn't figure out who."

"He was," Roberts said. "He was killed in a bad deal."

"Yeah, but by who? They never cared to figure that out, did they?" Elias said, his voice getting higher and louder. "And you told this man…You told him not to investigate because I'm too fragile or somet'ing? I can't handle it? Dat's what you t'ink?"

"No, I wanted…I don't know. I just wanted to protect…"

"My modda. Dat's what you wanted. To protect my modda!" Elias shouted.

Someone rattled the doorknob, trying to enter the law office. We all froze. Roberts inhaled and stepped between us to open the door. Lucy and Marge stood there. Marge held a handbag and Lucy had a large manila envelope.

Roberts smiled big. "Hi, Lucy and…!" He snapped his fingers.

"Marge," Lucy said.

"Yes! Marge! I was just finishing a meeting with, well, you know Boise, right?"

Marge said nothing.

Lucy said, "Can we come in? We have an appointment at ten o'clock." She looked at her phone. "We early."

Roberts stepped aside, pushing the door back and spreading his arms, almost hitting me in the process. I stepped back, bumping a chair. Elias looked like a fighter in the fifteenth round after taking an uppercut to the jaw.

"Please, early's better than late, I always say. Please go right into my office."

The women scuffled into the office. Roberts reached for his office door.

"Please have a seat. I'll be right in." He shut the door then whispered at Elias, "We need to talk about this."

Elias picked up his backpack and headed for the door. He paused, staring down at his hand grasping the doorknob. "No more doing things behind my back in the name of protecting me. My mother said that shit to me so much, and it ain't not'ing." He pursed his lips, then repeated, "It is nothing."

I followed him out, shutting the door on Roberts before he could say anything else. Elias stood with his hands over his face for several seconds. I leaned against Roberts' Audi. The metal felt hot. It felt good. It pulled me into the moment.

Elias removed his hands and glared at the office door.

"He had to take that client. He needs paying customers," Elias said.

"Are you going to be an attorney?" I asked.

"Maybe. I go back and forth. They help and they hurt. I want to make a good living, but I want to make a good living," he said. "Hard to do both."

I nodded, not knowing what I could say to allay his concerns. I uttered, "I understand," then went back to feeling the heated metal while I watched his eyes for some hope.

He finally squinted at me, "So you and my pops were what, besties or somet'ing?"

"We lived next to each other. You know the neighborhood where he lived with Auntie Glor?"

"I met her once," he said.

"Maybe we can go see her sometime," I said. "I called her Auntie, but she was his grandmother, which makes her your great-grandmother."

He shook his head now, then banged his open palm against the trunk of the car with a *clang*!

"This ain't no family reunion. My pops is gone and seeing my great-grandma ain't fixing dat."

"Then let's fix it. Let's get the jerk-off who did it," I said.

"I'm interested in order. That things are kept together. You know, right. That people get along. That laws work for people," he said. "You're talking revenge."

"No," I said. "I'm happy to bring the law-breaker to justice for his crimes, but I'm running out of options. I need your help."

"Incarceration won't bring my pops back. I know who did it, but I'll be in da mud if I want to kill that snake."

"Who?"

"Phil Gardelin. He's the one who got pops into that life. I don't want to do that though."

"Did he get him out?" I asked.

Elias squinted at me, his nostrils flaring slightly. "What do you mean?"

I sighed, then continued, "You said Phil Gardelin got him into dealing. That's a fact, right?"

"Yeah, pops told me that. He introduced us when I was interested in that business. He said that guy was like his mentor."

"So you have first-hand knowledge that Roger was taken into the drug dealing life by Gardelin." I pressed my palm against the hot metal. "What makes you think Phil Gardelin took him out of this life? What evidence do you have for that assertion?"

Elias' mouth popped open, then snapped shut. "I jus' know," he said. "My father was gonna take over this area. It was a battle for control of this market." Elias waved his hand over the town like a politician giving a speech, "He done it, trust me."

"You feel this in your gut?" I asked.

"No, people told me he threatened him."

"That's more significant. What people?"

"I don't remember. Just other guys around," he said.

"Can we talk to any of them?" I asked.

He shook his head. "No, they don't talk to me anymore since I went into this." He cocked his head toward the office. "They call me cocky-law-sucka because I didn't take revenge and I ain't interested in defending criminals."

"How does it make you feel knowing he's out there free?" I asked.

"I told you already, I believe in order, not revenge. I want him punished by the law. I want justice," he said.

"So revenge and justice aren't the same?" I said.

"No," he said. "If you don't understand that, what are we talking for?"

"I understand," I said.

"I want to kill him, but that would just prove that my father deserved it. He didn't. He provided a need to people who want something for a price. How's that different from everyone else?"

"It's not, but if you really believe that, why aren't you a drug dealer too? It's easier and faster than studying law."

"Alcohol's legal, but I'm not a bartender. It contributes to people's problems. I wanna solve problems, create more order, not more chaos. Destroying is easy, building hard. What do you care?"

"Can you take me to talk to Gardelin?" I asked.

CHAPTER 52

Elias peddled his bike next to me, wiggling the front wheel back and forth to keep balance at the snail's pace. Cars ripped by as I walked, half in the street. Even the drivers in St. Thomas seemed to be in a bigger hurry nowadays. Perhaps I'd slowed down.

"This man ain't no joke," Elias said. "You knew my pops. Seriously?"

"We learned how to ride bikes together in the parking lot where the V.I. Courthouse is over on waterfront," I said, picturing my first bike and its sky-blue banana seat.

"That dumpy parking lot? They got fences round it. No way you could get in there without a pass."

"Everything's high security now, since 9/11. When we were kids, that place was just built. All the paint on the asphalt sparkling. The parking lot smooth as a seagull's feather. No fences." I crossed my finger over my heart.

Elias licked his thick, chapped lips. "What kind of bike did pops have?"

"He had one of those BMX models with the silver rims and black body. His was much cooler than mine, but it was really small. That was the style, riding a bike that looked too small. Like a big tricycle."

"Yeah, they still do that," Elias said. "The loser drug dealers."

I stopped walking. Elias was looking down at the dust and rocks, navigating the road's edge. He was twenty yards past me before he realized I wasn't by his side.

He turned and said, "What?"

I didn't move and could hear another plane powering up. We could see part of the runway through the trees.

"Don't say that," I said. "He was a good person. My best friend." I started to walk again and as I passed him I said, "I left him behind. Who knows what happened. We weren't there."

That killed the conversation for the remainder of our walk. We followed a small street leading away from the airport up into a hidden neighborhood north of the main drag. We arrived. Elias stopped in front of a ragged house with chickens and a rooster in the yard.

"I told you, you ain't ready for dis," Elias said as we stood on the edge of the silent property. "Maybe we should best leave."

The door opened as he uttered the last word. A man stood there in a tank-top and sweat pants. His hands were held behind him in a military-style stance.

"Wha' you want?" He said, his ample mustache bowing as his lips opened and shut.

Elias sighed, then started to approach the house. Gardelin's hands whipped from behind his back like cobras.

He gripped a black gun and assumed a two-fisted shooting stance, his weapon trained on us.

"Now you done gone on my prop'ty wit-out asking. Wha' your business is?" I held up my hands and Elias did the same, dropping his bike on the browning grass, then backing up into the street.

"Phil, it's me, Roger's son Elias."

A faint shadow of recognition crossed Gardelin's face as he studied Elias.

"Elias? Dat you?" At this Gardelin shifted his gun to me. "Who dis?"

"He grow up wit' pops. His name Boise," Elias said. "He want to meet you because you was pop's friend. Just want to ask if you know anything more about what happened to me pops."

Gardelin studied me a long moment, like a rancher examining livestock. Finally, he lowered his pistol.

"Can I put my hands down?" I asked.

Gardelin gave a huge grin that exposed a large gap in his front teeth. "I like he already. He know not to fuck wit' me. Yeah, put dem down. You know Elias, you need to learn dat kind of respect. As I recall, I had to put you over my knee more dan once."

"I rememba. I more respectful now."

"Good. Dat's good. Respect is the cornerstone of any relationship. Don't you agree, Mista Boise?" Gardelin said, his smile evaporating.

"Sure. Yeah. It's the cornerstone," I said, still reeling from the adrenaline rush. I hated guns, especially when criminals pointed them at me.

Gardelin nodded, his brown eyes twinkling. He seemed to relish life-or-death confrontation. He waved the gun around with indifference.

The black eye of the weapon crossed in front of my face while he said something to Elias and I ducked away. He ushered us around the side of his house and into the backyard. Stacks of open, wire cages housed more roosters and chickens. In the far corner of the dusty mess of dried corn pieces and bird shit, a couple of grey pit bulls strained against spiked leashes with deep chuffing noises. A wooden picnic table dominated the middle of the yard.

Gardelin shooed a chicken away and offered us a seat. He shot me another hard look, up and down, then seemed to decide I posed no threat. He disappeared into the yellow house and returned holding three beers.

I thought back on what little I knew of the primal antics of gang life. He would keep testing the rope, like the chained dogs that had known freedom too long to accept the chain as inevitable. Under the eaves of his house, something hung there on the side away from the sun. It looked like a small, brown pouch. White tufts stuck out the bottom.

"What's that?" I said.

Gardelin didn't turn to look where I pointed. Instead he took a swig of beer and gave a large grin. "Dat's good," he said. "So, you here about Roger. He liked to be called 'Force' by the people in his business."

"Force," I said, with a slight laugh. "Seriously?"

Gardelin leaned forward. "So, what so funny about dat? You show respect for da dead when you wid me." He nodded to Elias. "Dis was da man's blood. His only son. You no joke about he fadda's chosen title."

"Sorry," I said. "Elias, sorry if that offended you."

Elias looked down at the table and took frequent, short sips from his bottle, saying nothing. I thought it over and realized this too was a test. Maybe I'd passed, but maybe I was failing by not standing by my position. If this man had killed Roger, then why was he so concerned about showing respect?

"We came here..." I started.

Elias interrupted me. "You. You came here. I just tagged along because you don't know Phil."

"I'm hurt," said Gardelin. "Hurt that you weren't coming to see me for your own reasons. Didn't I always show you a good time, Elias?"

Elias darted a sip from his beer bottle.

A mix of stale pot and boiled potatoes wafted off Gardelin as he stood and waved his arms around wildly.

"What wid dis kid? You got somet'ing to say?" Gardelin hissed at Elias.

"Hey Phil," I said. "We just want to know if there's anything you can tell us about what happened to Roger. I'm trying to do what the police wouldn't and find out who killed him."

Gardelin pounded the table with both open palms and started laughing. The pit bulls barked in unison and the brown pouch shifted under the overhang.

"What you is, some kind of Sherlock or somet'ing?"

"A childhood friend of Roger's, trying to get a grip on what happened. I moved back and went to see him at his grandmother's house."

Gardelin held up a hand to stop me. "You talkin' 'bout Glor? Dat Jesus woman who raised him? You know Force was sick of her."

"Yeah, I went to see her," I said.

"Bet dat was fun. She give you milk? Woman crazy," he said, sitting back down. "You brave goin' to see she." He waved his hand up and down. "She don't know nothing about Force. She don't know nothing don't go on in dat church. She t'ink Jesus goin' come save her rass. Jah maybe. Force had enough wid dat shit. You know why he get into dis life? Because dis life where it happen. Survival of da fittest." He popped his fist into the palm of his open hand. "You be fuckin' or you be fucked. Dat's da only rules. Simple. Life easier like dis."

He took another swig of beer. "Now come straight. What da fuck you want to know about Force dat you ain't already know? He dead."

"We...I want to find out who killed him," I said.

"For what?" Gardelin said.

"Justice," I said.

"You goin' kill da killa?" he asked, leaning closer to me so I could smell the fresh beer on his breath and see his gold fillings. I stared right back at him, swallowing hard, but keeping my gaze fixed on his dilated pupils. Elias peeled the paper off his beer bottle in small strips. After a few long moments, Gardelin gripped my shoulder and smiled, then looked up at the sack beneath his overhang.

"Bats," he said. "Dey's fruit bats, but dey also eat insects. I keep dem happy wid dat water and papaya. Dey kill da insects so my boys," he pointed his open hand at the dogs, "ain't got to have bites 'cept when dey fight."

I nodded. I could feel something coming from deep in the past.

"He wasn't kill by no drug dealer. If he was, I would have know. No dealer. Force couldn't be killed when he ready," he said. "Not no way. Well, maybe by I-and-I."

I took this in. Elias looked up. His upper lip trembled. He was fighting his emotions. I needed to get him out of there, but we weren't finished. I might not get a man like this in such a talkative mood again.

"So, what do you think?" I asked.

"Ha, you want to know what I t'ink happen?"

"Yes," I said. "I do."

"Carelessness," Gardelin said, his mouth pouting as if he'd tasted bad fish.

I waited for him to continue, feeling that he needed to take his time with the narrative. Elias couldn't contain himself. "What dat mean?"

Gardelin, who'd been gazing off in the distance and squinting, brought his focus around on Elias. "He got careless 'cause of you."

Elias' eyes bulged. "What I have to do wid this? I ain't do nothing." He threw his arms wide as he stood.

"No, you do. He lose sight of da prize when you come round. He worry 'bout you."

Right then, we heard a car stop in front of the house. Gardelin picked his cell phone off the table and tapped the screen.

"Shit! We go!" he said, charging toward the pit bulls.

Elias hesitated as the dogs growled. I waved him on and he slipped by the snapping jaws. Behind the chicken coop rested a trap door that Gardelin held open.

"Get in," he hissed.

Elias jumped in, but I started to ask him what was going on. He used one strong arm to shove me into the pit, then dove in as the dogs' barks grew fiercer.

Inside the pit lay an arsenal of weapons. Plastic pillows of cocaine were stacked neatly in piles. In the sudden darkness, I heard a metal latch thrown on the trapdoor. Gardelin snapped on an exposed light bulb. A Bob Marley poster hung on the earthen wall below the bulb.

"Phil, what was that?" Elias asked, raising his voice. Using one hand, Gardelin grabbed Eilas' throat and squeezed. I broke his grip, but Gardelin stared into Elias' eyes and held his index finger to his lips as he raised a pistol in his other hand and tapped his temple.

"T'ink boy," he whispered. "You want be da one who kill me too?"

We heard two yelps and the barking ceased. Shelves covered the smooth earthen walls to hold the drugs, some canned food, bottled water, and guns. Gardelin's bunker.

Gardelin handed a revolver to Elias and cocked the hammer. He reached into the pile, checked the clip on a more modern gun, then clicked off the safety and handed it to me. He took a semi-automatic for himself. The one other time I'd held an automatic weapon, it disgusted me. This time, I was eternally grateful.

Gardelin tapped his phone screen. He scrolled through a series of video shots that surveyed his property. One man was in his house, rummaging through the kitchen. Two more examined the backyard, their backs to the camera mounted on the roof. There was an angle from the chicken coop showing another man walking right on top of the bunker. He stomped on top of the metal trapdoor. It clattered.

He called his mates over. Gardelin positioned himself beneath the trap door, aiming the gun upward. He instructed Elias and I to take up defensive positions out of sight of the trapdoor entrance.

The door rattled as they tried to open it. The latch held firm. They rattled it harder. We heard murmuring. The guys in the backyard all converged. Moments later the ones who were in the house joined them. Eight of them in total. They debated something. By reading his lips I could tell that the one who appeared to be in charge said "Fuck dis!" and yanked a round object from his vest.

"Is there a way out?" I hissed at Gardelin. "Or somewhere to hide?" He shook his head. We were trapped. Elias shrunk into the corner. I didn't want to die in this stinking, sinful bunker.

In those precious seconds, I made a truly commanding decision for the first time in my life. I shoved Gardelin aside as the other men above backed away from the leader who'd put his finger through the ring on the tip of the small, round pineapple. He leaned over the door to place the grenade above the latch and in that moment, my mind felt as deep and clear as the Caribbean Sea.

Gardelin fell aside. In one fluid motion, I unlatched the door, crashing upward using my shoulder. The metal door shot loose. I felt a wet crunch as it connected squarely with the thug's face. The grenade flew backwards. The pin snapped free, caught in the leader's index finger. All the men standing behind him froze as the grenade arced above in a perfect parabola. It struck the dirt next to the dead dogs. They started to run. Too late. The blast caught all the thugs full in the back. I plunged back into the bunker and the door clanged shut as I crashed in on Gardelin crouched below me.

The blast reverberated through the bunker. My head pounded. Elias screamed. A silent ringing, like we'd just left a rock concert, filled my ears.

Amazingly, Bob Marley still clung to the wall. Dust filled the phone's frame, but after a few minutes it cleared. The cameras showed two men writhing in the dirt. The others lay prone. The leader looked scorched, but relatively intact in his unconscious state.

I leaned back to take a breather, but Gardelin, a veteran of the drug wars, knew what came next.

"Cops," he said. Both Elias and I were paralyzed. Gardelin screamed, "COPS! WE HAVE TO MOVE, NOW!!!"

Through my fog, I heard him, but Elias still looked like he'd been hit over the head with a bat. Gardelin made it halfway through the trapdoor, when I called to him. "Wait, I need your help! Elias isn't moving."

Gardelin yelled over his shoulder, "Fuck dat! Dere was an explosion here. Dey comin.' I goin.'"

He took off, running as fast as he could through the yard and into his house. I shook Elias. Crippling fear held him motionless.

"Elias, we have to go," I said, shaking him by the shoulders. I spotted a bottle of water. I opened it and pitched water in his face. He blinked.

"We have to go," I repeated with an eerie calmness. He nodded, hugging himself. "You're okay. Let's go," I said, mustering all the calm I could from my last CPR training. He responded to my firm command and pulled himself up through the door. I followed.

The leader moaned. Gardelin stormed out of the house with two guns. Elias still held a gun in his hand. Gardelin shot the leader in the head.

"Le's go. You got wheels?"

"No," Elias said, rubbing water from his face. "I have my bike!"

"Don't you have a car?" I asked.

"Dey'll be looking for my car," Gardelin snarled at me. "Me house just blow up."

"You must have an escape route for these situations," I said.

He sighed. "We go."

Gardelin and I hustled off on foot, away from the main road. Elias snagged his backpack and zipped ahead of us, pumping the pedals of his burnt-sienna Diamondback mountain bike. We ran at full speed for half-a-mile and turned into a driveway leading into tall grasses on the hillside. Through the grass I made out blue and red lights spinning as six cop cars encircled Gardelin's residence.

At the end of the gravel road stood one house. It appeared vacant until a petite woman in a flowing linen dress sauntered out on the porch and leaned on the railing. She craned her neck, trying to see the commotion down below.

She spotted us and waved us up. Gardelin started jogging. Elias and I looked at each other. I chucked Elias' bike deep into the high grass, making sure it was completely obscured from view.

I limped up the hill, my knee aching again as the adrenaline wore off. The short-haired woman shot another glance down the hill, then snapped her fingers urgently as she ushered us through the front door, ducking inside and throwing the deadbolt.

"Philip, what dat goin' on down der?" She had a heavy island accent.

From the corner of the living room she grabbed a Louisville Slugger and slung it over her shoulder. She looked as comfortable as Mickey Mantle holding a bat.

"Fucking Semlis find me. I don't know how," Gardelin said.

"Ca' you stupid," she said. "Who dez fools?"

"Visitors. What it is to you?"

"It's to me becau' I going down wid your rass if dey fin' anyt'ing down dere," she said, pointing the business end of the bat at the blind-covered window. "I tell you no do dat deal wid Semlis. I done tell you." I assumed Semlis was the gangster who'd sent the eight goons.

Gardelin raised his hand over his head, ready to strike her. She stepped out of his reach and raised the bat like she'd just stepped to the plate.

"I told you woman, don't talk like dat to me. I ain't your fuckin' kid. I da man here."

They circled each other like wildcats. A hatred that could only be born of love. Behind me, I heard the deadbolt click open. We spun around in time to see Elias open the front door and shoot out into the afternoon heat.

"Shit!" Gardelin bolted after Elias.

The woman hollered, "Forget him! Philip!"

Gardelin chased Elias to the spot where his bike was and tackled him as Elias jerked the bike free of the bushes. Gardelin dragged him back into the house and the woman slammed the door shut.

"Where da hell you t'ink you going?" Gardelin growled. Elias' hands shook uncontrollably.

"I want to go home," he whined.

Gardelin gripped him by the collar. I heard the fabric rip as I pulled them apart.

"Let's just talk this out," I said. "Phil?"

Gardelin released his grip and glared at me. He stalked the sparsely furnished room like a caged beast. Animal print rugs and throws covered the hardwood floor and the lone couch. One wall featured a row of small, wooden African masks and on a round end table sat a single lamp made of green metal in the shape of a gorilla.

"No talks. Act! Dis man young, right?" He got right in Elias' face. "When I your age, I already earned enough to buy me modda dis house. You put your modda in debt with dis college learning." He pointed out toward the back of the house. "You in it wit politicians."

"Mr. Gardelin, we really didn't come to discuss your views on our society or the political situation of our economy," I said as gently as I could, still thinking of my intact spine and hoping that my actions at the house had purchased a little credibility. "He's a kid. He's not you. He likes school. Do you really have a problem with that?"

Gardelin dropped his head and let it loll around a long moment, then headed to the back door. In the back yard, he ripped a tarp off a motorcycle.

"You get him out," he said to me. "I lead dem away."

The woman said, "No Phil. What you talkin' about?"

He pointed the gun at the sky as he mounted the motorcycle, like he was posing for a photo in a western magazine.

"Shut up, woman. Dis a man's job, you not understand. I back tomorrow."

We watched wide-eyed as he sped away down the hill. The sound of the roaring engine faded. I turned to his girlfriend.

"You knew Roger?"

"Yeah, so?"

"Do you know who killed him?"

She laughed. "Dey say he kill by a dealer, right? Dat's da story?"

I nodded. Elias sat patiently. We had his rapt attention.

"Do you know something else?" I asked.

Her lips drew back revealing rotting teeth. She used-- probably crack. Bone-thin shoulders shrugged under eggshell-colored dress.

"Why I should tell you? Who you is?" she asked.

Elias spoke up then, his voice finally finding its strength again. "I his son. I want to know."

"All a sudden you want to know? What? You special 'cause your mama fuck wit Force?" She tried to laugh, but it morphed into a phlegmy cough.

She pulled a packet of cigarettes out of a pocket in her dress. "Fetch I matches in da kitchen. I talk better wit a smoke." She gummed at the filter, the end glistening with spittle.

Elias returned carrying matches. He lit one and held it to the tip. She sputtered as she inhaled. "T'anks boy. I ain't know much, but I know Roger ain't die from no drug deal."

"Why Phil don't tell us that?" Elias asked as he set the matches next to the gorilla lamp.

"'Cause Roger better off dead and buried. You two diggin' up da past. Phil ain't much about da past. You best go outside and get ready." She pointed the orange tip of her cigarette at a palm tree-shaped clock on the wall. "Been almost ten minutes."

"Okay, but…" I looked at the desperate look on Elias' face, "…that is we need something if you have it. We need more than who didn't kill this boy's father. Do you know anything else? Please."

She took a long drag. She let the smoke out in a plume, then we heard two gunshots.

"Now, go now!" she said.

"No, not without an answer," I insisted.

Elias didn't move either, except to wipe a drop of sweat from his forehead.

"Talk to he modda," she said as she glared with bloodshot eyes at Elias. "When it ain't business, next stop be family. Now, get da fuck out my house before take my bat upside your skulls. You got bad ju-ju."

Elias nabbed his backpack and we sprinted out. He jumped on his bike, barreling down the hill at almost tumbling speed. My knee screamed. I ignored it as best I could, but it slowed me down. Elias kept squeezing hard on his brakes so I could keep pace. I waved him on.

"Just go, get outta here. I'm fine," I said. He gave me the *are you sure* stare over his shoulder and I nodded again. He released his brake and swerved around a rock, rounding the bend and disappearing. Fear flooded through me as I wondered how long I could keep up the charade. I was in no shape for this game.

Gardelin's street. Two cop cars blocked the way out. As I rounded the corner, I spotted two policemen questioning Elias. They were so focused on him that they never saw me limp through, then I ducked behind a tree.

Elias must have come around the corner so fast there was no way for him to avoid detection.

Henry, my homicide detective friend, popped into my mind. What would he do in this situation? By helping his kid, I'd be helping Roger. Nothing came. No plan. So, I walked out into the open, whistling, my hands stuck deep into my pockets. My whistle sounded strained and uneven to my terrified ears.

The cops turned in unison, the smaller one grabbing Elias' arm to make sure he didn't get away.

"Who're you?" the larger one asked, simultaneously pointing at me using his left hand and tensing his right hand on his gun. He snapped off the leather strap.

I steeled myself and kept walking like I hadn't heard them. The cop drew his weapon and pointed it at me. I froze. No amount of play-acting could hide my paralyzing fear.

"I said, who are you?"

One thing remained clear in my mind, be as vague as you could get away with when telling the cops a lie.

"Takin' a walk," I said, mustering all the nonchalance I could, which wasn't a lot.

"Take your hands out of your pockets."

I started to withdraw my hands and he squatted deeper. The younger, shorter cop mirrored him like a good sidekick. That's when I noticed Elias' bike thrown to the side. "Slowly," he said. "Easy, like in the movies."

I relaxed a little and my mind kicked back into gear. I thought about rhetoric and its power. According to the Sophists, the art of rhetoric was both beautiful and infinitely functional, allowing the user to dazzle a listener and giving him the ability to get away with anything if the words were used properly. It allowed thieves to talk their way out of prison sentences and otherwise irrational, untrustworthy shysters to become senators. Rhetoric would have to do because running was out of the question.

"You got something to say?" The taller cop patted me down as I held up my hands. He pulled out my wallet and checked my identification. "Boise Montan-gue?"

"Montague. Like from the play," I said. "You know Romeo?"

"Romeo? I know Romeo." He smiled and turned to his partner. "Romeo's last name Montague?"

His partner laughed but didn't let go of Elias. "Nah. He last name was somet'ing like Samuels or Stevens or somet'ing."

He turned back to me. "How you know Romeo?"

I smiled big. "You know, I just moved back here from California. It's this actor out there. Never mind. So, what did my little cousin do now?"

"Dis your cousin?"

"Yeah, he my cousin," I said. "Elias, what you doin'?"

"Uh?" was Elias' succinct response.

"You going to see Elyse again?"

He stared at me, still not with the program, so I spoke up. "He doesn't want to admit that he's out here to go see this honey. His mother said she was off limits."

Sweat poured down my forehead. If it had been five degrees out, I'd have been sweating anyway, but luckily it was ninety-three and everyone was dripping wet. I swallowed hard and walked over to Elias like I was terribly concerned.

The younger officer gripped Elias' arm firmly. For a short man, he had large hands, completely encircling Elias' bicep.

I had to be convincing here, like Elias and I had a long history. I'd taken two acting classes in L.A. I wasn't a good actor on stage, but out here in real life, who the hell looked too hard at your performance skills?

I slapped Elias hard across the face, something I always thought was ridiculous because it happened all the time in plays and movies, but never in real life. In fact, I'd read in *Vanity Fair*, slapping the face was rarer than punching. Slaps startled people, and since reading that, slapping had become my go-to method of throwing authority figures off their game. Startled, the younger cop released Elias, whose hand floated instinctively to his cheek.

"Owww!" Elias barked.

I fought the urge to laugh. "Your mama's gonna blame me if you get that girl pregnant. I told her I'd look after you."

The younger cop looked very confused. He pulled out a white handkerchief and wiped his pimpled face.

The larger, balding cop remained unfazed. "So, you cousins?" He had his hands on his hips like he was taking control of the situation again.

I ignored the question and continued my barrage on Elias, who still had nothing to contribute verbally. "That girl," I pointed up the hill for emphasis, "been wid half da boys at dat school, you hear? She might've got something. You ever think about that before you pull it out?"

The younger cop yanked his partner away and they whispered. I continued my verbal assault on Elias, pretending I was blind to the cops' exchange. Out of the corner of my eye I saw the larger one nod reluctantly as the younger one gestured like an Italian talking to a hot girl. The youngster walked over, picked up Elias' bike and wheeled it over to us. He squeezed my shoulder in an effort to get me to stop.

When I didn't, he yelled at me, "Shut up! Stop it! We have other things to do and you need to clear dis area." The cop pushed me away and gave Elias his bike. "Please, go away."

I held my hands up in the air like, fine, we're gone, jeez. As he walked back toward his partner, he muttered loud enough for me to hear, "I hate dez fuckin' family fights. Dey's loco. Radda have drug dealers dan family fights."

The bigger one gave him a slow nod and they resumed standing in the shade of the only tree around. As we ambled away, I held fast to the handlebars to keep from collapsing.

Elias leaned over and whispered in my ear, "What was that? You almost got us arrested."

My eyes burned and I closed them.

"Just don't let me fall," I muttered back. Through my shoes I could feel sharp rocks jabbing like tiny knives.

CHAPTER 53

I recovered, but Elias kept shaking as I set him on the picnic bench outside the university café.

"Wait here," I said.

Ten minutes later I returned, carrying a decaf for me and hot tea for him. A mild breeze swept through the buildings and created a draft, making it feel almost cool in the shade beneath the colorful umbrellas. He kept sitting there as the steam from his cup rose between us. I let it go on for a while, then said, "Drink."

He picked up the cup and sipped. "Keep drinking," I said, sipping my coffee. "You need to warm up."

Teens and twenty-year-olds moved around us like schools of fish, going from place to place on the picturesque campus.

"So, Elias, we need to talk," I said, turning my attention away from an attractive young student and back to him. "Keep drinking your tea."

He held the cup out. It was empty, so I went and got more. When I returned, he looked at me with focus for the first time since we'd entered Gardelin's bunker.

"I'm hungry. I really need to eat."

"Sure, sure, no problem." Inside the café I ordered food. We sat in silence until a woman set down four pâtés, fried dough pockets containing meat, fish, or veggies. Caribbean empanadas.

"Not sure what you like so I got one of each."

Before I could point out which was which, he grabbed one and devoured it. I snatched the salt-fish. He polished off the other two before I'd finished. I ordered another. The flaky golden dough had always been a weakness of mine.

"Your mother is Noa's sister, right?"

He looked over the rim of his tea cup, then gingerly lowered it to the table.

"Yeah, all right, she's my aunt, my mama's sister."

"Does your mother know what happened to your father?"

"No, they split up long before that," he said.

Elias leaned back and rested his right hand across his stomach, clenching his fingers. He rolled his neck around like fighters do before the bell sounds.

"I'd like to speak to her," I said.

"She's not here."

"Is she on vacation?"

"She doesn't live here," Elias said.

He rested his knee against the side of the table and leaned back. Some of that young man swagger returned as the shock wore off.

"Where is she?" I said.

"St. Croix."

"Why?"

"Job over there pays better, so she went. I stay my junior and senior years with my aunt 'cause I didn't want to switch schools," he said, rocking back and forth. "You could call her. I have the number."

Calling someone worked when there were no alternatives, but I had options. I wanted an in-person reaction when I hit her with my questions.

"Looks like we're going to the land of Crucians," I said.

"I'm not going anywhere with you," he said as he dropped the chair back onto all fours. "You do what you want, but I'm not going."

"Your mother's not a drug dealer," I said. "Is she?"

"I'll give you her address."

"You don't care about figuring out what happened to your dad?"

A dark cloud crossed his face.

"You know what, screw you, Mr. Montague. Stop questioning me about how much I care about my father. He was a fucked up guy who sold drugs and got killed over it. What the hell do you want me to do, let my life become consumed by a need for the truth about something that really doesn't matter?" He waved his hand around and almost hit a passing student in the face who ducked away.

"Sorry," Elias muttered, but she didn't even look. "You see that, you got me going crazy. We almost died today then you had to lie to keep us from getting arrested. I tried that life, it wasn't for me, okay?"

He started to stand, but I put my hand on his shoulder.

"Hey, I'm sorry, Elias. I don't question your love. I don't."

291

He looked like all those guys whose fathers leave them whether it's because of death or work or to start another family with a new set of kids and a younger wife. He needed a safe place in the world, a logical place, or he'd make a quick turn into a cell. Even in St. Thomas, being a young black man could be hazardous to your freedom.

"Can you give me her contact info?" I asked.

"Yeah, I'll share it from my phone. What's your number?"

I gave it to him and after I received the shared contact, we shook hands. He was more mature than I first thought.

"Do you want to know what I find out?" I asked. "Or you want me to leave you alone?"

He shrugged, then said, "I got class in twenty. I goin' go study."

Students were eating and laughing all around me as I watched him sulk away. He walked like his father, but a little less arrogant. Maybe that would keep him safe. Maybe not.

CHAPTER 54

We called the local seaplane "The Goose" when I was growing up and used to fly back and forth from St. Croix to St. Thomas. The take-off and landing were still as much fun as I remembered. Water splashed onto the windows and beaded off as we "taxied" to the ramp, riding up onto the concrete "runway."

My family had left St. Thomas in the middle of my sixth-grade year to move to St. Croix. I'd never forget arriving in the classroom of The Newman School in mid-January. The teacher introduced me to a sea of strange faces.

I made one friend the first six months. An Italian kid whose father worked for Hess Oil and he'd only moved there six months earlier. He had about as much success fitting in as I did, mostly because of his strong accent. The fact that he wore glasses so thick it looked like his eyes were underwater didn't help either.

He moved away at the end of sixth grade and I never made another significant connection with anyone in St.

Croix. We left after eighth grade and I'd never thought about coming back. What could've made Becca Hariri move here, even for a job?

St. Croix was the antithesis of St. Thomas. Flat, over twice as large, fewer people. It had two small towns instead of one hub. Cheaper and sleepier, the beaches were less picturesque and the people scattered. The Florida of the Caribbean, without the excitement of Miami.

I left the seaplane depot and rented a car. After a small breakfast, I headed to Becca's address. It was out in the country halfway between Christiansted and Frederiksted.

On the winding road to Judith's Fancy, I passed my old school. The campus looked small, but well-maintained. I headed west on Northshore Drive, winding through tall grasses, past a small lake with reeds taking over. Frogs croaked as I zipped past.

The address led me to a small bungalow on the water, made of cinderblock and wood. A simple, brown beach cottage that probably was once a vacation home for some rich white family from New York or a rental, also owned by a rich white family from New York. I heard barking from inside. The door opened before I knocked.

"Can I help you?" a short, Lebanese woman with jet-black hair and thick eyelashes asked.

Her pouty lips almost blinded me with their sparkly pink sheen. She wore sensible two-inch pumps and white pants that hugged her curves. The woman had sex appeal and she knew it.

"I'm here to see Becca," I said. "I'm a friend of Elias."

She squinted at me, then leaned out the door to see if anyone was in my car or hiding behind me.

"Okay. What do you want?"

"To talk. If you are more comfortable we can go to a restaurant," I said.

She studied me. "Nah! Come in. If you try anything," she gestured to a black and gold Doberman Pincer sitting behind her like a statue, "he will kill you."

When I reached my hand forward the dog growled. I snatched it back.

"He's not the friendly type, but he won't hurt you unless I say the word," she said. "You Boise?"

The question threw me. "Uh, yeah. Boise Montague," I said, holding out my hand. She had a solid grip, giving me nothing more than I had already learned: don't fuck with this woman. Her long, black nails dug into my skin on the back of my hand a little, like she wanted to make a point.

"You look confused, but you shouldn't be. You've blabbed your name to all my family."

"Oh right, you mean Elias."

"No, actually Elias and I haven't spoken in seven months and fifteen days. I mean my nosy sister," she said.

"She's not that bad, is she?"

She strutted down the stairs and into a living room featuring art deco style sculpture and paintings. The space wasn't large, but packed with stuff. I felt like I was in the lobby of a Vegas hotel on the strip. A giant sculpture of a standing dog made of some kind of white plaster dominated the center of the room.

She skirted around the sculpture over a thick, off-white rug that reminded me of a polar bear's pelt and into the kitchen. Her hand rested on the brushed chrome handle of her side-by-side refrigerator. I knew the model: a Viking.

The damned thing cost over three grand. Repairs cost more than any refrigerator I'd ever owned. A buddy of mine in Marina del Rey owned the same model and bitched about it all the time, but it was considered one of the best on the market.

The rest of her kitchen was appointed with similar high-end fixtures and appliances. What the bungalow lacked in size and exterior landscaping, it made up for with her luxury interior. Why not? She looked like a woman who savored the finer things.

"Drink?" She flicked her bangs out of her eyes.

"You have Guinness?"

"Isn't it early for that?" she mused.

"Yes, but this isn't your everyday morning. I haven't been here in decades."

She surprised me again by producing a Guinness and setting it on the counter. After a long tug, I belched.

"'Scuse me," I grunted. "Don't love flying."

"You took The Goose?"

I nodded. "You're well-dressed for a Saturday morning. Were you expecting me?"

"I work on Saturday. I'm leaving in twenty minutes, so talk fast."

"I want to know anything you can tell me about what happened to your ex-husband."

"First off, I've never married."

"You had a kid together. That's almost deeper, wouldn't you say?"

"I kept Elias clear of that man for as long as possible and if I had my way, they never would have met." She walked over to the window and looked out at the beach.

"Nice place," I said.

"Yeah, it's quiet. I like quiet." She took a sip of coffee and turned to me. "So, is that it? You could've called."

"No, there's more. A woman said to me, talk to you about this. She had some idea you would know more about what happened to Roger than the cops, Phil Gardelin, and your son. That's why I'm here."

"Yes, well, what do you care about Roger? And who's this woman?"

"Don't know her name. She's Gardelin's girlfriend."

"Sandra used to be, not sure who is now. Been a while. So what about you and Roger?"

I told her about growing up with Roger and my shock at finding out he'd been killed. I also explained I didn't believe it was as simple as the cops wanted it to be.

"He was a bad guy," she said. "Can't you just leave it at that? Go investigate someone who needs justice. What Roger got, from whoever he got it, it was justice. That guy killed people with drugs to make money. He's not the kid you grew up with." She moved closer and I heard the click of her dog's paws on the tile as he followed her. "Yes, he's dead and he was your friend, but that person died long before the Roger I knew passed."

"So then tell me what you know," I said.

Dana had rubbed off on me. I was prepared to have this woman dislike me. Short of that pincer attaching his teeth to my flesh, I'd question and probe. She poured the remainder of her coffee into the kitchen sink, picked up her purse, and headed for the front door.

"Not now. I have work. Maybe another time, Boise."

She pulled a car cover off her black Porsche convertible parked in the tiny carport. She balled it up and dropped it into a box behind the house.

Tailing her in my rental to Christiansted, I watched as she did her job at the concierge station at the Vineyard

Hotel. She helped people with a smile. The men at the hotel all had a lot of questions for Becca. She seemed like a friendlier person here.

It used to bother me when I believed people were always the same, but after Evelyn died, I accepted that we're different every time someone different is in front of us. Might as well be better whenever you can, even if it's only for money. I respected her for that. She watched me out of the corner of her eye. I made no effort to conceal myself as I sat reading *The Daily News*.

After her shift ended, she disappeared into the employee area. She never came out, but I'd situated myself in the lobby so as to see what her car was doing too.

I stared out at her glowing Porsche 911; midnight blue contours swelling and dipping even as it sat unmoving beneath the hotel's parking lot lights.

Before I got up to follow her, I made a phone call. Miguela Salas. I asked her about Roger's finances. At first she was reluctant to indulge my delving further into her client's affairs, but as I laid out my theory, her tongue loosened. Then, when she heard the whole thing, she agreed to email copies of the financial documents to my phone.

Minutes later, I spotted Becca strutting to her Porsche at the same moment my phone dinged, notifying me of the incoming email from Miguela Salas.

Back at Becca's bungalow, I pulled up as she got out of her car.

"We meet again!" I said joyfully.

"You don't quit," she said. "Perhaps my dog can persuade you to leave me alone."

"What's his name?" I asked.

"Jesus," she said.

"Wasn't he a pacifist?"

"Let's hash this out, okay?"

"Sure. Can I buy you dinner?"

She swiveled her hip slightly. Becca moved like a dancer: smooth and elegant. She was very different from her harried sister Noa.

"You're already dressed for it," I said.

"No, let's talk here. If you need to eat, please go and come back."

I said I could wait and followed her inside. I looked at my phone and saw I had a message from Dana. I asked to use her bathroom and listened to it.

I came out and hit her with a question right off, "So, Becca, when'd you leave St. Thomas?"

"A few years ago," she said shrugging out of a sequined jacket she'd put on at work. The kitchen smelled like freshly-microwaved chicken. She grabbed a sharp knife and began cutting up an apple. Jesus ate the chicken from a large silver bowl next to the refrigerator.

"Did you leave a week after Roger was killed?"

"I really don't remember specific dates that well," she said. "It wasn't long after."

"Why then?"

"I got a job over here."

"Why didn't Elias come with you?"

"He didn't want to switch schools. Hard to change in the middle of high school."

"What was he, sixteen?"

"Yes," she said. She took a bite of the cut apple and offered me a piece. "Mangos will be ripe soon." She nodded out the window at a tree in the yard next door rimmed with greenish-orange fruit. "Then I can eat fresh fruit again."

I sighed. "You don't much want to talk about this, do you?"

"If you cared about whether I cared, you wouldn't have followed me today. You wouldn't be here now." She took another bite then continued. "Yes, I moved here to get away from that place and to start a new life. I couldn't be in Charlotte Amalie anymore. My son didn't share that sentiment. St. Thomas has more energy. A young person likes that. It's the center of this little world. I prefer the fringe."

"But why not tough it out for a couple years so you could stay with him?" I asked.

"Have you ever been laying under the blankets in your home on a cool night? You're perfect. Your body has no aches, you feel warm and surrounded. You're drifting off, then suddenly, it's too much. You need to be out from under. You feel like you're drowning. You need to feel the cool air on your skin, but you weren't sweating, nothing was openly wrong. That's why I left when I did."

She brushed a lock of black hair out of her face and looked me full on. Determination shown through. A decision made.

"So, what have you and Elias done in the meantime?" I asked.

"A mother finds a way," she said. "Please help yourself to something in the 'fridge. I'm going to change." She looked around the room as if making sure there was nothing for me to steal, then shimmied through a sliding bamboo door into her bedroom. Jesus stopped eating and followed her in. She shut the door.

I had my first "a-ha" moment then. She came out of the bedroom wearing a loose top with no shoes. Her meticulously pedicured toenails boasted black gel nail polish with a flower painted on the big toe of her right foot.

"I'm gonna to go," I said. "Can we talk tomorrow?"

She hesitated, then said, "Sure. Happy to help in any way I can."

I sat in my car and called Elias.

There were no street lights. The natural darkness and the beating of the ocean through my cracked window gave me a feeling of security. Like it would all be okay.

His voicemail picked up and I left a message. I was a boulder on the precipice. I needed to figure out which way to fall and time was short, but for the moment, I felt relaxed in the dark beneath the sound of the waves.

CHAPTER 55

Elias called me back as I dozed in my luxury room at St. Croix's Buccaneer Hotel. Dana had sent a text that the other half of my payment was waiting for me at *The News* for pick-up, so I felt a little better about my monetary policy, hence the nice digs.

"What you want?" Elias said by way of a greeting.

"You sound tougher today," I said.

"What you want?" He repeated. "I goin' out."

"Don't you want to know how your mother's doing?" I asked.

"All right."

"Not great. She seems stressed out."

"Well, t'anks for calling."

I stopped him from hanging up by asking, "Exactly when did she leave to St. Croix?"

"You mean a date? I don't know, I wasn't spending much time with her den."

"Were you with Roger?"

He hesitated, then said, "Yeah, mostly."

"Did she like that?"

"I don't know." He sucked his teeth, then said, "How I should know what she like?"

"How do you know Phil Gardelin?"

"From my fadda. He bring me wid him when dey do business."

"Did you like that?" I asked.

"Yeah, I guess. Yeah. He make me part of things. It feel good," he said.

It hadn't cooled off so I shuffled to the ice machine. I plopped a couple cubes into a glass of tap water and swallowed it in one gulp.

"You still there?" Elias asked.

I finished swallowing then said, "I'm here."

"Dat's it? I need to go," he said.

"Tell me, when exactly did your mother leave and why didn't you go?"

"Man, I didn't go because I was in da middle of school. I no want to leave for another school."

"I get that. Was it before or after Christmas?"

He was silent for a while. As I was about to ask if he was still there, he said, "Right after. Listen, I got to go. My friend outside to pick me up."

CHAPTER 56

The front desk called at noon to ask if I was staying another day. Moments later, a knock at the door roused me as the housekeepers came looking to clean the room.

"Shit! Can't you read the do not disturb?" I grumbled as a tiny woman in a housekeeping uniform opened the door.

"Sorry, sorry," she said backing out and bowing slightly. I felt bad, but busied myself clearing out. I'd never actually unpacked and my head hurt. After showering and dressing, I checked out. The maid glared at me from the room across the hall. She looked away when I tried to apologize. On the bedside table I left a guilty ten dollar tip.

As I pulled up to Becca's bungalow, she was loading a bag into the trunk of her car.

"Going somewhere?" I asked.

She jerked up, startled.

"Going to see my son. You got me thinking that I hadn't seen him in a while."

"You left after Christmas," I said.

"Excuse me?"

"St. Thomas. You said you couldn't remember when you left. It was Christmas of 2011. Does that ring a bell?"

She nodded cautiously. "Maybe that's right. I need to go. My flight's at two-thirty."

"Have a nice trip," I said.

She stepped inside the sleek Porsche 911 as I held the car door open for her.

I tailed her to the airport, then followed her inside. I bought a ticket on the same flight. Her head remained buried in her cell phone screen. She never spotted me sitting two rows away.

CHAPTER 57

Becca's father picked her up in a beige vintage eighties Mercedes. I tailed them to a cinderblock house on the east end near Red Hook in a cab. The house looked like every other one in the development. A two-story job on a quarter-acre lot on the side of a hill. Everything from the fences to the exterior walls was whitewashed and had brown trim. If you didn't look at the address number, you could easily wander into the wrong house on any given evening.

Noa met them at the door. Elias must have been inside already. I paid and the cabbie sped away. Standing on the side of the road, the occasional car passing, I contemplated my next move.

Family dinner on a Wednesday night. A reunion with Becca. Did I want to be the jerk who came uninvited? Noa's father already had questions about my presence in his daughter's life. I watched for half-an-hour, then decided it wasn't the correct course of action. I needed to talk to Elias alone.

At that moment, Elias walked out the front door. He paced back and forth, holding his phone. He touched the screen twice, then pocketed it and marched back inside. A minute later, he came out again, looked up at the sky and pulled out the phone. He selected something on the screen, then my phone buzzed.

"What did you say to my mother?" he asked.

I ducked behind the nearest house and leaned around watching him as I held the phone to my ear. I probably shouldn't have answered, but there we were.

"I wanted to figure out what she knew," I replied. "I think she's involved and wanted to get away from here to avoid the situation. So, she moved to St. Croix."

I heard him swear under his breath.

"She doesn't know anything. I didn't know you were going to attack her!" he protested.

"I didn't. I just wanted to get the timeline straight," I said.

A rusty Volkswagen Beetle puttered by and back-fired. Elias' face lit with recognition as the noise echoed over the phone. He gazed out and spotted the car.

His eyes drifted to the area near my hiding spot as I ducked back behind the house.

"Shit!" I whispered and poked my head out in time to see him pocket his phone and start barreling toward me.

A car honked and swerved around him as he charged into the street. The driver yelled something and I stepped out, scared he'd get hit.

"Elias, watch out!" I yelled.

He didn't even slow down as he approached and launched himself at me. I slammed into the ground. My gunshot shoulder howled and my lower leg twisted awkwardly under my hip as he pinned my arms beneath his knees. Rolling slightly to the side, I managed to straighten my leg as he gripped my shirt collar in both hands.

"You can't do this!" he yelled, spit from his mouth sprayed my face. "Leave us alone! I don't wanna know anymore. You got it! I don't want to know. Leave us be!"

He rolled off of me and laid on his back in the gravel and dust. The rocks were still warm although the sun had sunk below the distant green hills.

He laid there, his head swinging side to side, chest heaving.

"Leave us alone, leave us alone," repeated as tears streamed down his dusty cheeks.

I'd gone too far. I was that asshole who can't keep his nose out of good people's business. I'd shoved him into a corner. And, like a cornered animal, he was lashing out.

Noa came to the door and squinted into the deepening darkness. She yelled for Elias. I saw my mother standing in the doorway, yelling for me to get back in the house before a car hit me in the chest and collapsed a lung.

My mother loved to talk about collapsed lungs, her go-to calamity. I'd come home and get a swat across the back of my head as I tried to scoot by her. She'd swear under her breath that I didn't have the sense god gave an iguana.

Elias fell silent and laid still. I started to get up and he held me down using one arm. I gave no resistance and collapsed back on the gravel.

"Not yet," he said. I laid there, his dusty hand print on my t-shirt. Over the smell of evening moisture, a dove flew west in the fading light, making that soft twittering sound they made.

Noa returned inside.

"What's going on?" I said, leaning on my elbow. Elias still didn't move. His chest rose and fell like a ship in a stormy sea.

"She's leaving. She came to say good-bye," he said. "It's my fault."

"Why is it your fault?"

His eyes glazed over.

"Elias. Hey, Elias?" I shook his shoulder.

"What? Get off me!"

He scrambled to his feet and sprinted across the street back into the house.

I called Dana. "I need a favor," I said. "You have any contacts at the airport?"

"Maybe. What about?"

"I need you to find out what flight Becca Hariri is on tonight or tomorrow, maybe even Friday."

"Sounds serious," she said.

"Does this take long?"

"It's late in the day, but I'll push it. Expect a call within the hour. Where are you?"

I texted Dana the address. After twenty minutes, I stole toward the house. Mr. Hariri's vintage Mercedes rested in the driveway. Papers were stuffed into the crevice between the center console and the driver's seat. When I tried the driver's door, it eased open. The smell of coffee assaulted me. This was definitely Mr. Hariri's car.

My phone buzzed as I leaned into the car. I jumped, banging my head on the edge of the doorframe.

"Owww!" I groaned. It was Dana. "Perfect timing."

"You okay?"

"What you got?"

"Nothing, my contact's on vacation and his assistant's a prick. I've got one more try."

"Hold on, I may not need it," I said.

On top of the pile I found a printed itinerary. Becca's flight the next afternoon routed through Europe and wound up in Beirut.

"What are you doing?"

"Hi!" I said, looking up at Becca Hariri and giving her my best Brad Pitt grin. I left the line to Dana open, hoping she'd hear the exchange in case things got dicey.

"I'm calling the police," Becca said. She pulled out her phone and started dialing.

"You might want to think twice about doing that," I said. "In fact, what I'd prefer we do is talk this over inside, with your family."

I grabbed the stack of papers and my phone as I exited the car and headed for the front door.

"Stop! What do you want?" she demanded, her voice cracking.

Dressed in a cream-colored silk blouse, she looked so put together, like an actress on her way to an audition. Her hair was teased and held using hair spray. Skin-tight leggings accented her muscled legs. A Beverly Hills debutant, not a Lebanese immigrant living in St. Croix.

"I want this," I pulled out the photo of Roger and me as kids fishing. His smiling, sun-drenched face gazed at her in a sideways glance. "I promised someone I'd get justice for him."

"Who'd you promise?"

"Me," I said. "It'd be easier to let you go. To let you get away with it. It'd be easier on you and your son, but what about him?"

She stared at the photo. I moved closer to her, my boldness growing as my conviction that she killed my best friend became more than circumstantial. That, and my certainty she'd done it for money.

"I'm not going anywhere, so if you have something, go to the police and do what you need to."

"And you were just going to leave Elias here?" I asked. She glanced at the papers in my hand. "Yes, I know about Beirut."

"Elias is better off free from that world, even if he never spoke to me again. He's better off without me."

I felt a dark pity for her and at the same time disgusted, the way I'd felt disgusted by Earl DeVere aborting his own child to save his skin.

"Where'd you do it? I know he didn't die on that fucking beach. The police detective said in his notes he was certain it was done elsewhere and the body dumped."

She shrunk, leaning against the side of the Mercedes.

"What's going on out here?" Noa called out.

She stood with Elias on the steps leading up to the house.

"Ask her," I lifted my chin at Becca as I addressed Noa and Elias. "Maybe you'll get the truth." I turned back to Becca. "Just one thing, I know it happened at Auntie Glor's house."

Becca stared at me a long while, trying to read what else I knew. "How'd you know that?"

"Why don't we go there and I'll show you how I know," I said.

Becca sighed. "I wanted Roger to leave Elias alone. I wanted him to stay out of his life." She paused. "I thought talking to Glor might help. I went over there and she wasn't home, but Roger was. I decided to confront him. I couldn't hold it in any longer. I knew it wasn't a good idea, but I'd had enough. He was turning my son into a drug dealer. Hanging out with Phil Gardelin. Dragging Elias into that cesspool."

Elias exploded, "Not true! That's not true! He wanted me to go to law school."

Becca stared at her son. "He said that?"

Elias shook his head. "Yes, he said that."

Tears filled Becca's eyes. "He never said it to me. Things escalated. We were in the kitchen. He was furious at me for telling you to have nothing to do with him. He started to come after me, so I grabbed a knife from the counter in the kitchen to defend myself. He seized my hand and held it there, right in front of his chest with one hand." Becca held her fist in front of her chest. "Easy as I'm holding this air. That's how strong he was. Using his free hand, he seized my throat and squeezed, then he shoved me to the ground."

Becca stopped and peered over at the porch. Her father stood between Noa and Elias holding a gun, probably *the gun*. The murder weapon.

"That's not what happen."

Behind Noa I saw the bright inside of the house. It looked warm and safe in there.

I checked my phone. It was still connected to Dana.

"Put de phone down, now."

I put my phone on the ground and my hands up. I left Dana connected, but realized my other mistake. I hadn't read through the other pages in the pile. Becca wasn't the only one going to Lebanon. Her father was leaving too.

I said, "You killed him." It wasn't a question.

"He choke my Becca. When she not come out for me take her home, I go in. Find him," he made a choking gesture with his hands. "So, I do what a father should."

"The autopsy says the knife wound to his chest was the fatal one, not the gunshot," I said.

"Which of you killed him?" Elias screamed. "Which one?" The question was directed at me.

"I believe your grandfather killed him. Becca, come on, admit it," I begged. "Your father killed Roger."

"Mom?" Elias moaned. "Mom, please tell me the truth."

Becca began, "I killed Roger, but…"

Her father charged over and belted her across the face with the gun. "Shut up!"

Becca spit blood on the ground.

Noa spoke up, "Papa, are you going to kill all of us? You forget I was there too. For support. Remember? You said, come to support your sister. I'm done hiding your secrets."

Mr. Hariri spun on Noa and marched to her, holding the gun in her face. "You, you woman, shut up! All of you," he turned in a circle, jabbing the gun at each of us in turn. "All of you disgust me. Inter-breeding with filth like him and him." He pointed the gun at Elias and me.

He returned his attention to Becca while pointing at Elias. "And now I have this half-breed negro in my family. Trying to carry my family name. And you," he turned to Noa. "Talking to this Boise in our store day after day. Don't think I don't know what you want."

He really did mean to kill all of us. Mr. Hariri looked at his grandson with barely disguised contempt. "Get up. Go get rope. Drawer right next to sink."

Elias hesitated, then hurried off.

Mr. Hariri glared at me, then his look softened and he contemplated his older daughter.

"Becca, you see, they will come for you. You must stop this nonsense and come with me."

"Lebanon?" I asked.

Mr. Hariri pointed the weapon at me. "You see, he knows too much."

Elias returned carrying clothesline.

Without looking away from Becca, Mr. Hariri said, "Do something useful, boy. Tie him up."

Elias bound my ankles together, then my hands.

Mr. Hariri stood over me and growled, "You threaten my family for this Roger who ruin my daughter's life? This man bad. He not care about people. I protect my family."

He spat at Elias' feet.

"This man take my daughter's virginity, then when he find out about this half-breeded boy he want to be part of our life!"

"I can't leave with you, Papa," Becca said.

Mr. Hariri whirred on her.

"What you say?"

"I won't go to back to that stinking country with you. I don't want to be covered with black cloth. I'd rather take my chances here, even if you give them the knife."

He blurted something in what I assumed was Lebanese.

She responded, "So what! I'm a westerner. I like cars and money. I like speaking English." She turned and said to Elias, "Your father cut me off. Like I was a dog. I struggled but couldn't get out of debt. I was going to lose everything!

So I went to talk to him. I didn't mean for this to happen. You must believe me."

Elias looked up from his hands, the hands he'd used to tie me up. "Mother, you should go with grandpa. If you stay, you'll go to jail."

Becca said, "No, I didn't do it. Right, Noa?"

Noa's face was a mask of pain. "Papa, you made her do it. You made her, you know you did. Like you made Elias tie up Boise. You made her stab Roger." She looked at me and said, "When I heard the gunshot, I snuck into the house and watched as my father held my sister at gunpoint and made her stab Roger over and over. He kept the knife and threatened to turn her in as the killer if she ever breathed a word or interacted with Elias. That's why she moved away. It was the only way she could stay away from her boy. Then, we took Roger's body from the kitchen and dumped it on the beach." Noa turned and looked at me. "You knew because of the piece of his red shirt on the railing, right? That's how you knew Roger'd been killed at Glor's house?"

A shot rang out. Noa collapsed to the ground, her hand over her stomach. Blood seeped through her fingers.

Mr. Hariri lowered the smoking gun and yanked Becca by the hair, pulling her face close to his. "You will do as I say. You will come with me. This disgusting mongrel's not worth your freedom."

Elias hadn't tightened the knots well. My hands were free. The ropes on my legs weren't tied at all really and in less than thirty seconds, all my bindings lay on the ground.

Seeing Mr. Hariri's attention was completely focused on Becca, I grabbed a stone from the rock-boundary around the flower bed. I ran, planning to bash him over the back of his head, but the small man spun around as if sensing my presence. At the last second, I hurled the rock at him as he leveled the gun at my chest. It hit him in the forehead. The bullet whizzed over me, and he dropped to the ground unmoving. Blood gushed from his balding scalp, staining the dirt black.

Seconds later, a police car raced up the road, an ambulance in tow, followed by Dana's Nissan. I ran over to Noa, removed my shirt and staunched the wound. Her pulse was weak, but steady.

She strained to speak. I held my ear close. "Audrey. I did it for Audrey."

CHAPTER 58

I dropped some pastries on Dana's desk. A couple other reporters ambled over, mumbling t'anks as they took a napkin and cradled a doughnut in their hands.

"So, you figured out it wasn't a drug dealer," she said. "You're the real deal, Boise Montague. Not many people would have thought of leaving the phone line open so I'd hear everything. You saved Noa's life."

"Ha!" I threw my head back imitating her. "I got lucky. You were the one who saved the day by bringing the cavalry. The ambulance driver said if Noa had gotten to the hospital five minutes later, she'd be dead. Also, I never had it figured till the bitter end. I really thought maybe Becca had done it to protect Elias or something noble like that. I mean, Roger was a drug dealer."

"Oh shut up! Did you really doubt your best friend?"

I scratched my chin. "No, I guess not really. I mean, like I said, Roger wasn't a saint, but he never seemed evil. And this was plain evil." I got up to get a cup of coffee from the machine in the corner. "This one's going to be all over the paper I hear."

"I have an exclusive with the guy who cracked the case, so look out Pickering, Dana's back! Getting a lot of calls on this one. The police aren't happy about you exposing their incompetence," she said with a large grin.

"Yup, trial's gonna be ugly," I agreed.

"That's the least of your problems. Living here isn't gonna be easy with the cops looking to string you up," she said. "You certainly have a way with people."

"Guess I better stick with my own kind," I said. "What have we got coming down the pike?"

"We? Look Boise, I know you can't go on forever without earning a living and this newspaper thing's not great on that front."

I put my hand to my chest like Scarlet O'Hara. "Are you firing me?"

Dana gave me a sober look. "You really are good. Why don't you hang a shingle?"

"You mean get an office with a sign?"

"Exactly. Do you have money for first, last, and a deposit?" she asked.

I thought about my bank account and concluded she was probably right, I'd better do it before my funds got too low. I had over a year's worth of cash stashed, but shit happens.

"All right, you got any buildings you recommend?" I said, a grin spreading as I realized a new venture might even be fun.

"We might have a spare office in this building. Let me talk to Pickering. Meanwhile, what about finding out what happened to Earl DeVere? That kidnapping case just keeps spreading like an oil spill," she said, moving her hands around her desk to illustrate.

"Not sure he's a worthy candidate for an investigation. Isn't he just a bad guy who was taken by other bad guys?"

"Yeah, you're right, we shouldn't waste our time on them," she said, biting into a doughnut and taking a sip of coffee.

CHAPTER 59

From the grandiose brick steps leading up through the wrought iron gates that framed The West Indian Manner, I could see straight down Kongens Gade to the base of Government Hill a half-mile away. Government House towered up there, gleaming and white.

To my right, Lucas's home, painted green and looking decrepit, sat lower on our smaller hill. Roger's house stood to my left, a little ways down the road that dead-ended at the Manner's southern entrance. A house like The Manner had numerous paths to reach its front door.

In fact, The Manner towered above the rest, only giving ground to Bluebeard's Castle which stood behind me to the east. Castles tended to have to the top spot on most hills.

I glanced back at The Manner. Although it needed a paint job, landscaping, new shutters, brickwork, and was over two-hundred years old, the structure had presence. It had housed kings and corpses in its illustrious history. It was solid, after all it had been through at least forty hurricanes. Now it housed a beat-down private detective who was considering staying on permanently.

I felt some peace about Roger. Living without him all those years, I supposed I could go on living without him, even in St. Thomas.

Turning back to look once more at Roger's former home, something nagged at me, something unfinished, but I couldn't think at that moment what it was. The red rag was gone, taken as evidence for the trial. The railing looked naked without it.

My eyes settled on the office buildings next door. The wooden Payne & Wedgefield sign bolted to the white concrete wall on both sides of the building loomed large.

My phone startled me by actually ringing. I hated the sound of a ringing phone, so I always kept it on vibrate. Somehow, the ringer had gotten turned on.

The screen pulsed "unknown caller" and I considered pressing the red button. Curiosity got the better of me.

"Hello," I said.

A soft giggle. "Hello, Mr. Montague, this is your damsel in distress."

I straightened up. "Celia! I tried to call, but the other number stopped working."

"Daddy made me get rid of it. No worries. I want you to know I'm okay, but a little sad." She giggled again, more nervously.

"Did you ever speak to..." I swallowed before continuing, as I pictured DeVere being dragged out of the car and the penetrating eyes of the man behind the mask, "...Uncle Earl?"

There was a long silence.

I almost said something, then Celia squeaked, "Uncle Earl came by, yes. He ate dinner with us a couple days ago. He and Daddy went fishing after that. They like nighttime fishing. They've been doing it forever."

She cried. Another call was beeping in on my phone. Ignoring it, I waited for what I already suspected. Her sniffles and sobs made my heart hurt. So much pain for a young girl to endure.

"Anyway, Uncle Earl, he...he had an accident on the boat. They like deep-sea fishing. He fell over and, well you know, like, he drowned."

Gripping the phone with both hands, I said, "Oh Celia, I'm so sorry."

She sniffled some more. I pictured her wiping the tears away from below her long, fine eyelashes.

"Anyway, I'm good. Daddy and I are going to the Maldives for a vacay with his new girlfriend. She's like twenty-five," she said.

I hesitated, then said, "Celia, are you happy? Do you realize those men who kidnapped you work for your father? Do you know why you were in that warehouse with an operating table?"

"Yes, I know. My baby. I'm too young for motherhood. That's what Daddy said," she sobbed.

"Well, yes, that's right. How do you feel about that?"

Rattling noises erupted as she adjusted the phone. I imagined her laying back in her teenager bed, frilly sheets and posters of pop idols adorning lavender walls. Her biggest worry should have been what concert she'd see that night or the best nail polish color for summertime.

She blew her nose loudly without a hint of embarrassment. "I loved Earl. He didn't hurt me. I suppose what we did was wrong, but he really was kind to me. Now, he's gone. I guess that's my world. My Daddy's world."

My brow knitted together as I shared her pain. The pain of the reality Celia lived with.

"What do I have to be upset about? I'm rich, I can have whatever I want." She paused, then said, "My Daddy loves me very much. But can I tell you a secret?"

"Yes," I whispered.

"I don't know if I can keep loving him."

"Celia…" I started, but she cut me off.

"Can I give you my new number? I'm gonna have to go now. You really are my hero. Maybe we can stay in touch?"

She sounded so sincere. I didn't have children, but if I did, I hoped they'd be like Celia. I couldn't fathom how Cecil had raised such a mature young woman.

"Of course, I insist on you giving me your number," I joked. "I've been worried sick about you for days."

She read the numbers to me and I saved them in my phone. She made small talk about her upcoming trip, then reiterated she had to go.

"One last thing, Mr. Montague, if it ever got unbearable here, would you come get me?"

I smiled, thinking that would be a job I'd have to enlist Sire Goode for help with. "You can count on it."

"Don't say it if you don't mean it," Celia said.

"I mean it."

CHAPTER 60

"Wait here," I said as I got out of Dana's car. "Once we're in the house, come in. It'll be a nice surprise."

Auntie Glor waited for me on her front lawn in full gardening attire. Her eyes glazed over as I explained the events of the night before.

She plucked a weed and threw it aside. "Somehow I knew. Something felt different in that kitchen from that Christmas on. It's the real reason I moved out."

"Becca's father killed your grandson."

"No, my grandson died years before that knife and that gun ended his body. The lord wanted him back before he went too far down Satan's path. Maybe that bigot saved him." She picked out another weed and pointed to her right. "Please hand me that trowel."

I gave it to her. "So you really think it's for the best? Maybe you should make an effort to get to know Elias. You might learn something about Roger."

She got up and put the trowel in her apron pocket. We went into the house. She sat on a stool next to the kitchen counter, the same one I'd sat on to drink milk on my last visit.

"I think eventually Roger was going to kill his own son by bringing him into that world," she said.

I shook my head soberly, then told her that she'd been duped by her own lack of faith. She'd shown so much faith in Jesus, but none in her own blood.

The PDF files Miguela Salas had sent me, showed Roger had put funds into a 529 Account for Elias' education. It proved Roger was plotting his escape from that life and wanted a better one for his child.

Glor stared, the white pages with numbers on them reflecting in her reading glasses.

"Sometimes people surprise you," I whispered when she looked up.

She placed her elbows on the counter. Her head dropped into her hands. She kneaded her scalp and she emitted a low whine.

A knock on the door.

"He's here," I said.

"Who?" Glor asked.

I opened the door and Elias walked in. She stood and looked at the boy a long time. Elias' mouth curled as he struggled with his emotions. Glor waved him over and enveloped him in her arms. I slipped out the door and stole away, hope in my heart for the last of this special family.

CHAPTER 61

According to Dana, a small, dingy office was available in *The Daily News* building. I could afford it, but I'd have to come up to the newsroom to use the john. She'd given me the business card for a sign-maker who I'd already called. I ordered a simple white sign with black lettering: "Boise Montague, Private Investigator."

That afternoon, I snuck back into Roger's house. After ducking under the police tape in the kitchen, I laid down on the cheap yellow and white linoleum. I scooted back, giving my legs room to stretch out in front of me, then pushed back a little further, accounting for Roger being taller. Above the sink, I saw what I'd hoped to see: the large portrait of Elias staring down at me.

After pulling the likeness off the wall, I lugged it back to my room. Lucy provided a hammer and some nails and with her permission, I hung Elias above my bed. It felt like home.

ABOUT THE AUTHOR

Photo © 2018 Miriam Sachs

Gene Desrochers lives and works in Los Angeles County. He is originally from St. Thomas. *Dark Paradise* is his first novel after a lifetime of writing short stories. He has a Juris Doctorate from Tulane Law School. His favorite activity is tennis. Gene believes the people you choose in this life are your family.

Please go to **GeneDesrochers.com** to sign up for Gene's newsletter and special offers on his future novels and short stories. Sign up now and receive a **free short story** starring Boise as he pieces together the mystery of a slain sailor on leave in St. Thomas.

Made in the USA
San Bernardino, CA
15 September 2019